# WEDLOCKED

# WEDLOCKED

*Emma Cooke*

POOLBEG

First published in 1994 by
Poolbeg,
A division of Poolbeg Enterprises Ltd,
Knocksedan House,
123 Baldoyle Industrial Estate,
Dublin 13, Ireland

© Emma Cooke 1994

The moral right of the author has been asserted

A catalogue record for this book is available from the British Library

ISBN 1 85371 326 0

Cover photograph by Peter Maybury
Cover design by Poolbeg Group Services Ltd
Set by Mac Book Ltd in Stone 9.5/12
Printed by Cox & Wyman Ltd
Reading, Berks

The Publishers gratefully acknowledge the support of

The Arts Council / An Chomhairle Ealaíon.

Emma Cooke was born in Portarlington Co Laois in 1934 and was educated at Alexandra College Dublin. In 1980 *Female Forms,* a book of short stories and *A Single Sensation*, her first novel, were published by Poolbeg Press to critical acclaim. A second novel, *Eve's Apple*, followed in 1985. Emma Cooke now lives in Killaloe, Co Clare with her husband, visited by a large family of children and grandchildren.

*To*
*Sarah, Nell, Tom, Joanna, Elizabeth, Matthew,*
*Kate, Martha, Stephen.*

# PROLOGUE

We have just moved house. An end to my
troubles, a fresh start, a clean slate, who
knows! This morning a letter written on
yellow paper, the colour of buttercups,
plopped onto the hall mat. It was from Jane.
It described her latest living arrangements; the
flat, her boyfriend, the baby, the sofa she'd
picked up in a market. The lines sang of
carefree happiness. She never once mentioned
her mother, but with Jane I always feel Ruth's
shadow attempting to push its way in.

Even so I appreciated the letter. It is good
to know that the young are so resilient. I
carefully folded it and crept upstairs and
tucked it away with the few mementoes I have
of Peter.

I have brought only the remnants of our

past life with us. As of today this is another stage of my existence. Jane's letter begins it with a good omen, a happy thought. I will use it as an antidote to what has gone before.

# Chapter One

18th July: Sometimes I feel as if I'm forced to go through life wearing a blindfold. There are so many things that I must not see. It's as if I've been caught up in an endless game with complicated rules. I'm not complaining, I've always been good at games.

Tonight we talked holidays. Clive plumped for Greece, Alan suggested Tuscany, Ruth wanted whatever Clive wanted and I opted for the South of France just to open things up.

Ruth was looking very beautiful, her hair bright gold against her black chiffon blouse, her long tanned legs enhanced by narrow gold-tipped shoes. We sat in our kitchen on the cane-covered stools. Bottles of gin and whiskey stood on the red tabletop. After his third Scotch Clive began to stroke Ruth's neck while I pretended not to notice. That's what I mean about wearing a blindfold. Alan, it seems, doesn't give a damn. Just as well; if he's annoyed he can be quite rough. At one stage he reached forward and tweaked my nose, then said with his devilish smile that makes me think he should be holding a pitchfork, "Wherever we go let's be certain we've proper king-sized beds. Remember, Dixie, the time we went to the Holy Land?"

How could I ever forget?

This foursome of ourselves and the Whites has been going on for more than a decade. Decade has an official ring to it. The sort of thing that gets debated in the Dáil, like divorce. Which shows how woolly-headed I get after a couple of drinks, because if there was divorce there would surely not have been a decade like ours and the Whites. Decades, decadence...

"Dixie!"

I smile as if I'm posing for a photo while Clive tops up my glass.

After Ruth and Alan left, Clive and I had one of our meaningless quarrels during which I knocked over a marmalade jar the kids had left standing with its top off on a side table.

This has begun to happen quite frequently. Clive and I, when left to ourselves, get cranky and quarrelsome. Maybe it's nothing more serious than middle-age. Perhaps we should take up bridge and fight across the card table the way my parents used to while playing draughts. "Your move, dear." "Must you take so long?" "Mean thing." "Sneak thief."

"For God's sake!" Clive roared as if I'd acted deliberately. Then he stalked out leaving me with the broken glass and sticky mess. A few minutes later he put his head around the door and said in a normal voice, "Don't forget we've an early start tomorrow."

Tomorrow our second child, Marie, is graduating as a B.Sc. in University College, Cork. So is her best friend, Tessa White, who is Ruth and Alan's second child. Our two oldest, their daughter Jane and our son Peter, are in Dublin studying architecture. As for the rest of them, they're still around the place, keeping the families together.

After I'd cleaned up the marmalade I mopped the floor. By the time I'd finished I'd stopped feeling so demented. The mindlessness of housework can be a balm on the soul.

Next I went upstairs and stood in front of the bathroom mirror scrutinising myself. I'm OK, very dark in a Mediterranean way, "voluptuous" is the word that men who fancy me use. But I'm not Ruth...

19th July: Only three of us went to the graduation ceremonies. Ruth stayed at home because Danny was sick. Alan came in our car. With just three of our foursome present the tensions of last night vanished. Apart from ascertaining that Danny's was only a childish sickness we didn't discuss the matter further. Danny is ten years old. He is not Alan's son, but Clive and Ruth's. Definitely a situation where the blindfold is necessary.

The graduation was the usual squash of hopeful kids and proud parents. By the time we arrived all the seats in Aula Maxima were gone. We crouched on the balcony stairs with other adults, our faces pressed against the banisters watching for our daughters' brief moments of glory. It was our first family conferring. Peter, although older, has still to finish his architectural studies.

While we waited Clive looked around with his professional eye and began to calculate gloomily how many would die if the place collapsed or fire broke out. I thought of Ruth being left with the two lots of children and our empty house next to hers. Then, to take my mind off such a grim prospect, I reminisced about Clive's own graduation.

The day that Clive graduated I met him straight after I'd finished work. I was secretary to the alcoholic owner of a small clothing factory close to where I lived in Dublin, on the northside, with my parents. I set out to meet him and do something unforgivable. Even before he showed up I was feeling sensuous and brazen. I was also desperate; desperate enough to press myself dangerously close to him as we swayed romantically under the revolving lights at the students' dance. Clive was a little bit melancholy because of his parents and I had a horrible feeling that he was going to say that he didn't want to see me anymore.

Later, with a clear crescent moon in the starry sky, we dashed hand in hand along by Stephen's Green. My mind was working on two levels. a. If I ran hard and fast enough I might shake Tristram's baby out of my body. b. I had to make sure that Clive came into our house with me.

"I love you, Clive," I said boldly on top of the double-decker bus and took his hand and placed it swiftly between my thighs.

"Dixie," he moaned and shook his head. Things were pretty tough for him at the time. His father had recently died and his mother was

4

terminally ill. His graduation lunch had been a roast pork and apple sauce affair in the Shelbourne Hotel with his uncle, Monsignor Patrick.

When we got to our house I knew my parents had gone to bed because the dog was locked, whimpering, into the back hall. I had to creep out and give him a bagful of dog biscuits to keep him quiet.

The next stage was still up to me. I unbuttoned my blouse and slipped it off my shoulders. Twenty-one years ago nakedness was still something of a novelty.

"You're beautiful," Clive kept saying, although his eyes, after the first few seconds, were tightly shut.

The smouldering coal that had been burning at my centre all evening erupted into a blaze that engulfed us both. We had sex, properly, with little preamble, on the black leatherette couch in our sitting room. The deed was done before the dog had begun to snuffle and scratch at the door. I felt that I was a very accomplished seductress. I was only sorry that Clive, when he was dressed again, looked so pale and a little sad.

"Don't worry about it," I said to him. "It was my fault too. I wanted it as much as you did. I couldn't have stopped if the Pope walked in. Anyway, I'm glad we did it."

"But..." Clive stammered.

"No buts," I said kindly.

"If you ever need anything, Dixie." He squeezed my hand.

Two months later I told him that I was pregnant. He made no attempt to escape. He has never been a vengeful person.

21st July: I took the girls on a picnic to one of our favourite spots. Once it was a splendid private residence designed by the English architect, William Godwin, for Lord Pery, Earl of Limerick. Bridget White came along as well as my youngest daughters, Beth who is sixteen and fourteen-year-old Anne. Bridget is Anne's best friend. One cannot move without the other.

I was doing my bit. Ruth was resting. Her oldest boy, Jim, was looking after Danny. Alan strolled in yesterday to say that Ruth wasn't feeling well. He wasn't looking too great himself. His face was very red and puffy and he had a scratch on the back of his hand. After a while he began to mutter about our two oldest children. Jane White and my son Peter are, right now, touring Connemara together, sleeping in a three man tent.

"Three man tent how are ye, I'd like to give both of them three man tent," he groused. "What do you think, Dixie? I think it's all wrong."

I groaned. Between both our houses we have nine kids. In Bella Vista we have Peter, then our three girls, Marie, Beth and Anne. Out in Evergreen there are Jane, Tessa, Jim, Bridget and Danny Molloy.

"I wouldn't worry," I pleaded. Privately I prayed Jane was on the pill. It was only as Peter was leaving the house that I'd discovered who he had for a travelling companion. I hadn't even told Clive. To divert Alan's attention I took his hand and led him to the window where I showed him the cock pheasant, tame as a barnyard fowl, which has taken to feeding daily in the flower-bed opposite our front door.

"God, you've a lovely arse," he said, fondling it. But thankfully it's holiday time. Kids are everywhere. I pushed him away and did what I did that day that Ruth came in and told me that she was pregnant by Clive. I poured us both large gin and tonics even though it was only half-past ten in the morning. After that I planned the picnic.

But the picnic quickly went wrong. Within minutes of our arrival the girls managed to climb up the parapets of the ruin and waved down at me. I covered my ears and screamed. I couldn't look because one of them was going to fall. It was a judgement. Part of me has always believed that some day there will be a judgement.

"I'm sorry. I suffer from vertigo," I pleaded as they helped me back to the car. I'd had a vision of limbs sticking through torn clothes, eyes gouged out, mouths awry, skulls split open. The works.

"You go on escalators. People with vertigo can't go on escalators, it gives them blackouts," Beth said crossly. At sixteen Beth is prepared to contradict everything I say.

"It's probably your nerves, Mum. You're like Mrs Connors," suggests Anne who, at fourteen, is still on my side. Mrs Connors, who does for us a few days a week, suffers from queer turns and odd moods. Sometimes she turns on the hot taps and lets the kitchen water run and run until the place is as steamy as a sauna. Recently I've come upon her pulling faces at herself in the mirror.

I shook my head and dismissed my bizarre

behaviour as a bit of maternal fussiness. Then I got the girls out of the car again. It was too fine to go home. We spread the food out on the grass. A helicopter droned overhead, making, I reckoned, straight for Limerick Jail. Order was restored.

I leaned back against the sun-warmed base of a stone tower. Squinting upwards at the battlements I could trace out the shape of a cross. Ireland, I thought lazily, I'd hate to live anywhere else.

Tristram Long used to call Ireland an evil-minded sewer. I sighed. Romantic, widowed Tristram Long. Tristram my dead lover who once owned a shop near our house. Tristram who switched the placard on the door to CLOSED and pulled down the navy holland blind when I came to him on those spring evenings while I was earning my living as a shorthand typist. I see him in his old-fashioned waistcoat, putting a record on his vintage radiogram in its walnut case. I feel the ache starting between my legs. He turns and holds out his arms and slowly, easily, we begin to dance.

# Chapter Two

6th August: Clive was forty-three this year. I gave him an exercise bicycle as a birthday present. In previous years I have given him an aquarium, bellows, a burglar alarm, a magnifying glass – he is not an easy person to shop for.

The bicycle is installed in the room that we refer to as the study although nobody that I know has ever studied in here. When the kids were younger it was a rumpus room. It was also the room where, in our wild party days, the wildest scenes of our parties took place. I used to spend hours decorating it with coloured lights, balloons and streamers.

This morning its beige walls, grey carpet and northern aspect gave it an air of solemn application. It is a room that holds strange memories. Once I came upon Clive and Ruth locked in a passionate embrace. He had her backed against the blocked-up door that leads into the old servants' quarters. They didn't see me and I tiptoed out again instead of shouting "Stop!" I had my own reasons. One of them was Ruth's husband.

We had only been in Bella Vista for a couple of months. The Whites had been living next door in Evergreen for not much longer. Our friendship had taken off with flags flying. Ruth was the quiet one, "deep" as my mother would have said. I enjoyed Alan's virile humour, his gamey eye. I could see he fancied me and I tingled when he came close.

We had met him because of Bella Vista. He was the auctioneer who handled the sale. "Sure, it's a bargain. Didn't I buy the house next door last month?" The argument was unanswerable. Besides, Clive's practice was at last making money. We were rapidly becoming affluent. A Georgian house was a suitable acquisition.

I still wonder if I'd have been prepared to carry on with Alan if it hadn't been for Clive's obvious attraction to Ruth. I'd certainly been happy to flirt with him. That particular evening I hadn't shouted "Stop!" either when he followed me to the kitchen for ice cubes and shoved his hand down the bodice of my strapless taffeta dress. I smirked when he said, "Big boobs turn me on." I laughed at his plámás and nodded when he talked about the importance of new experiences. After all there was such a thing as personal liberation. Since our marriage Clive had been the only man I'd slept with.

Today, I walked around the study touching various articles of family life which have drifted in. A tarnished pewter mug, a fuzzy dog with a nodding head, a blue glass fish with a chunk out of its tail. I wondered what would have happened back then if I'd accused Alan of molestation and nipped everything in the bud. Or made a fuss about Clive and Ruth and brought it all to a halt.

Supposing Clive and I had split up? I imagined myself living in some miserable bed-sit in a house with three tenants to every floor. Wintering out in a rabbit hutch, queuing for the bathroom, cracked linoleum, flaking walls, stinking drains. No thanks. It was like the time they held the referendum on divorce. Once I heard that the deserted wife would be left to the care of the Social Welfare people I decided to vote against it. I felt people could work these things out better by themselves.

I caught one of the pedals of Clive's bicycle and gave it a quick experimental spin. Then I went to make lunch, mix a martini, and whip up a pudding.

13th August: A cobweb thick as a rope dangled in the corner where Clive once kissed Ruth. As it caught my eye I reminded myself to tell Mrs Connors to dust and polish Clive's bike. He hadn't used it for weeks.

A picture postcard showing a donkey has arrived from Peter. He and Jane were "loving in Connemara." I hoped that the omission of the word "it" was a simple mistake. They're too young for a serious commitment.

I wondered anxiously if girls of Jane's age considered abortion as a real alternative nowadays. "Dixie, do you think I should have an abortion?" Ruth asked on the morning she told me about Danny. It was the first time I'd ever seen her so timid and malleable.

"No way." I'd been emphatic. The very notion went against the grain. Anything but that. If there had ever been a moment when I might have told someone of my own predicament after Peter was conceived that was it. Peter, my darling son.

Abortion! When Peter happened it was something that smacked of witchcraft in backstreets, crazed lapsed midwives venting their spleen on the human race. The word gave me the shivers. I'd spent one whole day travelling around the city on different buses. The top of a bus was the only place I could find to sit and think. At one stage, near the bottom of Grafton Street, I looked down and there was Clive, his T-square under his arm and I knew that there was hope for me.

"Abortion!" I'd managed to speak kindly to Ruth, to pour her another drink, to reassure her that we were civilised adults.

"I admire you, Dixie," she'd said finally. Then she'd looked scared. "Alan will hit the roof. He'll murder Clive."

"Oh no, he won't." My own strength and power thrilled me. I could have browbeaten Maggie Thatcher. OK. We were faced with a messy situation. Messy situations were my forte. After I'd talked Ruth down I kept talking.

I rendezvoused with Alan, I had sex with him, cajoled him; told him how generous he was and brave and good and understanding and anyway he'd always insisted that "live and let live" was his motto in life.

I waited up for Clive and we talked into the small hours. By the end of it all I felt like a macaw or a talking Teddy. I could keep on for ever if someone asked the right question or pushed the proper button. The one marked, "Remember how you felt when you got pregnant by Tristram."

15th August: Yesterday Peter and Jane came back from their camping trip. Today Ruth asked me to go to the circus with Danny and herself.

"Please – I just can't face it on my own, Dixie," she said in a shaky voice. It was Danny's tenth birthday.

We travelled in my car. Ruth appeared looking like the Christmas tree fairy in a flame red dress and white, high-heeled, strappy sandals. Her hair was freshly curled. I decided not to care about my own baggy denim trousers and faded sweat shirt. Besides, when we got up to the circus field she was the one who looked out of place.

All around us was ramshackle drabness. The ground was soggy from recent rains and Ruth's heels sank into the mud with every pause in the queue. Danny acted like he was ashamed of us both. All the other women were fat and jolly with tight perms and bosoms even bigger than mine. They sported cerise lipstick and plastic handbags. They had dimpled elbows and dresses that stretched in wrinkles from their armpits. By comparison we were a pair of boringly decadent rich bitches.

"This looks like fun, doesn't it?" said Ruth imploringly.

"It's stupid," Danny whined.

After that we were quiet while hurtful thoughts collected like black crows under a silver sky. Ruth is always hopelessly vulnerable where Danny is concerned. She started trying to entice him by pointing out the brightly coloured caravans, and the cute dog with a studded collar which she was sure was part of an act.

Danny grew mutinous. This place was boring, he was too hot, he wanted some lemonade, he wanted to spend the fiver I'd given him.

But Ruth had grown obstinate. "We'll get everything inside," she said.

I kept out of it and started thinking of other circuses I'd seen. An acrobat who could teach you new thoughts about gravity, a girl balanced on a pony's back, trapeze artists seizing each other from the jaws of death, the uncompromising stares of a chimpanzee family, sawdust, knife throwers, the lion escaping into the streets of Dublin, Tristram Long with his ringmaster's boots and whip teaching me new tricks.

"Sorry, sorry!" I hadn't been paying attention. Danny must have shouted a dozen times. I realised that the crowd around us had begun to disperse. People were grumbling. A woman with jangly gold earrings was closing the ticket booth. A clown with white tennis shoes stuck a notice saying HOUSE FULL onto the tent flap and Ruth had vanished.

I pretended I didn't hear Danny say, "Fuck it, anyway" as he rubbed his eyes. I can't bear to see children cry.

"It's Mama's fault," he said. His face was as grave as a High Court judge's. I never noticed before how much he resembled Clive. He's the spit of him.

14

"Don't be silly," I said briskly.

"She and Dada were fighting before we came out," he went on.

I didn't want to know about it. "We'll find your mother on the way home. Bet you anything," I offered. And I was right, Ruth hadn't gone very far. We caught up with at the top of William Street.

"Sorry, Dixie." She climbed into the car. I saw she was shaking. When we got to Evergreen I went in with her to have a drink. "God knows, we deserve it," she said seriously. We sat back on her velvet sofa with gin and tonics in our hands. I know this house almost as well as my own. The rooms are the same shape, the corridors as substantial, the windows are as fine and they look out onto similar vistas of shrubbery and flower-beds.

Ruth sighed, then sat back and squeezed her eyes tightly closed. "I wish, I wish, I wish," she said.

"Wish what?"

"Wish I'd been brave enough when Danny was born to let everyone know the truth about his father. I think it would have turned out better all round if we'd all been more honest and open."

"Don't be a fool, Ruth. Think of the kids." I reacted fiercely.

"I am thinking of them. Look at Peter and Jane," she said.

Then we sat in silence finishing our drinks.

20th August: We spent today in Kilkee. Our visit coincided with an annual festival. Scraggy horses ran races on the strand. Crowds shifted around the wheel of fortune. Foam whispered and nibbled the shoreline. Kilkee had been the only place we could afford to go to on holidays in the early years of our marriage. I spent several Augusts in dark draughty houses, knee-deep in nappies and wet swimsuits.

As Clive and I sauntered along by the bandstand he started to talk about our proposed holiday with the Whites. He mentioned Greece and became enthusiastic about columns and temples, building systems, classical proportions and recent discoveries about ancient heating methods. The stuff of architectural reviews. But suddenly I wanted something else. I groaned, saying, "I don't feel like that sort of trip at all. I'm sick of always going abroad with Ruth and Alan."

Clive looked as if I'd punched him in the stomach. A crowd were throwing mop heads at oil cans for worthless prizes. "Have a go, sweetheart!" A roulette man with a gypsy face and a leather hat leered at me. I told Clive I wanted to walk on my own and hurried up towards the rocks where swimmers bask between dips. There I perched on a slab and stared out over the green ocean and down at people playing racquets against the sea wall.

In the distance I could see Clive, across the crescent of the bay. He was wearing a white yachting hat I'd picked up for him in a Christmas sale. I tried to articulate the emotion I'd felt when he started talking about Greece, but I failed. Then Anne, with Bridget White in tow, called over the sea wall asking me to come with them up to the

Pollock Holes. They had splurged on shrimp nets and wanted to relive what they called their young days.

At six o'clock we all met up in Scott's pub where I contemplated the poster of Mrs Elsie Dyson, the Bovril Venus of nineteen-thirty-seven, which had been pinned against a shelf for as long as I've been coming here. I wondered what sort of complications Elsie had had in her private life. Did she have children and a lover? How did her husband feel about her exposing herself in a sepia brown swimsuit?

It was Anne who mentioned the smell, wrinkling her freckled nose exaggeratedly. We speculated in whispers as to whether it was air freshener or some deadly, ozone-destructive window cleaner. The mystery was solved when it turned out to be a bottle of cheap perfume which Clive had won at the mop-head stall and which had broken in his pocket.

24th August: I dressed myself up and went to the agricultural show which is held at the racecourse towards the end of August. The sky was calm and blue and routes to the entrance were choked with traffic. I parked halfway down the South Circular Road and decided that I would travel the rest of the way to the showground on foot.

Clive had not pursued the idea of an autumn holiday. However, brochures of new destinations appeared on the hall table every day. With the arrival of each one I became more determined not to participate. If all came to all Ruth could go off with the two men on her own. I didn't care. They could do whatever they liked. Even a solitary week in a health farm getting myself into shape (for what? I suddenly thought) seemed a more enticing prospect.

It was one of my restless days. I wished I was a man, out in the world, arranging things. Or, not exactly a man, but better educated so that I could aim for some exciting new horizon. A bit late in the day, Dixie, I chided myself as I abandoned making a lemon cheesecake at the whipping the cream and egg whites stage. I scraped everything into the bin, dressed myself up and left the house looking for something or someone.

My walk up to the racecourse brought me past the gate of Rosepark House. The main wall of the largest wing had been painted but the roof still sagged. Twenty years ago that roof used to worry Clive and me. On windy nights every creak and rattle convinced us that it was about to cave in and bury us alive.

It was the first house that we lived in when we came to Limerick. We could eventually have bought it for peanuts but it was too ungainly, too dilapidated, too ugly with its yard walls flush with the road. A back-to-front house, its imposing entrance porch facing out over grassy hummocks towards the racecourse.

Today I peeped through the bars of the small gate as the side entrance which leads to our old hall-door. There are highly coloured flower-beds where I'd had only weeds and a long clothes-line. Clive moaned about the clothes-line, asking me to remove the nappies at sun-down to make the place less of an eyesore on a summer's evening. A few years ago, in Spain, I saw a young woman with a tired stoop pinning up a line of those almost obsolete white towelling squares. Flags of surrender to drudgery. My heart went out to her.

"I suppose you'd like me to dig the garden too, while you sit around like Lord Muck," I'd shout.

When we moved into Rosepark House Clive swore that it would just be for a month or two. We ended up living there for five years. My stomach muscles clenched with an old ache as I gazed in at the display of hollyhocks and dahlias. Whoever owns that garden now has more spare time than I had. I wished them luck.

Clive once slapped me in that house and I went for him like a fishwife. Clive was more frightened by the incident than I was. He hates violence. (Maybe he's always been afraid to broach the subject of our splitting up in case I try to kill him.) Even at the time I didn't blame him for the slap. I had provoked him beyond endurance in revenge against a miserable house-bound day of cranky children and unending rain. I was sick of a draughty house with broken floor boards and inadequate plumbing. All the children had tummy aches.

"Next time I'm walking out," I warned, though I had nowhere to go except back to my ageing parents.

I remembered how hot and dry his hand felt as he reached out to me in apology. I remembered pushing him away.

"This is the end of the road, Clive," I'd said and we stared at each other in mute desperation.

"What the hell are we going to do?" asked

Clive softly.

But next day things had changed. It was as if our confrontation had acted as a catharsis. In the morning a phone call confirmed Clive's first big assignment. We were saved. We need never look back.

I moved away from Rosepark's gate and those shoestring years. Our problems are of a different nature now. At least in Rosepark House we were, willy-nilly, totally involved in getting by. There was no need to look for outside excitement. A glance at our overdraft was enough to get our hearts racing, our hands to grab at each other for support.

And on good days the sun streamed through the front door and the children played long involved games on the front step. And there were minor triumphs; like Christmas dinner cooked in the poky kitchenette, and a woman who arrived on horseback for afternoon tea. There were flagons of cider shared with Clive in the woodworm-riddled sitting-room.

When I got into the showgrounds I could see the house facing me across the racetrack. It made me smile. It's such a cheat of a house with its bare rump exposed to the public road instead of its pretty facade. I stared at the window of what was once our bedroom and had an unexpectedly vivid recollection of Clive and I fumbling for each other through layers of flannelette as we burrowed for comfort in our freezing bed under a dangerously sagging ceiling. And a mouse that ran across our blankets as the city church bells rang in a frosty New Year. Our startled laughter. The kids with measles and myself pinning old sheets across the windows because we hadn't money for curtains. Was that happiness or was it just being young?

The first person I bumped into at the show was our bank manager, Brendan Collins. He naturally assumed that I was looking for Clive. He brought me into the bank's hospitality tent in supposed search for him. (I knew that Clive couldn't possibly be there. He had gone to Kerry to see a client.)

"Won't I do instead?" Brendan pressed a tumbler of whiskey into my tiny hand. This was an old line of his.

"Oh, sure."

"But when? When!" Brendan's moustache tickled my ear lobe as the golden liquid trickled through my body. It was very strong. My toes started to tingle right away.

"When what?" I joined the game, acting as if I didn't understand.

"You and me, Dixie. Anytime, any place. You name it." He rocked back and forth on the soles of his feet.

A man wearing a brown hat butted in saying, "God, Brendan, you're a terror for the women."

Brendan smirked. "What do you say, Dixie?"

"Don't let this chancer fool you, Missus." The intruder gave me a sharp nudge.

I looked at him. He had hairs sprouting from his ears and his nose was navy blue. "What makes you think I'm a Missus?" I asked. "I bet you don't know that I'm a millionairess in from New York."

"Right so." Brown hat looked at a loss and shuffled away.

"You bested him, Dixie. Fair dues to you. The biggest horse dealer in County Limerick," Brendan said admiringly as we watched him go. "That's what I like about you," he went on, staring hard at me, "you're direct. You know what you want. And," he gave a heavy sigh, "did anyone ever tell you you were sexy?"

I burst out laughing. "Lots of times," I said. I felt reckless. What the hell! He'd be a change from Alan. And I'm sick of compromising. I'm sick of playing along with Clive and the Whites.

"You're a bit of all right yourself," I offered. And he was, in a pale brown suit with a red carnation in his buttonhole.

Brendan leaned forward. He has the greenest eyes I've ever seen. As green as woodland sorrel.

"Let's fix up a date," he said. "I don't often get the chance of talking to you without that gouger of a husband hanging around."

"That'd be nice," I said. It was the first time I'd felt cheerful for days.

"Good woman yourself," said Brendan. "I knew there was hope for me." He caught me and gave me a quick warm kiss, then winked and said, "I'll be in touch."

5th September: "Dixie, I hope it's all right for me to go off like this?" Clive sounded a little plaintive as he packed up for a trip to Egypt. He was travelling alone to an architectural conference. It was an opportunity that had unexpectedly presented itself and I had encouraged him to go on his own. It would divert him from the home situation. He and Alan have been carrying on like a pair of Victorian patriarchs about Peter and Jane. "Students how are you!" Clive grouses. "They get away with murder. When I think back to my student days!" Then he stops abruptly as he remembers how it worked out for him.

"Why are Mr and Mrs White making a fuss about Jane and me?" Peter asked me this morning.

Were they!

"Don't they like me anymore?" Peter's hair looks as if he's just done a job on it with a kiddie scissors. I patted his head.

"It's because of what we think the two of you were up to in that poky sleeping tent. It's been worrying me as well," I said.

Peter looked mystified and then affronted as he said, "Gee, you must have really dirty minds." Somehow, I felt unconvinced.

6th September: Grey, stormy day. I reached for Brendan Collins's hand as we walked along a cliff path high up over the Atlantic ocean.

"So Clive's gone off to Egypt," he said.

Rain began to spit against our faces and quickly thickened into a steady downpour. I tasted salt on my lips.

"It was supposed to clear up," Brendan said crossly. He was wearing a tweed jacket with the collar turned up and a check cap flat on his head. The weather made even his amazing eyes look colourless.

"This is bloody awful," he said after we'd struggled on for a few more yards. I marvelled at our optimism in heading out to visit the coast on such a threatening day.

He'd phoned me first thing this morning to say that he'd heard about Clive going abroad. His own wife, Phyllis, had left him at a loose end too. She was attending a bridge congress in Portugal.

"So how do you feel about playing hooky?"

I'd felt agreeable.

But as we stopped and faced out briefly towards the vast churning ocean all I wanted to do was to go home again. This was no day for grassy hillsides or dalliance in a honeysuckle-scented grove. We retraced out steps to the car, my wet skirt clinging nastily to the backs of my legs.

The car was parked outside a higgledy-piggledy bungalow. There was a large shed beside it from which came a raucous cackling chorus.

"Geese," said Brendan opening the car.

It sounded as if they were laughing at us. Brendan put the key in the ignition and turned it on to silence. We glanced at each other. He made a few more attempts with nothing more happening than a flutter of moths' wings. Driving here he had turned the lights on during a heavy shower and forgotten to extinguish them. The battery was completely flat.

After long loud banging on the door of the bungalow the inhabitants opened it. They sniffed at the weather conditions and were reluctant to come to our help. Brendan began to look like a man in pain. At last the rain eased and the couple agreed to see what they could do.

The man was a huge figure with a heavy black beard. He wore a torn red jumper and he had a broken wrist so his right arm was in plaster. I had the sensation of having seen him before as a brigand in a film about pirates. The woman was much younger. A proper goose-girl with a blonde pigtail hanging over one shoulder, her feet stuck into dirty wellington boots.

Because of his wrist the man could only give advice while the goose-girl and I grunted and pushed at the back and Brendan did what he could with the driver's door open, one hand on the steering wheel, his feet slipping on the muddy verge.

Just as we'd started to move the goose-girl screamed and jumped away from the car towards her own gate. A small child had come scampering full speed down the front path.

After two more false attempts we got going. I trotted after the moving car with the child's wails and the cackle of geese deafening my ears. We went straight to a pub and revived ourselves with several hot whiskeys. Anything further was out of the question. I was home at six o'clock. In time to empty the dishwasher and make potato salad for the tea.

7th September: I woke up feeling sore and bone weary. It took me a moment to remember pushing Brendan's car. I felt as if some vital part of my own anatomy had been burned out. So much for treats from your friendly bank manager.

I looked across at Clive's empty bed and pondered over something that has always bothered me. Why have I never been able to make a grand plan for my own life that actually worked? I can't even plan a successful day out. Today, not yesterday, was the one on which Brendan and I should have gone to the coast. The sun sparkled non-stop. In the afternoon I sat in the garden, watching for the pheasant which didn't materialise. Then I began to think about Clive. I remembered how scared I'd been on my wedding day in case he left me standing at the altar. I've always owed him for that. But I'm getting nervous. Ruth is beginning to worry me.

She has started telephoning the house and hanging up when I answer it. I know it's her because when the children take it she says things to them. I don't know what. "Nothing. She didn't want anything. She was just worried." They're infuriatingly vague.

One thing that has happened is that I've completely gone off Alan. The thought of sleeping with him gives me the creeps. I think of it as a bad habit which now disgusts me. I know that Clive and I don't have much of a sex life these days, but I'd rather be starved for it than continue on with Alan.

Our relationship was one of those things that happened without much thought. Like emigrating without bothering to discover anything about your destination. It's an adult affair and it has run its course. His swarthiness and macho charm seemed exciting when we first met. The idea of a real proper Lothario had always appealed to me. Alan seemed to be the genuine article, besides my nose was getting out of joint from trying not to sniff out Clive and Ruth's secrets. Now, even being charitable, I find him irritating and too much of a bully. I hope Brendan Collins asks me out again.

## Chapter Three

12th September: Clive has been away for a week and it feels like a lifetime. This morning was cold, the sky glassy, as I sat at the kitchen table drinking coffee and listening to the ticking kitchen clock. Finn, our golden cocker, lay hunched beside the range. I'd expected to hear from Brendan Collins but there has been no word. His wife must be back by now.

I wondered if Clive had met any attractive women on his travels. Of course, he's not as handsome as when I married him. His beard is thinner, his hair has receded, the tip of his nose has sharpened, his face sags after a late night or the act of love. I wonder what Brendan looks like after making love. Does it drain the colour from his eyes? Tristram Long used to get the shakes, but that was because of his heart condition. I was so young and foolish that I didn't believe Tristram's heart condition could be fatal until it killed him.

I wondered if it's as hot in Egypt as it was that September, some years ago, when we went to the Holy Land. That trip was different from our usual vacations. It came about because of a misunderstanding with Clive's uncle, Monsignor Patrick. He happened to visit us just as we were in the throes of deciding where to go.

Monsignor Patrick is a well-meaning, autocratic tyrant. He has travelled most of the globe and has contacts everywhere. He pounced on our latest guide books and decreed that we must visit Israel. In jigtime he had mesmerised us into putting our names down for a pilgrimage to Jerusalem followed by a stay in Tiberias. It was an up-market package deal being organised by some of his clerical friends.

All we could do was bow our heads and go quietly. Alan was in the process of negotiating a big property deal with Monsignor Patrick's religious order and Clive thinks his uncle is equal to the voice of God. Neither of them were prepared to tell Monsignor Patrick that the trip was not at all what we wanted and in Monsignor Patrick's world what women say doesn't count.

It was a very quiet holiday. Our hotel in Tiberias had no air-conditioning and paddle fans whirred all night. My dark hair and eyes made the Arabs mistake me for a Jewess. One time I got separated from the others and a group surrounded me. I was poked at obscenely and one nasty character hawked phlegm and spat at my feet.

I felt Jewish. I felt defensive and alone. My only feelings of kinship were for the uniformed girls who carried guns over their shoulders. Dark-eyed, sallow-skinned, smooth-lipped, glossy-haired, their hair even blacker than my own, they reminded me of my daughters.

Peter is the only member of our family who has pale skin and sandy hair. When he was born my mother inadvertently gave an adequate explanation. He was the image of her brother, poor Bertie, who went to Canada. The identical look around the mouth and eyes, and the same snub nose. Fortunately my mother never had any reason to think of Tristram Long as other than "that poor lonely widower with the handy little shop."

I have decided that all this harping back to Tristram is a bad habit that has crept up on me. It must stop. I never had time to brood in the early years. First there was Rosepark House and one, two, three little sisters for Peter. Then, when Anne was three months old, we moved to Bella Vista.

I remember staggering through those months in a state of permanent exhaustion. The three young children and the new baby seemed to have been sprung on me as unexpectedly as mushrooms. I was still in my mid-twenties. I spiralled from cooker, to table, to clothes-line, to potty training, round and round with corkscrew determination. Weariness streamed from my bones. Regret for anything was impossible. Besides, what was there to regret? Peter! Oh, no.

Alan and Ruth were next door. New house, new friends, new money, fresh possibilities. Gradually, it seemed it was possible to have fun and be married at the same time. Even after Danny was born it was still fun. Even the Holy Land, at the beginning, was fun.

The start of our stay in Tiberias was a joke. The place we stayed in was little more than a hostel. In the upstairs lounge there was a large communal refrigerator. The lounge was nothing but an open space furnished with green-topped tables and squeaky rattan chairs. After the other guests had gone to bed Clive and Alan would rendezvous in front of the refrigerator, ostensibly to get themselves some late night iced water. As soon as they were certain that the coast was clear Clive would dash off to Ruth while Alan made his way to my bed. Or, rather, the other narrow monkish couch beside my own.

"Holy God...this place is driving me insane. I feel like a Christian brother on a night out." At first Alan's grouchiness was comic.

Meanwhile Clive and Ruth...But I mustn't speculate on Clive and Ruth, I quickly trained myself during the fun years to sidestep any disturbing aspects of the situation. How could we solve it? All of us sell up and emigrate! With all nine children!! Time would have to take care of everything. Time was the great healer. Least said soonest mended. Men have died and the worms have eaten them, and so on.

But Alan's grouchiness changed into something nastier and more intense. He grew critical of me. I found him irritating. After his early morning bath he'd appear pink and squeaky clean as a doll on a toy shop shelf to whip off the sheet and pinch my bottom spitefully. "You snored," he'd say. "You're getting fat." Temper gave his chubby face a roseate glow. His breath blew cold puffs of peppermint into my face. "You're showing your age, Dixie," he said. Afterwards, when we came home, he was repentant and contrite. We've even had fun holidays since, but the Holy Land gave me a taste of Alan's nastier side.

On our last night Clive and Ruth went their own way and Alan and I headed together for one of the piano bars. There he left me sitting in a corner while he danced with all the young girls.

When the two English misses walked in Alan made for them like a bee to clover. One wore an ankle-length paisley dress and had a mop of deep gold curls. The other, whose hair was a rippling amber waterfall, was more casually attired in blue denim. Alan became very excited, see-sawing between the pair of them, his white shoes flashing faster than the piano keys, his paunch vibrating to the strumming of an orange guitar. Eventually, red-faced, his hair standing on end, the girls led him over to my corner.

"I hope your husband is all right," they said. "We were only having some fun."

"Fun." The word took on sinister connotations. Alan's head lolled to one side, like a man with his head in a tightened noose. His eyes had closed.

"We'd better loosen his collar." The girl in the paisley dress became brisk and efficient. She and her friend were nurses who had taken a year off to go tramping through the Middle East and on to Greece and Turkey.

Alan shook himself and sat up. I squeezed his hand. It felt like a lump of plasticine.

"Are you all right, dear?" My tone was mischievous and sarcastic. It sparked off flames of bright anger. Of course he was all right. What the hell was I talking about? Didn't I want to see him having a good time? I was worse than any wife. In the middle of his tirade the girls slipped away. I wished that I could do the same but I had to haggle for a taxi and take him back to our stuffy room. Once there the situation got worse. Suddenly Alan moved in on me roughly, without warning. His harsh breath blew hot and sour on my face.

I moved fast, jabbing my knee up hard between his legs. Our struggle became more silent and deadly. I remember the smell of the green tiled floor, a mixture of disinfectant and smoke. And a moment of fright before Alan released me saying, "Dixie, you're a dangerous bitch."

In the morning we were both subdued, until Alan, his mouth full of croissant, mumbled, "For once I'll be glad to get back to married life." We sheathed our swords and resumed our friendship. We would soon be going home. There seemed no point in turning our skirmish into a major battle.

24th September: Today as I went downstairs I heard a clicking noise coming from the study. I walked in and found Clive on his exercise bicycle. His eyes stared ahead and he pedalled through his own private dream. He's been in a filthy mood since he came home.

Last night, as we sat in our front sitting-room he got up from his chair, walked over to the wall and pounded a fist against the golden marigolds on the wallpaper. He looked lost. I felt sorry for him, but apprehensive. Later, upstairs, he came into my bed and tried to initiate sex. It's something we haven't done much of lately. When we do I try my best to please but last night I kept being distracted by night-time sounds. A tomcat's wail, a ship's hooter, something fluttering against a window pane, footsteps running along the garden path under our window.

At last he stopped, sat up awkwardly and said into the darkness, "I want a divorce." Just like that!

I immediately answered, "You know as well as I do that divorce is out."

"I'll move away," he said. "I'll go and live someplace else."

I knelt up and shook his shoulder. "Uncle Patrick would have a fit."

"We wouldn't be the first couple to split up," he said.

"You'll be in a state of mortal sin. Uncle Patrick won't be pleased."

"I'm not a bit religious anymore, I've lost all that," Clive said harshly.

"How do you think Ruth will feel if you smash everything up? How do you think she coped the time Danny was born? It was because she could continue on as Mrs Alan White. I know Ruth. You'll destroy her if you force her to change everything now. We've managed OK so far, Clive."

"We'll see," Clive whispered into the darkness while I trembled, not for Ruth's fears but for my own.

This morning I watched as circles of sweat widened on his white vest. I saw him as a reincarnation of a mediaeval monk flagellating his body until there was nothing left but a husk.

Clive: I have always pulled the wool over your

eyes. I remember the first time the four of us went away together. It was to Paris. On Sunday we lunched in the Flea Market. There was a fat waiter and an old fortune teller with a red skirt and wicked black eyes. We sat like conspirators around a bottle of green chartreuse. We had been in the city for two days and the tension between us was practically smoking. Suddenly you turned to Ruth and seized her in a passionate embrace, falling on her like a man who has just reached an oasis in a desert. The waiter, the fortune teller and some onlookers clapped and you, lifting your head, a shocked expression on your face, burst into tears. Ruth rested her head on folded arms. Under the table Alan's thigh rubbed against mine and our eyes met.

It was Alan who masterminded the rest of the afternoon. When we returned to our hotel he said without preamble, "Dixie!" and I was whisked off in the wrought iron cage of a lift to his bedroom. It was a small room, stuffier than our own. A blue shirt belonging to Alan was draped on a wicker chair. Ruth's red umbrella was propped in a corner. I had been with her when she bought it from a stall outside Galeries Lafayette. Alan opened the window and let in the deafening noise of a pneumatic drill. I found I was shaking with a wild rather sleazy excitement.

"Is this wise?" It was hard to sound sensible and shout. Our lunchtime wine and the green chartreuse made laughter bubble inside me. Then I hiccuped which made me giggle and all was lost.

"Jaysus, Dixie, lie down this minute on that bed unless you want me to have a seizure." Alan charged like a prize bull.

His hands were very hot and urgent; so was his tongue. By the time he was finished I was trembling from head to toe and being lapped by waves of ice and fire.

"You're a cracker. Anyone ever tell you that?" Alan lifted his head from the pillow. I shook my head lazily, feeling myself orbit in space. Then lightly I bounced back to earth and said, "What's going to happen now?" I didn't much care.

Alan gave my shoulder a smacking kiss, saying, "I've been watching Clive sniff around Ruth for months. This'll show them we're quicker off the mark than they are. Right?"

"Is that all?" I felt like a kitten being dipped into a bucket of water. "I thought you liked me. I like you," I said bravely.

"I'd fancy you anyway," Alan said lazily, "and there's nothing wrong with two mature adults having a good time."

Today Clive wasn't having a good time on his exercise bicycle. As soon as he caught sight of me he stopped and climbed off.

"Don't overdo it," I cautioned.

He stepped backwards onto a pair of clogs which were thrown carelessly on the floor. His face contorted as he picked one of them up and hurled it at the mantelpiece. It and the blue glass fish skidded along the wall and onto the ground. We stared at each other. Then I went off to get a sweeping brush and a dustpan.

29th September: As a mother all I've ever wanted is the best for my children. Because of them I gladly make sacrifices. I also realise that life is freer than when I was growing up. People can do things openly now that were dark secrets for my generation. The rules have changed. I'm not complaining but I wonder if other people ever feel as muddled as I do.

When Peter and Jane headed off with rucksacks and tent for the West of Ireland all any of us did was grumble a little. And there was nothing secret about the trip. I suppose we were caught off guard.

When I asked casually, "Who's going with you?" and Peter answered with matching nonchalance, "Oh, I suppose Jane will," all I could manage was "Jane...Jane White?" What other Jane was there?

I tried to imagine myself and Tristram snuggled together under canvas. No way. Our world would have caved in and anyway Tristram would probably have developed bronchitis. I'd probably have ended up incarcerated in a home for fallen women.

A while ago Peter said we must have dirty minds because we queried the situation that was created by them sharing a tent.

Today he said, "It's only human nature, isn't it?" and, "Jane knows that if she's going to have a baby I'll help her to take care of it."

This was said to me while I was cleaning out a food mixer. At first I was so preoccupied with blades and grease spots that his words didn't register. Then it clicked. "Baby. What baby? Tell me I'm hearing things." I wasn't. Jane was pregnant. "No need to lose your cool, Ma," Peter said. "She's not dying. She hasn't got AIDS or anything. It's only a baby."

Later Jane called and he brought her upstairs. I listened as his door closed. After thirty oppressive minutes I could stand it no longer. I charged up, rushed across the landing and after the quickest tap pushed my way in. Peter and Jane were sitting cross-legged on the carpet playing Fish-in-the-Pool. By the expression on their faces I became convinced that the cards were a decoy.

"Of course we've been playing cards. What do you think this is?" Peter spoke as if I was feeble-minded while Jane gathered them into a pile.

Jane is very pretty in a different way from Ruth. It is a hazy, appealing, defenceless prettiness. Today she was all mussed hair and flushed cheeks. She wore a baggy sweater identical to Peter's.

"Hello, Jane," I said, trying to sound normal. "I'm a bit shattered by your news...if it's true... that you're having a baby. How are you going to take care of it? Have you thought about that?"

Peter sighed. His window was pushed wide open. I clambered past them and banged down the sash. The temperature in the room was arctic. "You'd need to keep it shut. There's a draught going right through the house," I said.

Silence and the slap of cards. Peter chuckled.

"Aaah!" Jane gave an anguished howl. "You're so mean. It's not fair. I can't win."

"I'm a genius," Peter said. I heard scuffles. When I turned round he was crouched beside Jane trying to give her a bear hug.

"I'm sorry, Aunt Dixie. We're in your way." Her voice came muffled through the wool of their entangled arms.

I loomed over them while their faces peeped up at me, smooth, wide-eyed, solemn, infuriating. "Is it all a joke?" I asked. "Is this something you're making up for a laugh?"

Jane pouted. "I'm sorry, Aunt Dixie. I don't want to be any trouble."

In the distance the telephone rang. It was Alan. He was stuttering with rage. He had to talk to me, myself, urgently. He was going out to look at a house in County Clare. He'd be glad if I'd come along. Had I heard the latest? Didn't that beat all? What the fuck did Jane think she was at, getting herself up the pole?

"I'd like to strangle that son of yours," he said in the car.

"Not to mention Jane," I shot back.

He groaned, "Bugger it! Ruth's going round the bend. She was bad enough beforehand. Come on, I've got to get out of here."

Our destination was a property a couple of miles outside Lisdoonvarna which Alan had for sale. The last occupants were two cantankerous brothers who died within a month of each other. It was in pretty bad shape, but there were some details that Alan claimed would sell it.

The bedrooms all had wrought iron fireplaces with art deco tile surrounds. The windows were finished off with deep low window seats. And there were presses and cubby holes everywhere. This, it seemed, would compensate for lack of heating and rusty plumbing.

The last room we went into was a back kitchen. The sort of place where people would once have prepared mash for hens, stored fuel, steeped household linen, or boiled up a broth for workmen. There were still the remnants of a stove in a corner. Close to it was an old-fashioned mangle. A galvanised washtub with its bottom rusted away was propped against the opposite wall.

Our kids hadn't been mentioned since we crossed the threshold. As we stood in this gloomy chamber I was just about to bring up the subject when Alan said, "Dixie, let's..."

I wasn't paying attention. "I'd like to kill the pair of them," I said ruefully and at the same moment Alan pounced.

His face was flushed and his eyes grew narrow and piggish. Over Alan's shoulder I could see a small picture of a recent Pope tacked onto the shutter of a poky, cobwebbed window. Its faded gaze was still hawk-like and withering. I screamed and screamed again.

There was an iron bar propped against the wall. Luckily I managed to grasp it and thwack it across Alan's back. He faltered and I managed to wriggle free. We stood panting. My coat was streaked with white.

"Bloody marvellous," I said. "What are you trying to do? Kill me!"

"You're the one with the poker. What's this, the League of Decency?" asked Alan furiously. "Since when did you get so fussy?"

"Forget it," I said but I was suddenly shivering.

"Come on. This place is giving me the horrors," he announced.

We went from there to a hotel. The place had

been tarted up with red moquette and brass trimmings. Alcoves were padded with cretonne leatherette and matching velour. I remembered the place from the fun years when it had been the genuine article, full of priests on holiday, and four-course lunches, maroon and white tiled floors, sparse bedroom furniture. The bar had been noted for its high-quality Guinness.

Today Alan returned his pint with a complaint. The frothy top was pancake thin. The tonic I poured into my gin had lost its fizz. We drank in silence. I was sorry to be there, sorry for myself, sorry to have placed myself in such an invidious position.

"What about Jane and Peter?" I ventured. The silence was too much for me.

Alan shrugged sullenly.

I picked up the brightly coloured list of cocktails priced at four pounds each. "What would you like?" I asked, reading from the card, "Family Special, Dirty Mother, or Secret of the Sea."

Before Alan could reply we were approached by a young, dark, spruce manager in a grey suit. Could he inquire if we were interested in a room for the night at a very special rate? As we glared at him his salesman's smile faded into a frantic facial tic and he ran for cover.

30th September: After lunch, while I was putting the plates into the dishwasher, Peter came up behind me and told me that he wasn't going to go back to college.

"Why not?"

"You know why." He sounded petulant.

"Because of Jane?" I felt more at a loss than ever.

"It's because I want to live a real life."

"How are you going to manage that? Digging ditches? Breaking stones?"

"Anything would be better than college," he said.

I took a deep breath. If I said anything I'd say too much. I pushed past him, feeling a deep affinity with ostriches.

I hurried up to the privacy of our bedroom. I had a million things to do. I had to go into town to shop. Suits of Clive's needed to be collected from the cleaners. I tugged open the wardrobe door and looked at my clothes. I wanted to howl with rage. I had to get myself into town and then come home and prepare a chicken for the pot. Coq au vin was on the menu for tonight. I wished something good would happen, a nice surprise, an unexpected treat. I wanted to spoil myself.

I dallied in front of the dressing-table mirror, searching for straggly eyebrows, fresh creases, grey hairs. Give me another ten years and I'd be a sly silver vixen. Our dressing-table is a long, built-in affair, taking up a large part of one wall. Its fluorescent lighting made me look like a blanched and withered prune. It highlighted the tiny lines webbing my eye sockets. I experienced the nervous frisson women of my age get when they look into a mirror and find their mother's astonished face looking back at them.

"I'm afraid your father is going to get very upset." My mother's face mouthed my mother's words. On an impulse I gathered up all the tubes and jars, the creams and salves, cucumber balm, witch hazel, eye drops, ear drops, sun screens and other beauty aids and stuffed them into a plastic bag destined for the bin in the back yard.

My mother is a victim of Alzheimer's disease. I hadn't visited her for weeks. When I do go it seems to make no difference. She doesn't know who I am. At least I wasn't going to have to explain this kettle of fish to her. I rehearsed what I was going to say to Clive about Peter's newest announcement.

I knew that I'd end up by trying to put the situation in a favourable light. I'd say how the young need to experiment, to find themselves. I'd suggest that if we were not paying college expenses we should give him some financial help. As for Jane's baby...that was going to be a more delicate matter altogether. I felt old wounds opening. I saw Clive's face the night I told him that I was having a child.

I stood in the backyard after dumping all my cosmetic gunge and shivered. I wanted to think clearly but my thoughts were held in an awful trembling paralysis. "History repeats itself." "Life's a sick joke." My mind zigzagged uselessly. I contemplated shaking Peter into some sort of maturity by telling him the true story of his own conception and the very notion gave me stage fright. Surely, I'd atoned for all that by now.

My past flashed through my mind like a tape being rewound. I'd cheated Clive right at the beginning and he'd been too honest himself to suspect me of lying. It never occurred to him that Peter could be anybody's child but his. "I'll do my

best, Dixie. I promise you that," he'd said. Once
he said tentatively, "I never knew it could happen
after only one time." And immediately he put an
arm around my shoulders and said, "Don't ever
hate me for it, Dixie. Man is not long out of the
jungle. I'll make it up to you." He was so very
much more decent and civilised than I was that I
wanted to cradle him in my arms and kiss him
better. I'd tried to repay him by being so tolerant
about Ruth, by giving him carte blanche. But
maybe I'd just made everything worse.

I suddenly had a feeling of a shape waiting to
move from the shadows. It was similar to the
terror that gripped me the day in July when I took
the girls picnicking except that there were no
parapets or towers, only the dustbin and our own
green back door. I hurried round by the side of the
house to my car. The navy blue blinds on Peter's
bedroom were pulled down. They could stay
down. He and Jane could do whatever they
wanted to. I couldn't cope with this all on my
own.

I drove into town with the car radio blaring
pop music and walked up and down streets
crammed with people I didn't know. I watched
the young ones with their tattered jeans, baggy
jumpers, and spiky streaked hair. I watched how
they openly embraced and nuzzled noses. My
children's generation. A new breed.

I followed one couple into a cheap coffee place.
They sat opposite each other fondling hands, their
legs entwined under the table. He wore dark green
leather trousers, she had leggings patterned like a
zebra's hide. "She's very lucky and she's very

unlucky," the boy said. I wondered who they were talking about. It might even be Jane.

"Her mother nearly killed her," the girl said. I wondered how Ruth felt about Jane being pregnant. My son and her daughter. I decided ruefully that there was an element of poetic justice about it. Then someone rapped at the misty glass front of the coffee place. It was Brendan Collins, wearing a grey anorak that should have belonged to a Methodist clergyman. He pressed his lips in a kissing motion against the glass and right away I stopped feeling like a middle-aged frump whose children had got beyond her.

# Chapter Four

1st October: Ruth contacted me. A tearful phone call pleading, "Dixie, I'm having a bad day. Will you drop in?" and so on.

It didn't suit me at all. I was in the middle of cooking mincemeat to store in the freezer. Dried fruits, carrots, lemon juice, cooking apples, cinnamon and mixed spice simmered on the stove. The kitchen smelt of Christmas.

"Ruth," I tried to sound patient, "you'll have to be more explicit."

All I got was a whimper and Ruth saying, "I'm just back from visiting Mother."

I switched off the saucepan and left it cooling, walked down the drive from our house and up the one leading to White's. Ruth was waiting for me on the porch. She wore a pale purple tracksuit of some velvety material and clumpy triple-tied Adidas. I made a joky remark about jogging around the circle but she just stared at me blankly. I noticed how thin she had grown. She was skin and bone. When she turned around to bring me inside I saw the nasty bruise on her left cheek. It was a considerable bump. Her cheek was swollen and lumpy.

"What happened?" I demanded.

She pulled a face. "Walked into a door." She was close to tears.

"How did you manage that?"

She blew her nose on a tissue, evading my eyes. "Easy. Being awkward." Then she began to wring her hands. "It's not a bad bruise, not as bad as this business with Jane. I couldn't even tell my mother. She'd have a fit! Dixie, how could they be so stupid?"

"I don't know. I've been asking myself the same question."

"I'm disgusted. And neither of them seem to give a hoot. Jane says she's old enough to manage, that she knows lots of others in the same boat. She even says she wants the baby, while she's young— young! She's not even out of college."

"Peter's announced that he's not going back," I said.

Ruth gave me a bleak blue stare. "And I suppose you didn't object. You think he can throw it all back in your face. How does Clive feel?"

"I don't know," I admitted, it was a subject we hadn't thrashed out properly. Both of us had become overheated in seconds when we tried. Ruth moved ahead of me like a sleepwalker and, when she stumbled, it crossed my mind that she was either drunk or under sedation.

I followed her into her drawing-room. The fire was lighting, the room smelt of furniture polish, the cushions on the sofas were plumped and precise. She stooped over a big bowl full of cyclamens on a white marble table and snapped off a wilted bloom.

"How's Clive? I haven't seen him for a while." Her voice was flat and listless.

"He's pretty sore about all this, naturally," I said.

"Sore! So he should be. They've had everything, good education, lots of opportunity, the pill. They're not ignoramuses like we were at that age." She began to shake and sank down onto a sofa, saying, "Well I'm appalled. I'm disgusted. And I hold you responsible as well, Dixie. I'd have expected you to have some control over your son." She snapped this out like lines she'd rehearsed for a play.

I controlled my temper. "It takes two to make a baby so don't start any of that blaming one person rubbish," I said.

She ignored this. Instead she said harshly, "They don't give tuppence about us so why should we care about them. I hope they have no luck. I hope they live to regret everything."

I was shocked and frightened by her bitterness. "If that's all you can say I'm sorry I came in," I said.

She leaned back against the sofa cushions and closed her eyes. I waited but I felt that we had reached an impasse. When she made no move except to give a low trembling moan I walked out.

Ruth's antagonism softened my own feelings towards the young ones. In Bella Vista Jane, with her hair scraped back, the front falling into a fringe, her cheeks rosy, sat on one of my dining-room chairs as awkwardly as a palomino pony and said, "We're truly sorry about all the trouble, Auntie Dixie." She spoke seriously. When she cried tears splashed down her face.

"We'll work out something." My words came automatically. I had no idea what I meant. I didn't know which was the worst prospect: Jane trying to manage a baby or Peter as a dropout. It was a pity the Whites had ever come into our lives.

I thought of Paris. It all seemed so simple then; a bit of fun between friends. Four big children in search of excitement. All of us had married young. In our early twenties we had so little money and so many responsibilities that it hurt. The world around us was swinging. In Paris we suddenly pushed our cell doors and found that they opened at our touch, the keys had not been turned in the locks. Even the taxi drivers aided and abetted us. "Look, so beautiful!" said one.

"Oh yes, beautiful buildings," responded Clive.

"Ah, mais non, les femmes!" and that hoarse masculine Gallic chuckle.

It was true. We were beautiful then, Ruth and I, arms encircling each other's waists. Ruth's red chiffon scarf was caught by a quick breeze. My round sunglasses glinted in the sunshine.

Our hotel, a small place behind the Galeries Lafayette, was a perfect setting for our lovers' intrigue cum bedroom farce. We were guarded by a pair of middle-aged ladies in deepest black. Our tiny rooms were enlarged by mirrors. A romantic glow came from the pastel-coloured glass inset into the windows. Our tubs matched the one in which Marat was stabbed by Charlotte Corday.

After Alan had made the initial move we didn't

waste a second. Our high double beds were used as vigorously as trampolines. And we ate—oh what appetites we had! Oysters, escargots, sweetbreads in cream sauce, kidneys with tender pink centres. We were dazed with food and drink and the sights. We became extravagant. Clive bought me a fluffy pink angora jumper. Alan bought Ruth a pretty black fur-lined mack. Ruth and I bought ourselves shiny pointy-toed boots in the flea market.

We had our own rules. They came into being without discussion. We were all aware, for instance, that if Alan were to buy me gifts, or Clive to buy them for Ruth, we would have in some way endangered the arrangement.

We were laughing at the world, laughing at the pimps trying to sell us tickets for porn shows, laughing at the idea of "the most beautiful girls in the world."

"Impossible," said Ruth, "they haven't got Dixie and I."

Happy and weary we grinned at the photographs in the seedy foyers. Groups of lesbians in erotic entanglement, a naked woman on a man's back. Oh, we were titillated all right; but it only made us rush back to our rooms on winged feet.

Then, in the morning, full of earnest good humour we shopped for our children. A red sweatshirt for Peter, a cute striped bag that folded into a purse for Jane and so on down the line.

12th October. I grew more apprehensive. All I could think of were hardships and difficulties ahead. Ruth contacted me several times. Her attitude had become more venomous. I wanted to ask Clive if we could take Jane in for the duration.

I watched and waited at the breakfast table looking for my chance but it didn't come. The telephone rang, the man who occasionally does the garden arrived, Clive announced that he wouldn't be home for lunch, someone upset a mug full of tea, Finn whimpered at the back door. He had been in a fight and had a huge gash in his side.

I bundled him into my car and spent the next two and a half hours in the vet's waiting room. I passed the time by pondering on how family life blocks vital channels of communication. I would get no chance of serious discussion with Clive today. Perhaps my signs of the zodiac were positioned adversely.

The dog attended to, I stepped out into the street again. He had been given an injection and was still doped. I had to carry him in my arms. The car was parked a distance away; downhill, luckily, along by the docks. Even so, I was soon red-faced and sweaty. I was glad I had worn an old jacket but I regretted the warm woolly hat that I'd used to cover my lank hair. I'd had to cancel an appointment with the hairdresser because of the injured dog. A sideways glance into a plate glass window showed a dowdy, lumpy drab. Was that me? Then I saw Ruth coming towards me, up the hill.

I composed my face into a series of expressions. Amused, mournful, carefree, worried. However, as she came closer it seemed that she wasn't going to pay any attention to me at all. She was dressed in a cream woollen two-piece that I recognised, and a leather jacket with fringed epaulettes that I did not. She looked like somebody on her way to an exciting lunch date. I remembered that Clive was not coming home. I frantically tried to compose some casual but penetrating words of greeting that would stop her in her tracks. Then it became clear that she either hadn't seen me or was deliberately ignoring me. Her eyes remained fixed straight ahead. She moved with unwavering precision on a straight uphill line. She could have been a robot. My actual words, "What the hell!" bounced uselessly off stone. Only the dog, who felt heavier than a sack of potatoes, moaned.

I reached the car with my mind in a muddle. I felt that I was the victim of a sell-out. Alan was part of it too. When I thought about it, he and I hadn't discussed Jane and Peter either.

It was a bad time to meet Brendan Collins, but there he was getting out of his car which was parked right behind my own.

"Dixie! Dixie! When did you turn into a doggie lady?"

"Five minutes ago. I hope you're admiring my hat." I made the best of it as I opened the hatchback of the car and removed the top part so that the animal wouldn't suffocate.

"Is it alive or dead?" Brendan was at my shoulder.

"Alive, but I'm not sure about myself."

"Let's see about that." He moved in at the speed of lightning and let go as quickly. "Sweet Jesus! You smell like you'd slept with a wolfhound."

"It's fear," I said. "Animal fear."

"Woof! Woof!" Brendan flopped his arms and my tiredness vanished and I didn't feel so lonely. I pulled off my hat and shook out my hair.

"I'm like the Wreck of the Hesperus," I said.

"Not at all! Me Tarzan, you Jane." I jumped into the car and Brendan raced round to rattle the driver's door handle. Then he was off, stepping quickly around the corner and out of view.

A mood of resignation set in as I drove home. Somehow or other I'd muddle along and it would all work out. Limerick, I thought. My resignation turned to a mad hilarity. "Limerick!"

I saw myself and Clive driving up O'Connell Street more than twenty years ago. It was the first time I'd ever set eyes on the place. Clive had come down ahead of me and rented an office and made arrangements with the horsy lady who owned Rosepark House. I'd been busy clearing up the loose ends in the flat in Dublin.

Peter was fractious after the long car journey and I was jiggling him on my lap trying to keep him quiet while I took stock of my new surroundings.

"Well," Clive's voice was cold, "what did you expect? New York?"

17th October: I suppose I had an unhappy childhood, it was certainly lonesome. It must have been if running down to Tristram Long's shop for messages seemed like a social outing.

"We just paired up," Jane said to me last night. She and I were sitting on the wooden seat beside our tennis court. Neither she nor Peter have gone back to college although lectures have started. Peter is adamant that he won't go. Jane has taken the first week off.

She was cheering me up. I had reversed the Fiat into Clive's boat trailer. The bumper had become wedged under the front part and I couldn't release it. I got out, kicked the car, cursed because I couldn't get down to Anne's parent-teacher meeting and shook my fist at Clive's boat which I blamed for my misfortune. He doesn't even need a boat. I could count the number of times per year that he goes sailing on the fingers of one hand. And my back was hurting me. It had been hurting me ever since I carried the dog from the vet's.

"Everybody has someone nowadays," Jane said diffidently. "It makes life easier if you have a partner."

I considered my own experience. I'd never thought of Tristram as a partner, only as a romantic secret. Our liaison began with jokes offered across bags of sugar and pounds of sausages. He was kind, his face creased into attractive lines when he smiled. Gradually I began to dress up, to pin a flower to my blouse, to prink in front of the mirror before snatching the shopping basket from the hook on the kitchen door and charging down for the tinned peaches, peas, or whatever my mother's finicky taste had settled on.

I suppose he was one of those men who give off a special aura that attracts young girls. His being a widower set him apart from the fellows you met in offices or at dances. He knew about women.

Sometimes we danced and sometimes he played his violin. Tristram. I must be the only person who called him by his proper name. Everyone, including his dead wife, knew him as Tim.

He was in his forties; lean, sallow and with teeth so perfect that they looked like dentures. I was very green. Even so I soon realised that the ache I got in my solar plexus the minute I stepped into his orbit was caused by love. When I told him he'd blinked and backed away saying, "No, Dixie. Easy on there. You're just a kid."

It wasn't just love, it was True Love.

"Please, Tristram." I was prepared to go on my knees and beg, for True Love knew no shame.

"You mustn't, Dixie. Listen, Dixie, you're too young."

Perhaps: but I was also besotted, obsessed, on fire, crazy. I couldn't contain myself. I stole the photograph of his wife that stood on top of the china cabinet in the sitting-room and, next day, tore it up into confetti which I scattered on the waters of the River Liffey. I wanted him to marry me. I didn't care about his bad heart or the gap in our ages. I wanted him to be all mine.

I started crossing the street to avoid speaking to my girlfriends. I found it difficult to show interest in their goings on, their silly crushes. Clive sought me out and I acted hard to get. It was only to give myself an alibi that I agreed to date him.

At last Tristram took me up to the double bed in the room over the shop. A month later he went on a protracted visit to his sister in County

Longford. He departed without warning. It was my mother who imparted the news, casually, over a tea of cold ham and pulpy tomatoes which she had had to go into Moore Street to buy. I already suspected that I was pregnant. I had no way of letting him know and, in his absence, became convinced that if he did find out I was having his child he'd never want to see me again. In my fright I suddenly saw Clive as my only hope.

Tristram returned to his shop shortly after my rushed wedding. Before Peter was born he had dropped dead while carrying out a box of groceries for a customer. The news gave me a vomiting attack that the doctor said was a normal side effect of pregnancy.

30th October: Peter and Jane are both hanging around the place. If anyone mentions work or study they curl up like hedgehogs. Clive says at intervals, "Well I don't know what to think!" Neither do I. Yesterday I walked into our bedroom and caught him saying, "Ruth, Ruth my darling..." on the telephone.

On an impulse, I called into Brendan's bank where Clive and I have our account. He asked me to join him on an oyster-eating excursion. That was how I came to be sitting in Moran's of the Weir in County Galway when Monsignor Patrick walked in.

It would have been a good day if it hadn't been for the Monsignor. I tried to introduce Brendan in an offhand, casual way but my crimson face betrayed me.

Instead of leaving us to ourselves, the

Monsignor, who was accompanied by two other clerics, sat down at the adjoining table and proceeded to engage us in conversation. He seemed to think that Brendan was a brother or cousin of mine. He damned the looseness of family ties in modern society and said how good it was to see people celebrating their kinship. He reiterated that it was a great pity that Clive hadn't been able to come with us.

"Will I ever get you into bed?" asked Brendan in a moment's interlude.

The small room off the main bar where we were sitting had been done up to resemble a log cabin. The priests were all smoking cigars which made it unpleasantly stuffy. Brendan had ordered mussels for us before our dozen oysters and after eating all that he insisted that we have another dozen for good measure.

"Does wonders for the you know what." He winked a tomcat eye.

We had drunk a bottle of champagne on top of double whiskeys. I suddenly felt very ill. My stomach churned; my head was roaring. Even my own perfume stank unpleasantly in my nostrils. Faces and oyster shells swirled in confusion before my eyes. I was sure that somebody said the word "condom." It made me giggle. Brendan was waving a wad of money and insisting on buying Monsignor Patrick and his companions a drink. The Monsignor was propounding one of his many theories. With every word he spoke I grew jumpier. He was blaming television for the decline in moral values.

My eyes had hardened into marbles. The day

was lost. I had no business here. "Brendan, it's time we were off." My voice was a useless whinge. A tray of fresh drinks had just that moment arrived. Brendan and the priests ignored me. I pushed my way past them and climbed the cold staircase to the draughty toilets. There I vomited and felt better.

When I returned Brendan was loquaciously describing the best place to buy black pudding. I stood in the doorway making getaway signs at him. I was about as efficacious as the town fool.

Eventually Brendan did get the message. We went outside to discover that, once again, his car would not start. The parting speech I had quickly composed in the ladies toilet and which I planned to deliver as soon as I got within striking distance of home evaporated into absurdity.

"It's not my fault, Dixie," Brendan defended himself.

"You should buy yourself a better car."

Rooks cawing in the trees struck a black note that echoed Monsignor Patrick and his colleagues who had emerged darkly in our wake.

I fell silent and let Brendan, the priests and the raucous birds settle things between them.

Finally we left Brendan's car where it was and travelled to Limerick with Monsignor Patrick. The other two priests headed off for Galway. I sat in the back seat. Brendan and the Monsignor conversed in front like characters in the second act of a bad play. Mouthing inanities, getting nowhere. Tears of disappointment blurred my vision. I was in bits. As we reached Durty Nelly's Brendan said quickly, "Dump us off here, please,

Father. There's a barman whose brother will go up and collect my jalopy tomorrow if I give him the word."

"And how about you, Dixie? I'm sure you'd prefer me to bring you back to Bella Vista!"

"No, thanks very much."

"Oh but you must..." Monsignor Patrick actually turned and focused on me.

I stared back at him daring him to ask for an explanation. He was the first to give in. "Well then..." His shrug was the tiniest of movements. "Clive and the children all well?"

"Terrific." I clambered out of the car and ostentatiously linked my arm through Brendan's.

"You gave him the run all right." Brendan was admiring as the Monsignor drove off.

"Good riddance," I said. We were pals again. I grew more cheerful by the minute. We went into Durty Nelly's and had several drinks. Brendan's corny jokes made me laugh so much I got the hiccups. I was beginning to enjoy myself. It was Brendan who dashed away and came back looking pasty. He caught my hand and held it, but his grasp was limp. "You're better than any woman I know in this whole region," he said.

And then suddenly my fecklessness abated. I wanted to leave at once. I was full of dreadful presentiments. It was six o'clock and I had to get home.

"You're fantastic...I mean that, Dixie." Brendan's words failed to hold me.

I spotted some Americans at the pub doorway paying off a taxi driver. I rushed over without even a parting word to Brendan and gave the man the address of the city carpark where I'd left the Fiat. When I got home I repented of my rudeness.

I don't know what I'd expected to find in Bella Vista. The house on fire, perhaps. But it was as I'd left it except for some more unwashed dishes in the sink.

As I cooked supper for the family my day resolved itself into a structure composed of enjoyable secrets. It was an old sensation, an almost forgotten one. I felt like a young girl. My heart was still foolish. I wanted to kick up my heels. I had found what I wanted in the unlikeliest spot. I was cheating the system. Great! It was the only way to survive.

The telephone rang.

"It's for you, Mum," said Anne.

I picked up the receiver.

"What do you want me to do...freak out?" asked Brendan.

"I'm busy," I said. Blue smoke was rising from the frying pan.

"Bitch," said Brendan. "You have me in a frenzy. You know that, don't you?"

I hung up on him feeling pleased.

# Chapter Five

2nd November: I'm becoming the spider at the centre of a web. This evening I went to a wine and cheese party with Clive. Its purpose was to raise money for homeless people.

I stood with a cube of cheese pinioned between two grapes on a little stick in my right hand. It felt like a miniature wand. I had a glass of white wine in my left. I waved my wand and wished an evil spell. At that exact moment Ruth lifted back her head, howled, lost her balance and collapsed in an awkward heap on the floor. It could not have been because of the cheap cooking hooch we had in our glasses. I had downed several and felt one hundred per cent well.

Doors slammed and people started shouting, "Where's her husband? Who's she with?"

Alan hadn't shown up with Ruth. She'd arrived after we did, alone, and made a beeline for Clive. That's when I started having bad thoughts.

The crowd formed a circle with Ruth, paws up, lying on her back in their midst. Her head was turned to one side. A stream of cloudy fluid trickled from the corner of her mouth. "She looks sick," somebody said. At once Clive dropped to his knees beside her. I felt embarrassed because I was immediately conscious of the gasps and titters, the sudden hum of comment but Clive seemed determined to let everything go by the board. And it wasn't as if Ruth had dropped dead, for heaven's sake! A few seconds later she was being helped to a chair. Looking at her I felt annoyed. I suspected her of trying to act the tragedy queen, behaving like a prima donna, probably because of Jane and Peter.

During the remainder of the evening I conducted several lengthy conversations with busybodies. My gaze dared them to ask my opinion as to what was wrong with Ruth. "Menopausal," I'd say if asked. Clive called me over to say that we were leaving and that Ruth was travelling home with us. I recalled the moment of her collapse and how I'd deliberately wished it on her. It was a weirdly rotten thing to wish.

Back at Evergreen I sat in the car while Clive brought Ruth to her door. They whispered together for some time. It made me feel very left out, especially when, as Clive got back in to the car, I saw him smile.

"You seem very pleased with yourself," I said nastily.

"Dixie, for God's sake, you haven't the faintest idea of how I feel about anything," he replied.

"I wonder if you'd be so caring if I was the one who conked out in public," I tempted him.

"Don't be stupid." He looked perplexed.

"Naturally I was sorry about Ruth tonight, I thought you would be as well. She depends on you."

6th November: My car travelled along a country road in the wake of Ruth's. I drove slowly making sure that I was far enough behind her to avoid being spotted. When she reached her destination I pulled into a laneway. Clive's car, as I'd known it would be, was already at their trysting place. I tucked my own so safely out of sight that I didn't even scare the rat that sneaked out of a brambly ditch to nose around the verge. It was a hare, bounding from a gap in the hedge and across the bonnet of the Fiat, that sent it scurrying off.

I got out of the car and by clambering onto the bonnet was able to see the figures of Clive and Ruth steadily climbing a hill. Ruth's head was bent. Clive had his arm around her shoulders. I reached back into the car and got out the binoculars. I could see their expressions. Ruth looked sullen. Then she was obliterated by Clive's embrace. My hands tightened on the binoculars. I knew I had no business here. It was a wild goose chase prompted by God knows what dark impulse. At least, it was better than staying home crying into my coffee.

I shivered as, clasped together they sank to the wet ground. They'd get their death of cold. Ruth should push him away. Ruth should leave my husband alone. I had enough troubles. This was wrong, this was barbaric. I couldn't look away.

The binoculars had misted over. I rubbed them on the sleeve of my coat and looked again. I was the first to see the man with the gun stepping from behind a tree. I focused on him; his rough red face and piggy eyes. As he turned his back to me and headed towards them I imagined his coarse mask-like face. I sat transfixed watching him bob and leer his way up towards my husband and his mistress. I discovered that in a way I was pleased. It served them right for behaving like animals. Somebody had to stop them. I saw Ruth get up and stumble down the hill while Clive spoke to the man. Then I climbed hurriedly back into my car and switched on the engine. It felt as if I had been there for a very long time. I had a bad pain in my left shoulder. It hurt as I swung the car to the right at the end of the lane and accelerated in the direction of the city. I was surprised how, at this late stage, I had started minding about herself and Clive.

Back in the city, instead of going into Bella Vista I let myself into Evergreen by the back door, unannounced. If I'd been asked I couldn't for the life of me explain my motive. I was tired and flopped into a chair in their empty kitchen. Not a child in sight, not a sound. Sunday afternoons can be amazing; even the largest family can disappear into some domestic Bermuda Triangle. It has something to do with washing-up. Our own house would be equally deserted. Of course if I had come around by the front entrance things would have been different. I would have seen Alan's car and guessed he was at home, snoozing, in fact, in his bedroom. I felt so foully misused that I might even have gone to him, woken him, taken advantage of his afternoon randiness. Instead I waited in the kitchen, among the remains of an Irish stew and dirty plates and saucepans. After a while I heard the hall-door slam, then Ruth's footsteps.

I braced myself as she approached, then she halted. A man's voice, which I was too surprised to recognise as Alan's, called out angrily. I hesitated wondering if I should make my presence known. The man, Alan, shouted again. I suddenly felt frightened. What was I doing here? I didn't want to meet Alan. I decided to step out quietly the way I had come, but I seemed to be turned to stone.

Then Alan started roaring filthy insults. He accused Ruth of prostituting herself down the docks, of being on the game again. I heard flesh slap against flesh. My own head jerked in sympathy, but I couldn't even manage a sympathetic whimper. I remained rooted, listening to scuffles, grunts, moans, more slaps, a louder cry. Something crashed to the ground. Ruth wailed. Oh God, what had I done? I wanted to stop him but it was how it had always been between them. I had known it in my bones from the first day. I thought of my own skirmishes with Alan – his roughness in the Holy Land. I had even known then. The spell was beginning to lift. Life seeped painfully into my limbs and I was able to move.

But it was too late. By the time I got to them it was finished. He'd dragged her into their bedroom. She lay against the foot of the bed as if she had been tossed there. She stared at nothing, ignoring me, not bothering to wipe away her tears. Her clothes were pulled to pieces, I saw her pale belly, her golden fuzz of pubic hair. I struggled with my breath, wanting to apologise. Words failed me.

"What the hell..." Alan turned towards me. We stared at each other. I was the first to look away, out into the orderliness of their garden. A circular bed of red roses still in bloom even in November. I imagined eyes peeking from the rhododendron bushes.

"You're mad," I shouted to Alan. He loomed enormously between myself and Ruth. I could hear her rasping breath and my own body trembled. Then his hand was in the small of my back and he was shoving me down the corridor. Suddenly I had the wit to turn and kick him in the shins. He grabbed me with a hairy arm and I felt its flesh sticky against my tongue as I sank my teeth into it. He roared as I ducked under his arm and raced back along the passageway. Ruth was still on the floor. I seemed to be moving in a haze of small black spots. I expected Alan to burst in and murder us both but he didn't reappear. I hurried to the kitchen for ice cubes. When I got back Ruth was leaning over the washbasin. Between us we cleaned her up. She pressed the ice wrapped in a face towel against her forehead and stared at me with her good eye. That bastard had really hurt her in every way possible.

Tears dropped from my eyes as I soothed her, promising her she'd be all right.

"Don't tell Clive," she whimpered. "I couldn't bear him to know."

12th November: Yesterday Peter and Jane headed

off to Dublin. They found themselves a flat with low rent, along the quays. They laughed at me when I said it was a bad area.

I withdrew two hundred pounds from some money I had stashed in a nestegg account and gave it to Peter. He plans to draw the dole and to earn some extra cash playing his tin whistle with a group of traditional musicians who play in pub gigs. Jane has been allowed back into college. Her pregnancy is looked on as an extenuating circumstance for her late arrival. She told the authorities some story about morning sickness and personal difficulties.

Peter maintained it was because she was a brilliant student.

I haven't seen their flat but I'm sure it's a dump. I sorted out plenty of sheets and towels, a spare electric kettle, the Slumberdown from Peter's bed, cups and saucers, cleaning materials, a floor mop, a draining rack. I ransacked the kitchen cupboards for packets of soup and tins of kidney beans and macaroni cheese. I also lent them my car.

"How's your mother?" I asked Jane cautiously before they left. I felt bad for not having checked out on Ruth all week.

"She's in bed," said Jane. "She's sick."

I felt even guiltier but I was reluctant to face Alan again.

I fought with Clive about lending Peter the Fiat. "He's not covered by insurance for Christ's sake," Clive exploded. He painted a picture of a crash; the cost, Jane suing us. "And her unborn child suing us," he added to make it worse.

It had a horror movie quality. By the time that Peter phoned this afternoon to say that they'd arrived safely I was almost hysterical. "I miss you," I wept into the telephone..."mind my car. Be careful. Put it in a car park. Don't go flying around with Jane, it's too dangerous."

"Gee, Ma...don't fuss," Peter sounded bored.

"Listen, buster," I said, pushed to my limit, "that's my car and I want it back all in one piece, otherwise we're all in the poorhouse."

There was a short pause then, "Gee, Ma! You sound like you're expecting trouble," Peter said, nervously this time, and hung up.

I went back to tidying the kitchen. My brain had shrivelled to the size of a pea. The old clothes woman called to the back door and on an impulse I ran upstairs, collected two of Clive's business suits, plus a pair of casual trousers and the sheepskin coat that he wears for site meetings. I shoved them into a plastic sack and threw them out the door to her.

"Take these," I was out of breath. "You should get good money."

When she smiled I saw that she was missing another tooth and her left eye had been blackened. "I wish I could give you himself as well, they're all bastards," I said in a flush of sisterly sympathy.

She flashed me a dark look, muttered her thanks and went off pushing her pram full of lumpy bundles.

"What an absolute bloody ghastly thing to do!" said Clive who discovered the loss ten minutes after arriving home from the office.

We stared at each other in fascinated trepidation. What's to become of us at all? When he'd gone I played with the idea of going in to see Ruth but when it came to the crunch I couldn't make myself.

2nd December: I got my Fiat back from Peter last week. Early this afternoon, as I drove along the Ennis road, it gave a half-hearted chug and stopped. I pounded the steering wheel and hissed imprecations. It had been giving trouble ever since I retrieved it. Clive keeps blaming Peter although I can't see how it is his fault. The car is just growing old. Like I will, I thought dismally.

I had been on my way to the shops but the only place close by was a sub-post office with its blue blind pulled down. The blind made me nostalgic. Tristram had a blind like that on his shop door. I could see him stepping nimbly past shelves of biscuit tins to give it one deft tug downwards and there we were enclosed in a romantic shade.

Tristram: I suppose that the most times we could have had full sex was five or six. I'd thought he was safely buried but this business with Peter and Jane has returned him to me. He appears in my dreams. I am caught in moments of total recall. Funny that Clive doesn't even know that he existed. But then Clive has never known me through and through; he has never suspected the lengths that I am capable of going to. It is one of his nicer qualities.

I climbed out of the car and the freezing air whacked my ankles. I wished I was wearing boots.

I would have to trudge down the road to a small corner shop. We'd have to make do with whatever it could provide in the way of tinned vegetables and boxes of eggs.

Other people's cars whizzed past me, uncaring. I saw Alan's blue Mercedes, the arrogant tilt of his head and wished fervently that he'd come to grief. I never wanted to see him again. I didn't know if Clive had had any contact with Ruth. I'd considered telling him the whole story from the point where I went into Evergreen but Ruth had begged me to stay silent. I could understand how she felt. The more I thought about Alan's brutality, the more it seemed like something that had infected us both. Involving Clive wouldn't fix anything.

"What's wrong with you, Dixie?"

I hadn't noticed the car pulling up. But there it was with Brendan Collins jumping out of the driver's seat and hurrying towards me.

"I'm just taking a walk," I said.

"You're crazy!" Brendan shuddered. "It's below freezing. You'll get your death. Hop in, gorgeous, and I'll take you wherever you want to go."

It was cold and I hadn't even a scarf. My ears felt frost-bitten already. I looked at Brendan. He smiled, his green eyes sparkling. I thought how nice he was and my heart lightened a little.

"Is this a pick up?" I asked flirtatiously.

"If you want it to be." His breath was warm on my face.

When I climbed in, the texture of his suede coat beside me felt as comforting as a family pet. I had an impulse to stroke it and the back of his head. Instead I shrugged myself inside my own heavy tweed and said, "What I really need is a hot whiskey."

As we sat on the red leatherette seats in the suburban pub I relaxed. Phyllis, Brendan's wife, had gone on another of her all-women trips.

"Do you trust her?" I asked teasingly.

"She shouldn't trust me when there's women like you around." We eyed each other, silently making a decision.

We wasted no more time. The hot whiskey was still a comforting tickle in my gullet when I was in Brendan's house, upstairs, in Brendan's bed, which had primly starched white pillowcases and a duvet cover splashed with startling scarlet poppies.

At first I was nervous, drumming my fingers along the knobs of his spine. "Will anyone find out we're here?" I asked, playing for time.

"Ssh..." He nodded at the cul-de-sac outside the window. "This place is as safe as a morgue."

He was so warm and alive, so fleshy and vibrant, that the description made me giggle and forget the outside world as he cupped my fat breasts in his eager hands. Then it was all harmony and delight, dark waters receding and the two of us encased in a golden sphere that finally burst soft and gentle as a soap bubble when Brendan pulled himself away with a contented moan.

"I won't tell you what I heard," Brendan said after a while.

"Go on. What was it?" I felt languorous and pleased with myself.

"About you and your neighbours."

A warning bell tinkled in my brain as I said, "Some busybodies with big mouths, talking?"

"Those kids of yours. Makes me glad that Phyllis and I don't have any," said Brendan. "The White girl must be at least six months gone."

"Four," I said. I didn't know whether to be relieved or furious. "It's no concern of yours anyway," I added.

"Sure what harm is it. You're very close friends, aren't you...the Whites and yourselves?"

"Not as close as we used to be," I replied. My amorous mood evaporated. I jumped out of the bed and hurried into the bathroom and stood under the shower squeezing spongefuls of hot water over myself with, I suppose, Phyllis's sponge.

# Chapter Six

9th December: Brendan woke me up to the realisation that life was going on elsewhere. I had other children besides Peter, other responsibilities. "What are you going to do with yourself? You're sixteen. You'll have to start planning your future," I shouted at Beth over the whir of her hairdryer. I had had a letter from the head nun in the morning post explaining that it was necessary to know what career path she hoped to follow. Applications would have to be made to the relevant courses early in January.

"I'm trying to read," Beth yelled back turning another page of *Adrian Mole's Diary* with her free hand.

"You've to make your mind up straight after Christmas." My voice cracked with vexation. She kept on reading. "Do you hear me, Beth?"

She sighed deeply. "What difference does it make?"

I stepped towards her and tried to grab the book but she held it out of reach and glared up at me. Her eyes brimmed with tears. "Leave me alone."

I lost my nerve. I didn't have the energy. I marched out of the room, pausing to say, "Well at least you can make your bed."

As I crossed the landing she ran out and shouted after me, "I'm going to be a geologist. OK?"

When I was Beth's age I wanted to be an air hostess.

"What did you want to be when you were sixteen?" I asked Brendan Collins this evening.

He cleared his throat and said gruffly, "A ship's captain."

"A ship's captain with sea-green eyes. Would you take me as cabin boy? I'd be a great cabin boy, ship's mate. We could go round the world." I was so excited that I couldn't keep quiet. We'd met up at a Christmas cocktail party given by a local solicitor and his wife. It was one of those affairs with huge amounts of people crammed into every nook and cranny of a large modern house with a startling number of small rooms. Brendan and I had managed to rendezvous in a niche in a panelled room that was furnished with an outsize sideboard and a number of tub-shaped chairs. We stood leaning against the cream striped wallpaper, glasses in hand, facing each other. Every so often people pushed trays of savouries under our noses. Voices buzzed all around us. A fat woman with glasses and a red knitted suit was grumbling about her husband's socks to a skinny brunette in black and white silk. I'd never seen either of them before.

"I'd love to make love to a ship's captain," I

said dreamily.

Brendan's eyes twinkled into mine and then his expression changed as he glanced over my shoulder. "Here's Phyllis," he said. "Take it handy, Dixie, like a good girl."

I turned around and saw her in a neat navy ensemble, a look of passive bewilderment on her face that made me feel mean. What, after all, did I know of her and Brendan's private troubles?

"Phyllis..." I crumbled the remains of a water biscuit on a paper plate between finger and thumb racking my brains for some neutral comment.

"What's on your mind, Dixie?" There was an ominous lift to her voice.

I was saved by a tiny woman with a blonde wig and a red Fair Isle cardigan tugged over a pink chiffon blouse. She pushed her way past us to catch Brendan by the elbow and crow, "Brendan Collins, the man of my dreams! I've been looking everywhere for you."

Phyllis and I both laughed falsely and I made a quick getaway to where Clive was talking business with other men in the kitchen.

14th December: "We've no money," Clive announced out of the blue at lunch time.

"You mean we're broke!" said Anne who is a logical child. She stared solemnly at her steak and kidney pie through newly acquired thin-rimmed glasses. Then with a toss of black curls she bent her head and began to eat it very fast.

"Don't gobble," I said.

"I'm serious. I may have to close down the office," said Clive.

Everyone grew very quiet except Beth who gave a noisy yawn and pushed away her plate. She looked very pale.

"Are you all right?" I asked.

She scowled. "I'm feeling sleepy. I don't want to go back to school."

Anne giggled. "Maybe you're pregnant. Like Jane! It's supposed to make you feel knackered."

"You know that I didn't get the new City Hall job," said Clive after Beth and Anne had been banished.

"Does that matter?" To tell the truth, I don't pay much attention to business. It seems as boring as politics.

"Matter? Jesus, Dixie! It was only the last straw."

There seemed nothing to be done right then except go out to the kitchen and ask Mrs Connors to slice a pear over the meringue and cream we were having for dessert.

"I have to visit Brendan Collins this afternoon. Ask him for a decent loan to tide us over," Clive said as I put his portion down before him.

That certainly put me into a Christmassy mood. "Tell him I was asking for him," I said lightly.

When Clive and the children had gone their various ways I wandered upstairs. Peter's room had a desolate unused air. I wondered about Christmas. Would he come home? Would he stay here? Some abandoned architectural magazines lay on the table beside his bed. I picked one up and glanced through it. Perhaps I should bone up on this, learn more about Clive's work. I came on an article about a new prison in England. The construction work was being done by the inmates. The notion had sinister connotations.

I dropped the paper and hurried across the landing to the teenage tackiness of Beth's lair. From there I could look out at our garden and across the hedge into Evergreen. Ruth's prison. The blinds in her room were pulled down.

I couldn't bear to stay indoors for another second. I flung on an anorak and hurried outside. My wallet was in its pocket. I made a mental note to return it to my handbag later. It contained two or three hundred pounds. Over the years, as Clive's fortunes improved, I had formed the habit of keeping a well-lined purse. An escape fund of a sort; enough cash to let me take a trip to Dublin, for instance, anytime that life began to drag.

The garden was gripped in wintry neglect. The man hadn't been for weeks. Moisture dripped from the huge expanses of tangled shrubs. The glass of the greenhouse behind the tennis court was shrouded in a sour glaucous film. Flower pots in the border beds held nothing but weeds. I had some vague notion of calling on Ruth, attempting some sort of woman to woman overture. That awful Sunday made it seem cruel to ignore her and yet when I thought of approaching her I froze.

As I reached the top of our drive a queer raggedy fellow stepped from behind a tree. He wore a moss-coloured woollen cap pulled down as far as his eyebrows. His face was swarthy but everything else about him was the same colour as his green wellingtons. He reminded me of a wicked gnome. There had been a number of violent incidents in the locality recently. I held my breath and waited for him to produce a gun. I hoped frantically that Mrs Connors was still in the house. Otherwise...all sorts of horrid possibilities sprang to mind.

"I'd like to enquire if you'd have any gold sovereigns for sale, Missus," announced the gnome. I do have a sovereign on a chain which I was actually wearing at that moment. He had obviously spotted it.

I shook my head negatively and made a move to pull the collar of my anorak tighter.

"I pay the very best prices. One hundred pounds minimum for the genuine article." He gave a huge sideways sniff.

"Go away." My voice was hoarse.

"No harm intended, Missus. Only trying to do a little seasonal business. A lady like yourself," he leered showing bad teeth. "Christmas is an expensive time with a big house. Family and all that. Let's say two hundred pounds now. That's my top offer."

I was being very foolish. But suddenly Clive's lunch-time grousing seemed ominous. And two hundred pounds! I didn't even like sovereigns as jewellery and with Clive in his present mood I would need cash. I was married to Scrooge. Happy Christmas! Come the New Year I was going to treat myself to a little of life's luxuries. Health farm, beauty treatment. My skin was like mud.

"I'd have to get two hundred, minimum." I exposed the coin with the young Elizabeth's shiny profile.

"If you would take it off now, Missus, till we have a proper look?"

Feeling stupid, I fumbled, removed my gloves and fumbled again while the gnome kept his eyes fixed intently on my face. Just as I'd unhooked the chain a noise behind me made me whirl around. Two more gnomes, woolly hats, wellies and all, stood with their faces pressed against the window of the family sitting-room. I froze. I'd been duped. It really was a hold-up. Or, at the very least, the place was being cased. A hand tugged at my anorak. I turned back to face the original gnome. He was nodding comfortingly.

"Don't mind the lads. Sure, they're with me," he said. I could see what an idiot he took me for.

I curled my fingers over the coin and spoke as nastily as I could, "Get out of here this minute. Get out before I call the guards."

"All right, Missus. Whatever you say. But if you change your mind..." He pulled a greasy looking card out of a trouser pocket and presented it.

I ignored the gesture, turned on my heel and marched smartly away, right around the house and into our backyard. Mrs Connors was there pinning a wash onto the line.

I could feel myself beginning to shake. My face was burning. This was no time to call on Ruth. I was probably in worse shape than she was. I put my hand in my pocket to take out the sovereign. It had been a gift and I was ashamed of the mean petty impulse that had made me consider parting with it. It took me a few seconds to realise that my bulging wallet had been whipped.

25th December: This evening I speculated on the possibility of an alternative existence. Was there some point at which I could have taken a completely different road or was Tristram always the hidden presence pulling my strings? Tristram with his seed ripening in my womb making me set a trap for Clive.

And if Clive had been free how would things have worked out between him and Ruth? But I think it was myself and Alan by our connivance, presenting them with a fait accompli in Paris, who were the real instigators of their relationship.

Anyway, I've had a straight talk with Clive. I've persuaded him to book a holiday someplace, anyplace, with Ruth. I've convinced him that even though the foursome has ended I have no wish to spoil anything between himself and Ruth. But there were certain conditions.

"Such as...?" He was wearing a red polo-neck jumper that the children had given him as a present. It made him look wishy-washy and vulnerable.

"You're not to leave me permanently." I had stated my price.

He studied me sadly and said, "I'd feel like a rat."

We were sitting amid the debris of our Christmas dinner. I poured the last of a bottle of claret evenly into our glasses and lifted mine in salutation. "You're not. I'm so serious I've even collected some travel brochures for you. I know you're dying to get away."

"Dixie," he looked worried, "how's Alan going to take this?"

"Call Ruth anyway and suggest it," I said, feeling gallant.

A few minutes later I heard him on the telephone. After that he went out. As soon as I had commandeered the family into helping me to clear up I let them return to their seasonal games of Monopoly and Scrabble and flopped in front of the sitting-room fire. I thought about Brendan. We'd snatched several more afternoons in his house while Phyllis was involved in a run of pre-Christmas bridge club activities. I had seen them at Mass today; Brendan in a snazzy suit with a pink striped shirt and a flashy flowered tie. I guessed that Phyllis had chosen his outfit.

"She likes things done properly," Brendan said last time we were together. "She's awful particular. It's because she spent ten years in America. She can't understand the way we let things slide here. She even tells me what colour underpants to put on."

I glanced at them hanging on the bedpost. They were buttercup yellow and toned perfectly with today's duvet cover which was a splurge of daffodils.

"Which does she choose first," I asked, "the bed linen or the underclothes?"

We were sitting up sharing a glass of gin and tonic between us.

"For God's sake don't spill it," said Brendan. "She's got a nose like a sniffer dog. She doesn't believe in more than one sherry."

I rested my head on his shoulder and said, "Poor Brendan!"

"Ah, I don't know," he said. "Maybe it's better

for a wild person like me to be married to somebody quiet."

My reverie about Brendan and myself was rudely broken by Marie and Peter who charged into the sitting-room. They carried mugs of coffee and slabs of buttered toast.

"You'd think you'd never seen food!" I said.

"Peter's had an argument with Jane," said Marie.

"Shut up. It's not your business," said Peter.

Jane was staying with us instead of in Evergreen. She was, through some sort of unspoken agreement, sleeping with Marie in the back bedroom. "She'd rather stay here," Peter had said and I hadn't probed further.

They'd all arrived at the same time on Christmas Eve. Eleven o'clock. Marie with Tessa White on the late train from Cork and Peter and Jane in the back of a car driven by some musical friend.

"Peter got a card from an ex-girlfriend and it had kisses all over it, Jane's jealous," said Marie.

Peter snorted. He was dressed in a long black de Valera style overcoat which he'd picked up in a second-hand shop. "It's stupid," he said.

"You shouldn't upset poor Jane," I warned.

"Cool it, Ma. You sound like she does," he said.

"It's your fault she's pregnant," I snapped.

He drained his mug then got up and slouched out of the room.

Marie wrinkled her forehead. "It's not Peter's fault that Jane's gone fat and bossy. She was always bossy, even when we were little." Then she grinned and jumped to her feet. As she passed my

81

chair she leaned over its back and tapped my skull
and said, "Relax, Ma. Don't you worry your little
head about them. It'll work out fine. Anyway, I
think Jane really wants to be a single mother."

A few minutes later I passed her bedroom door.
It was slightly open and I could hear herself and
Jane chattering away like a pair of magpies in a
tree.

9th January: Clive and Ruth are on one of the
Canary Islands enjoying sun, sea and sex. I didn't
even bother to enquire which island they had
settled for, but I sincerely hope that they're having
a good time. I really do. I checked the temperature
in the newspaper and noted that it was in the
high seventies.

Crouched behind the evergreen hedge that
separates the Whites' garden from ours I witnessed
their departure. Ruth stepped out from the pillars
of their porch, which is identical to ours. She and
Clive hugged each other quickly and then they
were gone. There was no sign of Alan but as
Clive's car turned to drive away I glanced at one of
the house's side windows and saw, with his face
pressed against the glass, woebegone as the little
matchgirl, Danny in his pyjamas. I hope that he's
getting on all right. I hope Clive's ear infection
has cleared up. It is something that afflicts him
from time to time. (I remember, once, in Rome,
trying to find a compliant chemist on the Feast of
Saints Peter and Paul).

I returned to our own house after the happy
pair had departed. Over my pink satin nightie I
was wearing the blue check woollen dressing gown

which I'd bought for Clive the time he had his appendix out. In our bedroom I suddenly felt happy and free. I struggled out of the dressing gown, whipped off my nightie and pranced in front of the wardrobe mirror. Not bad. Breasts still suckable, waist still there. I flexed my upper thighs feeling their power. Then I went to the telephone and dialled Brendan's bank.

"For fuck's sake, Dixie—excuse me, excuse me. No harm meant—tell me, how can I take the day off?"

It wasn't what I'd hoped for. "Have you been drinking?" It wasn't what I'd meant to say at all. I'd been going to issue an invitation: a meal here. Cooked by myself. Vichyssoise, stuffed pork, potatoes au gratin, vegetables and trimmings. Followed by my home-made gateau. I had even decided how I would explain the occasion to the children.

"I have not." Brendan left the words "You silly cow" unsaid. He sighed heavily. "What can I do for you?"

"Nothing...sorry." I was glad he couldn't see me, starkers, legs held knock-kneed like a tremulous schoolgirl. "I just rang up for a chat."

"Well...nice of you to call. See you around." He spoke very crisply. I replaced the receiver and dragged on some clothes, then hurried down to the kitchen and boiled myself an egg.

The kitchen was very quiet. The children had gone back to school. Marie was down in Cork at a twenty-first. There was just myself and the kettle singing on the solid fuel cooker. I felt lonely. I felt middle-aged. I felt ugly. I felt abandoned. I had only one life to live and I had played it all wrong. Peter and Jane were back in Dublin. Their Christmas visit had been full of upsets. I made my way into the sitting-room, opened the drinks cupboard and looked at the bottles. Maybe the answer was there. First step on the road to a home for chronic alcoholics! I knew of other women who had used that escape route, but the idea nauseated me. I made out a shopping list. Programming: that was the thing. I had no wish to end up in a madhouse for drunks.

It was a horrible, sleety, gusty morning. I thought of Clive and Ruth winging their way into the sun and felt noble and strong as I sent them my blessing. I imagined them in bed together. I hoped that they were whole-hearted about it. The way Brendan and I had been the other afternoon. That's right, Brendan, not Tristram. Tristram had been kid's stuff. I was a big girl now.

I had to shop. I shoved the car key into the ignition, turned on the engine, put one foot on the accelerator, the other on the clutch and let go...wham! I drove smack into one of the pillars of our porch.

It immediately slanted in like the leaning tower of Pisa. I scrambled out and approached it gingerly, expecting the whole edifice, complete with overhead balcony which leads off our own bedroom's ante-room, to crash down on my head. Nothing stirred, nothing even creaked. Dimly, from a distance, I became aware of a telephone's trill. I opened the hall-door and charged towards it as if I expected God to be on the other end of the line.

"Sorry about that, Dixie love," said Brendan's voice. "You got me at a bad moment. I had some of the big boys in the office. When can we meet? That is you, Dixie, isn't it?"

# Chapter Seven

11th January: I am expiating my sins. This evening
I applied myself to turning out cupboards and
scouring seldom-used pots and roasting tins to an
unnecessary brilliance. I cooked a huge vat of
spaghetti sauce, ladled it into foil containers and
stocked it in the freezer. Mrs Connors will think
I'm going berserk. In fact I'm trying not to go
berserk. I have had a terrible fight with Peter; not
about Jane but about Brendan Collins and myself.

OK, OK, the whole murky mess was my own
doing, but there was an element of bad luck, ill-
fate, about the thing as well. At least the porch
pillar is fixed. I was woken this morning by the
sound of hammering. I had managed to engage
two workmen who arrived on time and in spite of
pouring rain they had it back in place in jigtime. I
was ecstatic and grateful. They were angels of
mercy straight from the Golden Pages. I didn't
even query the exorbitant cost but paid up
without a murmur to their obvious derision.

The next part, the bad part, of today involved
Brendan whom I'd invited for lunch. Beth and

Anne had gone on a special New Year educational trip to Galway city. Marie was still with her friends in Cork. It was one of Mrs Connors's free days. I was able to laugh at myself as I prepared for Brendan but inside I was like a little girl getting ready for her birthday party. I don't often have Bella Vista completely to myself. Whenever I do it seems full of trembling shadows and thrilling possibilities. Today, even the oranges and lemons in the bowl on the sideboard glowed and caught the eye as enticingly as forbidden fruit.

My lover was coming to eat lunch with me. "Eat lunch", I rolled the words luxuriously against my palate. "Sleep with" seemed innocuous by comparison. I rescued the last hardy blossoms, some pink carnations, from Christmas flower arrangements and placed them in a Waterford crystal vase. They graced the dining-room table which I had stripped of its workaday baize cover. I placed the flowers in the centre of the table and set two places.

Brendan arrived on the dot of one-thirty.

"Come in here, you," I said, pulling him into our hall, glad the builders had finished the porch so fast. "Kiss me, kiss me quick."

He was red-faced and out of breath. He lunged at me, crushing my plunge-necked green satin blouse against his business suit. "You'll kill me," he murmured, pressing his lips into my hair and then against my face, "you're a desperate man-eater, Dixie, under all that suburban codology." He let me go quickly and stepped back. "We could have a lot of fun together if things were different. You know that too."

"I've opened a bottle of champagne. Let's celebrate," I said gaily. It had been a gift to me from Clive and the children last Mother's Day.

Brendan stepped forward again, caught me by the elbows and gave me a little shake. "Don't you know what I'm trying to tell you, Dixie? I'm a working man. I can't get mixed up in this sort of business." He released me, stuffed his hands into his pockets, walked over to the window and looked out at the trees.

I went over and stood quietly beside him. After a moment he reached out and caught my hand. I found, for some unexplained reason, that I wanted to weep.

Then Brendan spoke quietly. "I'm being moved, Dixie. They're shifting me up to County Mayo. To the back of the beyond."

At first I thought it was some sort of joke, but gradually, as he elaborated a bit more, I believed him.

"But why?" I kept asking. "Why?"

"Don't forget me, Dixie," he said in the middle of it all. "I won't meet many like you up in Connaught."

I leaned against his shoulder and stroked his shirt front. I could feel his ribcage. I opened a button and slipped my hand under the poplin.

I gave his belly a little pinch and said, "Flab!" Then suddenly we were kissing each other again, and pulling at each other.

I just managed to gasp, "Upstairs!" and then I was climbing upwards with Brendan's hands reaching to touch and pat and hurry me on. Choking and laughing I popped a button as I wrenched off the blouse I had paid eighty pounds for only yesterday in a local boutique.

"Is this your bed or Clive's?"

"Mine!"

Our voices failed us as flesh pressed against flesh. I was lost in an enchanted forest thick with snakes and wizardry.

"I'm going to die," Brendan moaned while the cosmos whirled into nothingness. Then he lay gasping like a spent fish and I caressed his shoulders. I opened my mouth to tell him how I felt but before I could speak Peter charged into the room shouting, "There's something burning in the oven."

I shoved Brendan aside and shot up holding the blankets close and shouted, "God almighty, I forgot all about the noisettes of lamb." How do you explain to your twenty-one year old son that you are perfectly entitled to go to bed with your bank manager? As the full implications of the situation hit me the sweat on my body turned to a film of ice. "How did you get in?" I asked foolishly.

"I've a key." Peter held it up. Then he stared up at the ceiling. I could see his Adam's apple bobbling furiously in his throat. Brendan buried his face in a pillow. We hadn't even pulled the blinds so there were no merciful concealing shadows.

"What are you doing?" Peter said in a shrill voice. "Why is he here? There's nobody around. I thought you'd all gone out. Oh, Jeez..." He scrubbed his forehead with a clenched fist. "This is awful."

I felt weak. My mouth had a sour taste. "Wait..." I stretched out a bare arm but he blundered, muttering, from the room.

Brendan and I dressed swiftly, without speaking.

"I'll stay if you want me to. To hell with the bank," he said as I combed my hair.

I shook my head.

"Well..." he shuffled his feet, "I'll be in touch."

I waited until I heard him crossing the front hall before I went to find Peter. He was in his room lying on his bed fully dressed, his arm covering his eyes.

I pulled up a chair beside him. The room was dark and silent. There were clothes and papers scattered everywhere.

"Go away," he muttered.

"It isn't all that serious," I said. "It's something that just happened. It never happened before, and it certainly won't happen again," I added unscrupulously.

"I don't know what you mean. Where's Dad? Does Dad know about this?"

"You know he's on a trip," I said weakly. The story Clive and I had agreed on was that he'd to go away on business. Ruth was supposed to be up in her mother's place.

Peter sneered. "So where's everybody else?"

"Different places. They're in Galway. Marie's in Cork."

"So you had it all nicely arranged. Pity I forgot some stuff and came back. I'm allowed to collect my own belongings, I suppose. If I'd known about you and that creep I'd have telephoned."

"Pity you didn't."

"It's disgusting." His face puckered and I felt my cheeks blaze. "You're too old, Ma."

"I'm thirty-nine," I said lamely.

"That's what's so awful."

"Peter," I said, "let's just forget all this."

"Forget! Do you know you never even told me the facts of life! You left me to find all that out myself. You did. You did. That's how bad a mother you are." His words came out in a rush.

I knew that was unfair and untrue. "Peter, listen to me," I said.

But he wouldn't. He ranted on, his accusations growing wilder, his theories more absurd. I was a monster. I was selfish. Everybody pitied him for having me for a mother. Jane had told him once that Ruth thought I was two-faced. Everybody thought I was two-faced.

I tried to keep calm. I tried to count while I took deep breaths. But then I snapped. I called him a brat. I told him that if it wasn't for him I'd have had a proper life. I told him that it was because I was pregnant that I'd had to marry Clive. The one thing, the only thing I didn't say was the name of his actual father. (I've often wondered how Mary explained his parentage to Jesus.) But it was Tristram's son who sat up in the bed to listen. With every sentence the image of Tristram grew more clearly manifested in Peter. The same gaunt line about the cheekbones, the thin arms and long bony fingers. The musician's frame, fine-boned and delicate.

As I spoke he seemed to shrink into himself, sitting huddled on his blankets. Then he gripped

91

the middle finger of his left hand between his right forefinger and thumb. He tugged it and the joint cracked. The gesture brought me right back to the beginning. I had a queer feeling that life hadn't moved on at all, this was just a mirage. The reality was myself, my mother's shopping-bag clutched in my hand, and Tristram sitting on a black leather chair saying, "Sure, it wouldn't be fair with a little bit of a girl like yourself..." And doing the exact same thing.

I took a deep breath and, forcing my voice to gentleness asked, "How's Jane? Is everything all right?"

Peter plucked at a fraying hole in the knee of his jeans and said, "She doesn't want me. She says she can manage better on her own."

There was nothing to be done but go downstairs with my heart heavy as a lead weight in my breast. When I reached the bottom step I realised that my eyes were watering from smoke as well as emotion. The oven was still on full. The noisettes were nothing but a few charred and smoking crumbs, like the tail-end of the lava flow from a recently erupted volcano.

12th January: I had a restless night and was wide awake, drinking tea, at six-thirty a.m. Peter was still in the house. He had come banging on the bathroom door last night while I soaked my troubles away in verbena-scented suds. "Use the downstairs one," I called and was answered by a grunt. We'd had no other communication.

During the small hours of the night I racked my brains trying to think of some way of putting things to rights. I was upset and terribly unhappy. I wished that I had died at an early age, in a car crash or, perhaps, a fire. I wished that the past in general and yesterday in particular could be wiped out. I recalled the fact that our Fearsome Foursome with Alan and Ruth had managed to survive without so much as a curious stare from any of our children. I marvelled that my liaison with Brendan, two mature adults who knew exactly what they were doing, should so quickly fall victim to youthful puritanism.

At nine a.m. I made my way to the kitchen. Beth and Anne were racing around gathering their things for school and fighting over the only scarf that could be found. There had been a row between the seniors and juniors after yesterday's school outing and they seemed determined to carry on the struggle at home. Beth paused just long enough to inform me that she intended to go to University College, Galway, in the autumn.

"You won't go anywhere if you don't grow up a bit and work much harder," I threatened. But it struck me that in a few years' time even Anne would be leaving home. I suddenly saw a vista of idle hours and silent rooms. I was going to hate it.

The girls pushed each other out the back door and raced by the kitchen window, tapping at the glass as they passed it. As if on cue Peter entered lugging a battered khaki haversack. He had a bundle of architectural text books under his arm.

"I'm selling these." He threw them down on the table as if he expected me to protest.

I felt apprehensive. "So you're heading off," I said.

"Yep."

I looked at him. I called on Tristram's shade. I considered my present predicament. Past, present...it was all so inexplicable.

"Peter," I said, "what happened yesterday meant absolutely nothing."

He remained silent.

"You must know that you, the family, all this is what really matters."

He shrugged.

"I want to do something," I said. "I can give you some more money. I have a little. Not much." Ruefully I remembered my stolen wallet.

"I'm not going to tell Dad if that's what you're afraid of," he said.

It flashed into my mind to tell him about Clive and Ruth, their relationship, the fact that they were not in the Canaries. But then I was afraid that he would just cite it as something else caused by my iniquity. "Keep in touch. Promise me that," I begged. "And let me know about Jane. No matter what happens between you two I'll still be the baby's granny."

"Stop interfering. Jane and I are all wrong," he said aggressively.

I closed my eyes and took a deep breath trying to subdue my fears. "It's a pity, a big pity," I said.

"What is?"

I felt as if every utterance of Peter's placed another plank on top of the barrier he was raising between us.

"This baby." I was desperately trying to break through to him.

But he wasn't prepared to throw me a crumb.

"You're merely going on your own experience." he said. "Just because you didn't want me, because you had to force Dad to marry you, doesn't mean that Jane feels that way. She just wants to have it on her own. She says she'll cope better. She just doesn't want to waste her life being married."

"Married to you, you mean."

He flinched. "Married to anybody. And I appreciate that. That's her privilege. I'm still her friend. We'll always be the best of friends."

"That's not true about my not wanting you!" I shouted. "I don't know where you got that idea. I wanted you so much that I married Clive even though...even though..." I couldn't go on. My face felt like a big pink streaming sponge.

"I'm not listening." His gaze was baleful as he swung his haversack over his shoulder and picked up his books again. Then he was gone, leaving behind him nothing but a bright empty circle that shimmered and sparkled through my tears.

15th January: Clive arrived home yesterday with his face and arms tanned to a dull copper. He also had a nasty tummy bug and elected to put himself in quarantine by sleeping in Peter's room. I asked him how Ruth was and he said, "At least she hasn't been puking her guts out." That was the end of our conversation about the holiday.

All he managed after that were monosyllables. Then he lay against his pillows, groaning and sifting his way through paperwork that had come out from his office. It seemed that there was bad news everywhere. A builder had let one of his clients down badly and Clive was being blamed for recommending him. Another client had changed his mind about renovating a hotel. Instead he was selling up and emigrating to South Africa. Bankruptcy, it seemed, was halfway up our driveway.

I was affected by the numb lack of interest that engulfs me when faced with depressing talk. Then Clive said, "And that so-and-so Brendan Collins wants me to clear the office overdraft by the end of the month. It's January, for Christ's sake! What architectural office makes money in January!"

"I suppose it's because he's moving up to Mayo," I said unthinkingly.

If business affairs make me stupid they sharpen Clive's wits. His eyes narrowed. "I wonder why you say that? What's the story?" He lost his invalid's complaining voice and sat upright looking at me with cold eyes.

I acted the innocent, saying, "It's just something I heard." But I realised that he wasn't fooled.

"I know exactly what's been happening. You've been carrying on with Brendan Collins. Somebody hinted something. That's why you were so anxious to see me off. You wanted a free hand." Clive's voice was definite and razor sharp. He paused, waiting. Then, with a quick catch of his breath he moaned and clutched his stomach in agony. The paella he had eaten on his last night away was wreaking its revenge. He clambered out of bed and staggered on buckling legs to the bathroom.

Feeling mutinous, I hurried downstairs. I longed to offload some of my secret troubles but there was nobody to talk to except the dog and the cat.

"Oh Tristram," I mourned, "I did truly love you. I'd have done anything for you but I was too young. I wanted more than I could have. It wasn't natural. You saw that, and you did your best in your own way. But if you're out there anywhere give me a sign."

I waited while the tick of the wall clock grew louder and louder, then with a sudden hissing splash some soup I had put on for Clive's benefit boiled over.

I rescued it and poured some into a mug and went back upstairs with the firm intention of letting Clive see that he had no right to question me. My life was my own affair.

I found him asleep with his mouth slightly askew. Even in repose he was frowning. He looked exhausted and unhappy and I noticed that his beard had a liberal amount of white which had been made more noticeable by exposure to the sun. Looking at him I felt disheartened. What lay in store for us? I didn't begrudge him Ruth but was that even the right thing? I had a sneaking feeling that the holiday had been a disaster.

I went into our own room and thought of Brendan sharing my bed. I supposed it had been a rotten thing to do. And then I decided that it would be foolish to become intimidated by my own failings. I didn't want to be wicked but life itself kept putting obstacles in front of me like rocks in the path of a stream, deflecting it from its straight and narrow course. And then I thought about Tristram. "You'll have to find yourself a young man," he'd said sadly after making love to me. He'd been so much older than I was that I'd accepted his words as unwelcome wisdom and found myself Clive and by doing so cheated everybody. And I'd drawn Ruth into it and Alan... The thought of Alan made me gloomier than ever. He was a brute. The best thing that could happen would be that he'd drop dead this minute. His shadow had become a shameful blot, distorting my vision when I wanted to think straight.

This brooding was superseded by a vision of myself, in my rightful place, ending up as an ageing bag-lady, mad as a hatter, shunned by my children, sitting on a sagging bed babbling nonsensical platitudes to a collection of holy statues. I shuddered, what else was there? Everything was ruined. I knew it. Even feeling penitential was no good. Blast Brendan Collins for causing that row with Peter! I had too much on my plate as it was. I was ready to give up.

"What's wrong with Dad? What's for tea? Can Bridget and I heat up pizzas?" The girls saved me. I wanted to hug Anne and Bridget.

"Oh, heavens yes, my pets," I crowed. "Whatever you want. And there's chocolate cake, and figrolls and help yourselves to lemonade."

"You're in a very good mood," said Anne grinning and giving a little bounce. "I suppose it's because Dad's home."

"Exactly," I said, "and he's not as sick as he thinks he is."

26th January: Several times a year Monsignor Patrick arranges what he calls "a little treat" for

Clive and I. It was one of these that brought us to the Abbey Theatre tonight. We drove up in Clive's car. Unfortunately we were delayed for thirty minutes by a garda checkpoint along the way. A bank in the midlands had been robbed. It was spouting rain and Clive began to curse as we waited under the dripping hedges for our turn to open our boot and say where we had been at two o'clock precisely.

"It isn't important," I kept insisting as it gradually seemed that we might arrive at the theatre after the curtain had been raised.

But in Clive's world anything that concerns Monsignor Patrick is important. By a marvel of short-cutting down side roads and alleyways he managed to get the car into a car park ten minutes before the deadline. It was an underground place, dark, damp and evil smelling. I could imagine a murder taking place right there. I had no time to check on my hair. Clive rushed me down the road, paused and took a deep breath as we reached the entrance, then placing his hand under my elbow, led me in as if he could hear the wedding march, to where the Monsignor was pacing up and down with his hands behind his back, looking important.

"So Clive and your good wife." Monsignor Patrick seldom uses my first name. He even managed to look surprised to see me. There was no more time for pleasantries. We hurried into the auditorium. I made sure to move quickly into our row ahead of Clive which meant that he was the one trapped beside his uncle.

The play started immediately but the head of

Emma Cooke

the person in front of me partially obliterated my view of the stage. I simply decided to sit and relax rather than be craning from side to side. A large head, with a good growth of hair. A man's head with a habit of leaning a little to one side. Then, as I scrutinised it more carefully and realised that I was looking at Brendan Collins, I thanked God that the dimmed lights concealed my scarlet cheeks. Phyllis was with him.

I was relieved when, at the interval, the Collinses hurried out of their seats before anybody else. We made our way to the bar more slowly. "A good play," Monsignor Patrick pronounced. I nodded and twisted a button on the purple banquette where I was seated beside him. The button came away in my fingers and I felt as guilty as a seven-year-old child.

"I see a friend of yours is here, Dixie," Clive said in a silken voice, coming back with three glasses. I pretended I hadn't heard. Then I saw Brendan detach himself from the crowd. He had two drinks in his hand. Our eyes met and he gave a little nod. Like a person under a hypnotist's spell I stood up and glided over to him. I had a sudden idea that the pair of us could just walk out the door and never come back.

"You know Dixie Molloy, don't you, Phyllis," Brendan said as I approached him. My feelings were a compound of terror and joy. I wondered if Phyllis was going to confront me with playing around with her husband, right here, in front of Monsignor Patrick in one of the temples of Irish culture.

"Yes," said Phyllis. "I know Dixie." Her

100

expression was safe and unconcerned. She was elaborately dressed in a ruby velvet cocktail suit with a ruffled white shirt. Her blonde bouffant hair and her stiletto heels made her look tall. I concentrated on the face-powder lodged in the crevices around her chin. Far in the distance I could hear the bell ringing for us to return to our seats.

"You'll have to excuse us..." Phyllis tugged at Brendan's sleeve.

I looked at her and felt the tension between us. "Will I see you soon?" I asked Brendan provocatively.

Next thing Phyllis was pushing her face up against mine and calling me a dirty bitch.

"What's this?" asked a gleeful voice. I was aware of faces staring and people backing away from us.

Then I felt a sharp pain in the centre of my back. Clive had stepped up behind me and administered a vicious jab which nobody except myself noticed. Brendan and Phyllis hurried towards the exit door.

"That's it. I've had enough," Clive hissed as he escorted me back to our seats. The Monsignor had taken my place this time. Clive pushed me in to sit beside him. As we sat down he turned towards me, pressed his lips together, raised his eyebrows but made no comment.

I sat breathing heavily, feeling mutinous. I registered the fact that Brendan and Phyllis had not come in for the second act. I didn't care what the Monsignor thought. He had never liked me. I remembered him when Peter was born. "And how does Clive feel about this little stranger?" He stared into the hospital cot as if he was experiencing a bad smell. Then he glared at me. "You took us all by surprise, Dixie," he added. And then, "It's sad when a young woman fails in her duty." But I was young and frantic. "Clive is thrilled. We both are. We wanted a son." My voice was cheerful as I unbuttoned my night-dress and gave my exposed nipple an encouraging squeeze to the Monsignor's obvious disgust.

28th January: A few years ago we and the Whites would automatically have paired up to go to the Architectural Association's dance. Getting ready for tonight's affair I found myself hoping that if they did turn up they'd be sitting at the opposite end of the ballroom. I wouldn't be able to bring myself to dance with Alan if I found myself thrown into his company. I was nervous about what he might say or do. Perhaps he'd bandy my name about in the men's room if I didn't fawn over him. I imagined him making coarse remarks, telling grinning lechers what I'd been like in bed. If he put a hand on me I'd collapse or throw up. And as for Ruth, I still felt bad for running out on her that Sunday, although I didn't know what else I could have done other than sending for the guards or an ambulance and that would have opened a proper can of worms.

One thing I hadn't expected was that the Collinses would be with our group. "Oh sure. I know the Molloys well." Brendan got to his feet, a big grin on his face, as our host introduced us. I wanted to slap him. Instead I said, "Seen any good plays lately?"

When I'm discomfited I become garrulous. That is my chief recollection of the architects' dance. The sound of my own voice in my ears jabbering away. Our host was the head of the Munster branch of the Association. A Corkman whom I'd never met before and who clearly thought that Clive was married to a madwoman. I was placed beside him and could read his opinion as if it was written in six-inch letters on his forehead as I soliloquised to him about the menopause, men and mistresses. Meanwhile, strong liquor flowed like a stream in full spate.

Across from me, Clive, when he wasn't staring in the direction of Ruth who was at the other side of the ballroom, looked increasingly anxious.

Another thing I do sometimes when I'm tight is complain about food. Tonight I sent back the vegetables because there was cheese on the cauliflower and also I got a blackened potato. And my turkey was underdone. A clot of blood was clearly visible next to the thigh bone.

"Salmonella," I informed our group. "Highly dangerous."

Soon other plates of uneaten dinners were being handed back.

After the meal and speeches dancers massed on the floor. I wasn't surprised to see Clive's chair empty and find him resurfacing with Ruth pressed in his arms. I only hoped that Alan didn't materialise. It was a relief when I saw him heading in the direction of the bar. I was so glad I even turned my head and smiled at Phyllis who bristled like a wheaten terrier. She and Brendan had been at the other end of the table during the meal. Then I got to my feet and swayed to the chair Brendan had vacated to dance with the host's wife.

"Lishen, Phyllis..." I began and realised I was tipsy.

"Is there something you want to speak to me about?" she asked coldly.

I had some vague intention of explaining away the incident in the Abbey Theatre. I also wanted to say something about Brendan, how he and I were a mere flash in the pan, about how I wouldn't have dreamt of becoming involved if I hadn't realised that she and Brendan were anything but wrong together. All I managed was, "Phyllish, I'm very fond of your husband."

Before I could go any further Phyllis had taken hold of my forearm. She has freckled skin which was not enhanced by the pink chiffon folds of her dress. I noticed that her diamond ring was as big as a gangster's knuckle-duster and wondered if her own money had paid for it. Her nails were very long and sharp and I felt my skin bursting under them like the skin of a ripe pear.

"Brendan is all the world to me, you bitch," Phyllis said. "I've nobody else. I'm not like you. I don't have children so you'd just better keep away from him. It's only for a month. We'll be gone out of here for good by the first of March." She spoke in quick staccato sentences staring ahead of her as if she was a TV news reader who was having trouble with the idiot board.

"Children aren't everything," I said, sobered by the thought of Peter. I'd been trying to make contact with him in Dublin, but had failed. I'd no idea what he was up to or, even, if Jane knew where he was. Jane was back in college again, pregnancy and all.

Phyllis loosened her grip. My arm looked as if it had been bitten by a small nasty dog. "People who say that don't deserve to have them," she said and I felt her hatred like a shock of cold water making goose pimples break out all over me as if I'd been cursed.

13th February: Tea, toilet paper, cornflakes. Words that make a strange epitaph. Tea, toilet paper, cornflakes, written on a coil of white paper that still curls from a holder with a funny-face schoolmaster's head on top. Anne got it for me several Christmases ago. I use it all the time.

Tea, toilet paper, the cornflakes didn't matter. Spaghetti with meat sauce for supper. I thought I heard the telephone but when I opened the kitchen door it had stopped. I thought I heard a ring at the door but when I opened it there was nobody on the step.

I went back to the kitchen and the transistor radio. News headlines: an earthquake in Algeria. I switched it off. My purse was in the sitting-room. I went to get it. I had never noticed how dark and heavy the furniture was. Auction furniture bought from Alan in the early days of our acquaintance.

I imagined I saw people flitting past the window. I remembered the men who looked like gnomes. I hurried over and pressed my face against the glass. The only trace of life was our marmalade cat skulking through the laurels.

I decided that it was my own restlessness that was causing my unease. A heavy drizzle started as I hurried out to my car. Before I left I shouted up the stairs that I would soon be back. Faint echoes came from Beth's and Anne's rooms.

As I parked my car in town I was annoyed to discover that I had forgotten my shopping list. T is for Todds. I needed tights. As I passed the cosmetic counter I was attacked, there was no other word for it, by a demonstrator with a perfume spray. She squirted it onto my wrists and throat. It was one of the floral bases which go rancid and sour on my skin. When I roared, "Bugger off!" she rounded on me and told me that I ought to be ashamed of myself. It was one of those incidents in which stupidity accelerates into absurdity.

"A woman of your age," the demonstrator scolded. "Using words like that in a family store. You should be ashamed of yourself."

I was trembling as I escaped and my mind had gone completely blank. I forgot to buy tea. I always forget the essential thing. Driving back over Sarsfield Bridge I remembered and made a detour round by our local supermarket. The place I go to for emergency purchases.

As I flew down the aisle to collect the packet of tea I noticed one and then another woman backing away from me. No wonder with that stinking stuff making me smell like a tomcat.

At the checkout the owner attended to me. He charged the purchase, put it in a carrier bag and as he handed it to me suddenly said, "Oh dear!" His eyes met mine for an instant and then swivelled away.

I headed for home wondering what had bothered him. Of course this suffocating smell... It was getting up my nose as well. It was the aura of melancholy decay. I'd scrub it off immediately. Jump into the shower, use the bar of Opium soap that I'd been hoarding for months. Maybe I'd even call Brendan to come over and wash my back. Have a last fling. Give the girls money to take themselves into town for Kentucky fried chicken. Bolt the hall-door so that Clive couldn't get in. As I fantasised I began to hum.

I was still humming as I drove up to the hall-door. The first thing that struck me as unreal was the poker faces of the people assembled in the front hall. They were just standing there, staring at me and my shopping bags. Not a flicker, not a sound. It took a few seconds to realise that one of them was a woman guard. She was brown-haired and sensible and her flat black shoes shone like polished marble but what she was doing there was a complete mystery.

I looked harder. They weren't poker-faced, they were scared. Beth and Anne were as pale as if they'd seen ghosts. My gaiety fizzled away. Oh God! I'd had a premonition before I went out. I remembered my pilfered wallet and those evil gnomish men. I shouldn't have left the house at all. We'd have to get a proper alarm system installed.

"Dixie," Clive materialised. His voice sounded funny. It sent flutters through my stomach.

"We've been burgled, haven't we?" I said quickly.

"It's not that." He shook his head. "I'm sorry,

Dixie." He reached for my hand and squeezed it.

I felt bewildered. I said, "For God's sake, why the long faces? Did you think I was lost?"

There was a commotion as Anne suddenly turned and charged back across the hall and up the stairs. "Anne! Anne!" I pushed in after her and stood clutching the curled end of the banisters.

The woman guard came and stood behind me and I grew more suspicious. I was forced to blurt out, "It's Peter, isn't it? He's in some sort of trouble. That's why he hasn't been in touch. You mustn't be hard on him." I was thinking that whatever Peter had done, if I put the words into her mouth the punishment wouldn't be so drastic.

"Believe me, Mrs Molloy, we're dreadfully sorry," she said, but I wasn't prepared to believe anything.

"He's a good boy," I said.

"I think we'll go into the drawing-room," said Clive.

I wanted to stop him. The drawing-room is too cold at this time of year. If we're going to use it we have to light the fire.

"I had to buy tea. I find Barry's the best," I said chattily to the woman guard once we'd crossed the threshold. "It's as bad as trying to heat a cathedral in here, we definitely need a fire," I added. Then I ran out of small talk.

I saw that there was another, male, guard present as well. Then I thought maybe it isn't Peter they're here about. Maybe it's me. Maybe Phyllis Collins has had me accused of something; maybe I'm going to be arrested. Maybe the perfume demonstrator was Phyllis's sister.

"Sweetheart, you have to hear this," said Clive. He never calls me "sweetheart."

Even with the chandelier switched on the room was full of shadows.

"We'll have to get some table-lamps," I said. "I saw some quite nice ones yesterday. We'd need white bases to match the coffee table."

It was Beth who stopped me. She stepped forward and grabbed me and hissed, "Mummy, have you heard the news?"

"What news?" I pressed her head against my shoulder. "Don't I smell awful!" I whispered as she squirmed.

"It's Peter," she shouted.

When I looked at her face I was unable to do anything. I felt as if I had been drugged. I wanted to sit down and fall asleep.

"That's what they're here to tell us. It's on the radio already except that they don't say Peter's name." She pressed a palm each side of my face as if she was a little girl playing with dolls.

Then they were all around me, chorusing, shouting in my ears, "Peter. It's Peter." Intrusive voices clamoured, "They brought him to a hospital but it was too late. His injuries were too severe."

"I'm afraid, Mrs Molloy, that by the time they'd got help for him he'd gone to Heaven," said the woman guard.

I raised my arm as if to ward off a karate chop.

"Take it easy, Dixie." Clive came and put his arm around my waist.

"Your husband will be able to give you the full details," the male garda said.

All the muscles in my face felt paralysed. I didn't believe them, I couldn't. One significant fact registered, proving them wrong.

"Nobody knew where Peter was," I said.

"Unfortunately that area of the city had a bad reputation," the garda said. "He was set on by a gang while he was walking by himself."

"I suppose there are formalities. What exactly do you want us to do, guard?" Clive spoke without emotion.

I am eighteen years old. I have spent all day in a poky office typing letters and sorting files. The flickering fluorescent tube has given me a blinding headache. My boss keeps promising to fix it but he never does. Today is one of his blind drunk days. I find him sitting on the lavatory with his trousers down around his knees. "S-s-s-h!" He puts a yellow-stained finger to his rubbery lips when I walk in on him.

After work I rush home and nibble a slice of toast standing up while my mother complains about faulty eating habits. Diet is a word that still has heavily medical overtones. I feel cheerful as I change my clothes. But the waistband of my bottle-green taffeta skirt is already too tight and my breasts have definitely grown bigger. My nipples tingle when the cold air hits them as I take off my blue workaday jumper and pull on a puff-sleeved broderie anglaise blouse. If I let things run on any longer it's going to be hopeless.

Clive is standing outside the GPO in O'Connell Street reading the evening paper. He looks up as I run towards him. I sashay a little in my high heels.

# Wedlocked

My all-purpose mackintosh is a perfect cover-up. Lately I have started wearing it with the belt held hanging loosely in a knot at the back. (I don't think I was as pregnant-looking as I imagined. But my nervousness magnified all the initial signs.)

"Congratulations!" I press moist violet-coloured lips against his.

"I've got the dance tickets," he says.

We scrutinise each other. He'd said that if he passed his finals he'd grow a beard. By now it is a respectable fuzz.

"How did it go?" I ask.

He grins. "You really want to know? Uncle Patrick is fixing things so that I can go and work with a firm in Canada. It'll take about four months because of the formalities."

Suddenly the air is full of crows floating like parts of broken umbrellas carried on the wind. I'm so scared my heart thumps. If I scream they'll peck me to shreds. I'm blinded by blue-black feathers and grimacing because of the terrible stitch in my side. If Clive leaves I'm a ruined woman. I daren't let him slip through my fingers.

# Chapter Eight

17th February: Peter's funeral, twelve o'clock midday. Everything about it felt unreal. I kept thinking it wasn't happening, but it was, on and on and on.

18th February: "People shouldn't die," Anne said. She'd been crying again. I envy kids for the way they can cry.

Monsignor Patrick was the chief celebrant (celebrant?) at the Requiem Mass. His face reminded me of a huge peony rose blooming furiously against his vestments. In the cemetery he donned a funny black hat topped by a scarlet bobble that clashed furiously with his complexion. "The Lord giveth and the Lord taketh away," he intoned.

The Lord's not a mugger, it's the devil who took him away, I raged.

Last night I slept as if I too was dead. The nightmares will come later. The days have been full of people and I haven't been able to think. Jane was the first to come up and embrace me in the funeral parlour. She looked like a girl from a nursery rhyme. Her belly was a soft round sphere sheltered under a black smock. As she pressed against me I felt it changing shape.

"I don't know what to say, Aunt Dixie," she moaned. "Sorry. Sorry."

"Why did it happen?" I asked the police doctor in Dublin. He just held up the x-ray of Peter's skull. I could make out the long jagged line and a white explosion. "A broken bottle," he said tapping the white blur with a manicured nail.

In the funeral parlour I stood beside Peter, asleep, waiting for them to put on the lid. There was no trace of the wound. All there was was a pale boy with a string of rosary beads threaded between his fingers. All around me shuffling shapes murmured condolences. I thought of my mother in her nursing home and wished my own mind could go blank. I actually envied her her senile unknowingness, would have wished Alzheimer's disease on myself if it would blot out the horror.

"Laugh and the world laughs with you, weep and you weep alone." That was my drunk old boss's favourite quote. I couldn't weep. I couldn't feel anything. Even Alan left me indifferent. He was there dressed like a country gentleman in a greenish tweed suit.

"Oh God, Dixie, I don't know what to say," he said.

For a moment his face was naked, the bluster all stripped away. Ruth was a silent wraith beside him. We pressed hands automatically. I found no spark of anything, even animosity, between us.

We could have been shadows meeting on a wall. Jane's choking sobs as she stretched to kiss Peter's forehead was the one true note.

Then Clive and I came back to the house with the girls and Monsignor Patrick and everything was unbelievably commonplace. Burgers sizzling in the pan. The girls changing out of their black clothes into jumpers and jeans. Glasses of Coca Cola and scotch on the rocks to ease our sorrows.

25th March: Weeks have passed. Most of the time I have suffered from headaches but I try to avoid shouting at Clive and the girls. When Jane came to visit me I couldn't think of anything to say.

Today I went out with Clive in his car. We climbed a high hill beside a lake and spread raincoats on the ground. It was an ancient place, so old that it was used as a burial site in prehistoric times. The top of the hill was where they used to build funeral pyres. Clive took a pencil and pad from his pocket and began to sketch.

It was the sort of thing that we used to do when the children were little. We had even brought them here once upon a time. Suddenly I could see them, especially Peter in a fleecy blue track suit somersaulting down the slope.

It was more than I could take. I jumped to my feet, stretched out my arms and began to run. The wind whipped against my face. I was travelling faster and faster, out of control. The faint cries of birds wailed against my ears. I was becoming airborne, a leaf on the wind before falling into the abyss.

I came to with Clive bending over me, his gaze full of decency and dismay. My ankle was hurting like hell. He managed to pull me up onto one leg and with my arm around his neck we set off across the rough ground.

"What were you trying to do?" he asked.

"I'm sorry," I said. "I need my head examined."

Part of the area had been fenced off for an archaeological dig. It meant that we had to travel around yards and yards of post and wire to reach the car. I didn't care. The physical pain was a welcome diversion.

Driving back to the city I felt a sort of pleasure as the pain began to ease. It was a mild sprain and not a break.

"All right?" Clive took one hand from the steering wheel and stroked my chin. On an impulse I placed my hand on his upper thigh. We travelled for a while in silence. I moved my hand higher and felt him come alive as I fondled his crotch. (The night after the graduation dance came back to me. Peter, the way I had worried and how differently it had all turned out.)

"Hey..." Clive said shakily, "I'm going to crash if I'm not careful."

"Pull up," I ordered. "Stop the car."

We turned into a lay-by. There was nobody about. Clive reached for me. His mouth was hungry on mine. The clock rolled back. I could have him if I wanted to. We were both trembling. But the moment passed. As if of one mind we drew away from each other.

"How's the leg?" he asked.

"Agony."

He switched on the engine and I returned to my mourning.

5th April: I spent the last few days packing up Peter's things into black plastic sacks. It was like dismembering and disposing of my own body. My life's blood seemed to be oozing out of me with every old rock concert poster, pair of towelling socks, mud-encrusted football boot, yellowed copy books, odd bits of jigsaw, etc., that the drawers in his bedroom disgorged. Nothing could ever be as bad again, I thought as I put each item into its appropriate bag or box. Some of it would have to be dumped, some given to charity and a few small items went into a large flat box which I was going to put in my own wardrobe and leave there for ever. Precious things like old school reports and concert programmes. I tried to turn myself into a machine as I shook out faded denim jackets, searched their pockets, tore up birthday cards and made war on the junk in a wooden chest. Every so often either Beth or Anne glided in with a cup of coffee. They looked petrified. None of us said a word except Anne who came in one time to announce, "Mum, Mr Brendan Collins is on the phone."

I shook my head. I didn't want to know. Brendan has gone out of my life. He's better off up in Mayo. When I think of men I grow cold. My desperate effort to make physical contact with Clive showed me that my passions have been killed by frostbite. I shrink from even a peck on the cheek.

At last the job was finished. I took a shower

and changed my skirt and blouse, pulled on a brown cashmere jumper.

"What are we having for tea?" Beth asked from the bottom of the stairs.

I checked my watch. It was half-past four. If we hurried I could make it to town in time to shop.

"Chinese take-away if you and Anne come along and get it yourselves," I said.

"I want spring rolls," Anne said as we bundled into the car. It was the first time I'd heard her sound cheerful since the funeral.

As we drove towards the city I noticed a clutch of tinkers' caravans pulled in beside a boat club. For once in my life I envied them their nomadic existence. There was a garda checkpoint on the bridge which delayed traffic. In the back seat Beth and Anne speculated as to whether it was a bomb scare or a bank robbery.

"Maybe somebody's been murdered," said Anne. Then she said in a scared voice, "Oh, I didn't mean that."

In fact the guards were checking tax discs. The delay meant that it was almost closing time when I got into the supermarket. I had forgotten to bring a list and my mind went completely blank.

Tea, toilet paper, cornflakes. I began to shake as I recalled the minutiae that preceded Peter's death. I mustn't pass out, not here with everyone gaping. I charged along the aisles and ended up at the check-out with a box of filter papers, tins of dog and cat food and a large bottle of vodka. I couldn't think of anything else I needed.

Then I bought a local evening paper and sat in the car reading it while I waited for Beth and

Anne. I skimmed idly through the tribute paid to Mrs Phyllis Collins by the city's principal bridge club. Her expertise and the brilliance of her strategy would be sadly missed. However, they congratulated her on her husband's new appointment. I wondered if Brendan was going to miss me. He had been at Peter's funeral. I knew because his and Phyllis's names were on one of the wreaths. It struck me that I was parked in exactly the same place as I'd been on the day I'd met him while I was bringing the dog home from the vet.

Then Beth and Anne came racing around the corner with silver foil containers balanced in their hands, both of them laughing as if they didn't know what disaster was.

As I drove home I decided that the first thing I was going to do was pour myself a large vodka. I was sorry I hadn't bought tomato juice for a Bloody Mary.

I pulled up on the gravelled sweep and looked at the door. Afterwards I remembered looking at the door, at how yellow it was in the evening light. I noticed the four panels and the letter-flap had been pushed in. I tried fitting my key in the lock but there was no need, it swung open at my touch like a door opening into my head. I became confused. I tried to step back but I didn't and went inside only half-believing. My foot bumped against one of the plastic sacks which was just inside the threshold. Things were thrown on the floor.

"Oh Jesus!" Beth startled me by charging in behind me and racing to the back of the house. In the kitchen all the cupboard doors were open. Groceries were scattered everywhere. Beth's heel came down on an empty supermarket meat tray. She skidded smartly across the tiles and cracked her head against the table leg and wailed, "Oh shit!"

She got up, moaning and the three of us staggered through the havoc. Everywhere was a complete shambles. I deputised Anne to ring for the guards. They took forever to arrive. When they did show up they marched in and immediately picked out clues which we had overlooked. We had failed to notice the bootmarks on the lower panels of the front door and we hadn't spotted the splintered wood where a chisel had been used on its frame.

One of them picked a bunch of daffodils from a jar on the kitchen windowsill and let them drop back again as if he found them offensive. Beth had bought those flowers for me last week. Now she was leaning against a ransacked cupboard having an attack of the jitters.

"Is there any money in the house?" asked the younger guard. "If they find cash they don't usually make too much of a mess." He had a bunny rabbit twitch in his nose.

"One thing, Missus, you'll have to put Chubb locks on all the outer doors," interposed his senior.

I was too depleted to do anything except nod.

"It's a good thing you didn't surprise them. If you had, there'd have been a possibility of violence,' said the younger one after inspecting our ravaged sitting-room.

The older guard yawned and shook himself. "Usual stuff," he said pulling out a notebook. Then we were subjected to a bombardment of questions. How long had we been out? Did we have a proper alarm system? Was our insurance policy paid up? Did we ever think of keeping a dog?

"Finn!" shrieked Anne and Beth and they tumbled over each other towards the back door. They found him, dead, outside the boiler house.

"A sharp implement," said the young guard. "Cracked his skull."

As I vomited into the kitchen sink I thought of people who had survived the Holocaust. Had they survived or were they merely walking ghosts? I swilled away the mess, wiped my mouth and turned to face the uniforms.

When they had gone Beth made me a cup of tea which I didn't want, then we set about cleaning up. But the more we cleaned up the nastier what was left became. It wasn't work for the squeamish.

"I'll do it," I said as Anne and Beth began to cry. As well as the filth there was the vulgarity. Coarse words crayoned on the walls. A lurid suggestion pencilled on the back of the bathroom door.

"Don't read it. Forget it," I said busy with a Brillo pad as poor Anne, who had been the one to discover it, sat on the toilet seat, her face hidden in her hands.

The ransackers hadn't used the toilet, they had used our bedroom. I shouted all the bad words I knew as I scooped up the scabrous mess into paper and dashed pell-mell to the outside lavatory. But I didn't get sick again. I was too furious, angry enough to kill. I understood why people committed murder, I could feel the cleansing fire of retribution coursing through my body. My energy became dynamic as I wiped, sponged, washed, soaped, sluiced, rubbed, swept and hurled all the stuff on the kitchen floor into the bin.

And when the house was liveable in again I couldn't stop. I had to take a bath and wash my hair. I had worked myself into a trance. The bathroom was like an oasis in a desert. There was only myself, sounds of running water, the smell of verbena shampoo, tropical fruits on the shower curtain, towels the colour of pale sand.

I pretended that Peter was safe and well. The break-in hadn't taken place. I greased conditioner through my hair and sat on the lavatory lid while it formed a productive film around each hair shaft, around my mind.

The door was unlocked and Clive came in hesitantly.

"You OK?" His glance flicked over the medicine cabinet, razors, nail scissors.

"You must have had a bad shock," he said. "You should be lying down."

"I can't while my hair is wet," I answered in a similar, neutral, cautious tone.

8th April: Clive had gone to London to an exhibition and the girls were out in friends' houses. Jane, stepping out from the bushes, gave me a fright because I didn't recognise her. She'd taken a short cut between the houses. "I'm sorry about the robbery. On top of everything else it doesn't seem fair." Her face wrinkled in sympathy.

She'd had her hair curled, and with a black shawl over her flowered corduroy maternity dress and concern showing on her pink shiny face, she looked too earthy to be clever and academically inclined.

"I nearly didn't recognise you," I said.

She pulled a face. "I hardly recognise myself. Everything's been messed up, hasn't it?"

We went inside and I put on the kettle.

"You know, I can't even cook," Jane said, sitting down at the table. Then she surprised me by going off at a tangent, saying, "Tell me Auntie Dixie, did you and Dada ever fancy each other?"

The question was so ludicrous and so out of date that I snorted.

"You did, didn't you? Mama said something about it this morning."

"Jane," I said, "does it really make any difference?"

"Yes," she answered matter-of-factly and immediately afterwards, with a toss of her head, "shit...no way!"

"How is your father?" I wasn't going to seem annoyed.

"He's sorry he wasn't nicer about Peter. He send his regards." She lifted her head. "That's not why I'm here. These are displacement tactics, evasion tactics, so I don't have to face the real problem." She looked terribly serious and worried.

I unplugged the kettle, made tea, put out some biscuits on a plate.

Jane wrinkled her forehead. "I mean, should I

marry the baby's father?"

The biscuits slid from the plate in my hand onto the floor.

"You can't. Peter's dead, Jane."

"It's not Peter I'm talking about."

"What's this? Some rotten kind of joke?" I felt completely at sea.

"Oh no, Sandy's not a joke."

"Who's Sandy?"

"I was sleeping with him at the same time as with Peter. Well...more or less."

I picked up the biscuits, put them and the teapot on the table, got out mugs and sat down very carefully.

"Is this something you've just made up?"

Her face puckered and she turned away crying, "Aunt Dixie, that's awful."

At first I had a singing noise in my head as if I was going to faint. I found it hard to follow the thread of Jane's story, but gradually it fell into some sort of shape. As well as Peter there had been Sandy, there still was Sandy. She still liked him, kind of. He was a bit older.

She gave me some more bits and scraps of information. Then she went on to say that it didn't really matter anyway, all that rubbish about spermatozoa and so on, because it was a woman's decision. And she'd decided that the baby was going to be Peter's anyway. Sort of, if I understood what she meant, like a transplant in reverse.

"You're talking rubbish," I said.

"I'm not," her voice was gentle. "Because the baby has to be Peter's. He will be in some sort of way no matter what. It's because we had that lovely time together in the summer. Even if I did have it proved scientifically that he was Sandy's son he'd have to be Peter's as well otherwise there'd be nothing of him left."

"You don't even know it's a boy..." The lump in my throat stopped me.

"I do know," Jane said. "Besides," she massaged her belly, "I like boys better than girls." Her smile resembled the Mona Lisa's. A Sunday in the Louvre, the Whites and ourselves.

"And does Sandy go along with all this?" I was curious and fascinated.

Jane considered. "He mightn't exactly be thrilled, but he's never going to know. He never knew about Peter."

I experienced a frightening sense of déjà vu. It struck me that I was listening to an exposition of my own frame of mind from over twenty years back. A cave, a hearth, a hunter, a safe haven for a child, salvation.

"Don't do it, Jane," I said. "Getting married for reasons like that is bad news. I ought to know. I did it myself."

## Chapter Nine

24th April: Jane received my remarks about mistaken marriages with as much interest as if I'd handed her a lump of coal and told her it was a priceless antique.

"Oh dear," she'd nodded then yawned. "I suppose things were very different in those days." After that the subject was closed. She thanked me for my advice and left with a nonchalant wave. Then yesterday she turned up again to tell me that Ruth's mother had died suddenly.

"I'm very sorry," I said although I hardly knew the woman.

"Mama's shattered," said·Jane. "She doesn't know anything about arranging things or anything and Dada can't go up until tomorrow. I thought that maybe you might go with her instead."

"I'm sure she wouldn't want me along," I protested.

"Oh, she would. It'd be great, honestly. Especially if you came in and suggested it."

So, much against my will, I found myself in

Evergreen practically on my knees in front of Ruth, begging her to allow me to accompany her up to her childhood home.

We took my car. Ruth was very nervous and dressed to the nines in a fitted black costume that made her look terribly fragile.

"God, everyone's eyes will pop out when they see Jane," she said. "She's enormous."

After that we spoke very little. Ruth was still in a state of disbelief about her mother, with whom she had been discussing "Coronation Street" on the telephone the evening before she died.

I had taken the precaution of making a telephone booking for us in the local hotel. The place was what you'd expect to find in a small midland town off the tourist track. The receptionist was a dark dreamy girl dressed in a T-shirt and jeans. In the bar two rough-looking men sat at the counter cocooned in cigarette smoke.

Our bedroom was basic verging on dreary but it did have its own bathroom. It was a corner room with three windows. From the front one you looked out onto the main street. We could see an elderly man wearing a mackintosh and brandishing a newspaper as if he was swatting flies.

"That's my Uncle Michael," said Ruth.

"Well!" I put my suitcase down on the bed closest to the front window. "What do we do next?"

"He's coming here." Ruth started pacing up and down the room.

A few seconds later somebody hammered at the door. Opening it we found the receptionist in the corridor. "Whichever one of yous is Mrs White there's a man downstairs wants you," she said.

On closer inspection Uncle Michael was a tall ruin of a man with a red face, bulbous nose, bedraggled moustache and thatch of white hair.

"Hello, my dear. Everyone's dead or dying. Mildred was one of the best, the most patient of us. Is Alan with you?" His rheumy eyes swivelled towards me.

"Alan couldn't make it until tomorrow. This is a friend of mine, Dixie Molloy." Ruth's voice sounded weak and girlish.

"How long since you'd seen your mother?" rapped Uncle Michael.

"Christmas."

"She'd failed a lot since then. Pity. Always fond of Mildred. Life didn't treat her kindly."

Ruth looked ready to crumble.

I thought of my own mother, chasing will o' the wisps around a Dublin nursing home. I hadn't seen her for months. The nurses have told me that it doesn't make much difference, time has no meaning, yesterday and ten years ago are one and the same to her.

"You know what it's like," I said to Uncle Michael, "it's hard to make space for everything."

He looked displeased, but at that instant a man of around our age, wearing a black suit and a solemn expression, stepped smartly through the swing doors. He made a beeline across the lobby to Ruth and shook her hand.

"Ruth," he said, "I'm sorry for your trouble. Remember me? Alf Fletcher the undertaker. Don't be bothering yourself now, we'll take care of everything."

Ruth looked anxious. "I'm not sure what I'm supposed to do."

"My dad was always terrible fond of your mother, she was some lady," said Alf. "We'll make sure she only has the best. It's due to her." His quick inquisitive eyes darted from Ruth to me to Uncle Michael. "Have you been down to see her yet? She's looking lovely."

"I was the person who found her on the hall floor. She wasn't such a pretty sight then. Lucky I called for my usual little elevenses," said Uncle Michael although the question wasn't addressed to him.

"Well there you are," said Alf. His gaze flickered from Ruth to me and back. "Isn't it a good thing you didn't have to travel up all on your own. How's the hubby? I suppose we can expect him later. In the meantime you'll want to go down to your mother's."

"I'll be fine here," I interrupted heartily.

"I've already notified the daily papers. I took the liberty," Alf said. He lowered his voice, "Don't you fret, Ruth. Sure it was a grand way to go. It's what I'd hope for for myself. A quick death."

I felt a bitter taste in my mouth. I'd had enough of death. I shouldn't have let Jane persuade me to come up here.

Ruth left with Alf and I rested for an hour or so in the bedroom before following Ruth's directions to her mother's place. I had managed to give Uncle Michael, who had shown signs of wanting to linger in my company, the slip. I bought myself a gin and tonic in the bar, carried it upstairs, lay on my comfortless mattress sipping it and thought seriously of going back down for another one and another and getting well and truly pissed. The place had slipped into an afternoon stupor, the world was at a standstill.

I thought how strange it was to be here with Ruth. And then I thought it was the least I could do for her. I thought she'd probably much rather have Clive with her but it wouldn't do, it would look all wrong. I wondered how she and Alan were getting on with each other. The one topic I hoped she didn't bring up was that Sunday. It was best forgotten. I'd rather talk to her about Peter, or Jane, than that Sunday. At this point my thoughts began to wander. It must have been the midland air. Before I knew it I was sleeping as heavily as if I'd been drugged.

I woke several hours later and followed Ruth's directions down the main street to the market square and easily picked out her mother's house. It was the one with the procession of stiff-jointed old people shuffling up to the door. As I approached I got a cheery wave from Alf the undertaker who was heading towards the pub on the opposite corner.

Indoors it was very overheated and stuffy with cups of weak tea circulating and ash-trays full of cigarette ends. The old people's faces were the colour of shrivelled mushrooms under the glare of an overhead light. Ruth's mother, lying in her coffin in the room across the hall, was fresher and healthier looking than any of them.

"God has taken her home," said Uncle Michael leaning so close that his moustache tickled my ear.

129

He had brought me across to view the remains. Ruth and two pathetic old ladies with lolling heads sat on three chairs against the wall.

"My aunts, Dixie," whispered Ruth. She looked resigned and pale. I found it strange to be among all these people who meant nothing to me, people who had no idea who I was. Nobody in this room, except Ruth, would know my son had recently been killed. I realised how little we all know about each other nowadays. I'd never discussed my own mother's illness with Ruth. I didn't know if her father had been anything like mine, growing so cantankerous in his final years that I dreaded visiting him.

I felt a rush of sympathy and grasped Ruth's hand which was quivering. "Don't worry," I whispered, "I'm here." She nodded with lowered eyes and a tear splashed onto the back of her hand.

The rest of the evening passed with nothing more dramatic than occasional spurts of elderly sniffing. I resolutely put my own private sorrows on a back burner. We took the coffin to the church and stood around making melancholy small talk after the prayers for the dead had been said.

Afterwards, Ruth and I had a meal in the hotel followed by a few drinks. Upstairs we discovered that we were sleeping over the dance-hall. Band music vibrated up through the floorboards in loud throbbing chords. Ruth plunged into a mood of deep melancholy which the racket exacerbated. Sleep was impossible. We sat on our beds shouting desultory remarks. We should, we realised, have stayed in her mother's house. Carelessly I asked her if she felt that her mother's death would change her life in any way. I was thinking how I'd nearly forgotten my own mother's existence.

"Change my life?" Ruth said, raising her eyebrows as if wearily amused. "How could it? I'm stuck, Dixie, you know that."

"It's amazing how young ones like Jane seem able to cope. I've promised to help all I can," I said, speaking lightly.

Ruth seemed to be smiling. It was an artificial smile and yet when she leapt to her feet I didn't realise right away that I was witnessing the start of a violent tantrum. Even when she ran towards the bathroom I thought it was because she suddenly wanted to use it. She slammed its door and a second later I heard things crashing. I raced to investigate and found that she had bolted herself in.

I hammered uselessly against the panels while glass and ceramic crashed inside. The bolt gave just as Ruth lifted the top off the WC cistern and hurled it against the tiled rim of the shower.

Water cascaded everywhere. Ruth came to a stop, her shoulders heaving. I pushed past her and switched off all the taps.

"It's all right," I said. "Calm down. We'd better try and dry the place up."

Ruth shrank back from me as I refitted the cistern top. It had broken clean in two but held together like a jigsaw. Some shower tiles were also cracked. Our make-up lay trampled on the ground. She must have been doing a war dance. I rescued the dregs of my own Estée Lauder and a squashed lipstick. The useless destruction made me feel poisonous.

"I'm sorry," Ruth whispered wringing her hands.

"Forget it," I said. At least the music, which had drowned out the sounds of havoc and kept the management away, was about to stop. I could hear them playing the National Anthem.

"Dixie, what are we going to do?" whispered Ruth while we mopped and wiped with the few threadbare towels available.

"I'm just going to go to sleep if you don't mind," I answered grimly. In bed I made a show of pulling the sheet up over my head.

Ruth shifted her position a few times but she didn't speak again.

It was early when I woke and discovered she was standing beside me.

"What's wrong?" I sat up, alarmed. Her hair was on end and her face contorted. She clutched a pillow tightly to her chest. "Nothing, nothing," she moaned. "I just felt so badly."

"Lie down at once," I ordered and watched while she stumped across to her own area and planked the pillow under her head again.

I wished we had a bottle of whiskey in the room or that the bar downstairs was open. I felt that Ruth had actually been going to press the pillow down on my face. I blessed myself surreptitiously, an action which made me feel idiotic. Even so, I lay, not sleeping, waiting and waiting for breakfast-time.

10th May: It's flowery dress and cotton T-shirt

time. Exam time. Beth and Anne chew pencils over tricky text books. The tennis-court lies starkly black and white under the throb of the midday sun. On the other side of the house there are marks on the tarmacadam where Clive's boat rested all winter. He launched it at the beginning of the month and whenever he has time he goes on sailing trips up Lough Derg, leaving me here at a loose end. I never did go with him. I refuse to commit myself to the water, always preferring terra firma beneath my feet.

But I was glad when Jane called. It took my mind off other things. I had been sitting up in Peter's room (I won't call it anything else) on his stripped-down bed, thinking that it was going to be a rough summer.

This morning the postman delivered an envelope containing some student documents relating to Peter and a copy of his birth certificate. It had come from the university but there was no covering note, nothing. Bureaucracy has no heart.

In Dublin the search for his killers has been put on file and I know what that means. Here in Limerick the guards have not produced any clues as to who ransacked our house. I called to the barracks yesterday morning and got nothing more satisfactory than shakes of head and shrugs of heavy shoulders while they kept their eyes fixed on a spot over my head and mouthed platitudes.

"Who's side are you on anyway?" I'd been driven to ask.

It was a mistake. I saw it in their beefy faces. Next time we could all be raped and murdered but it was only to be expected.

"These big houses are a liability nowadays," said one of them, licking the point of a pencil and marking something on a notepad. The matter was obviously considered closed. I'd been trying not to brood but it was impossible. I came home and shut myself up in Peter's room leaving the girls to fend for themselves. They're getting very good at that. But Jane arrived at a moment when they were all elsewhere.

Jane's face was flushed and she was very ungainly. She had a collection of bags and cases piled on the doorstep. I lifted one a fraction and said, "You'll strain your back."

She groaned. "I don't care. I'm moving in with friends. They're renting a house up the road. I wonder could you bring me up. Would you mind?"

"Sit down first." I led her over to the seat by the tennis-court. The surrounding hedges were very green and glossy. Summer growth had thickened them into a dense screen. I used to love sitting out here but now I keep seeing murderous eyes gleaming through the dark spaces.

"It's good to have company," I said. "I get nervous on my own."

"Are you going to sell the house?" Jane turned towards me. "Mama and Dada have been talking about selling up...at least Dada has."

The idea startled me. "I don't know!"

"How about your man friend in Dublin?" I asked to change the subject.

"I'm not deciding anything until after the baby. Anyway, I'm being allowed back next year to repeat. It can wait until then." She smoothed the front of her dark blue Indian shop smock over her swollen belly.

"I'm scared," she said in a small voice. "I'll never cope."

"We all feel like that the first time." I rested my hand against her flushed cheek. "You're a big girl now."

She grinned ruefully. "I'm big all right."

I helped her to her feet and got her things into the car. "...And you're tough. Remember when you used to climb those trees? You always climbed higher than anyone." We turned to face the large copper beech at the edge of the lawn. At that second the evening sun caught its leaves and lit it up into a gigantic bronze lantern.

We held our breath. Then Jane said, "Peter could swing by his ankles. It's a wonder we weren't all killed." Her voice broke. "Oh, I didn't mean that. It sounded awful."

"Hush!" I made myself very busy loading her things into my car.

The house she was going to was about half a mile from our own. Some friends of Jane's who were going to Limerick Art College were its tenants. When she walked into the house ahead of me she was greeted with laughter and cheerful applause and cries of, "Here comes the fat lady!"

The kitchen reeked of chips and burnt grease. Tea towels and damp clothes festooned the backs of a motley collection of chairs. The room was full of young people. Girls with shiny eyes and spiky hair and boys who were all like Peter—pale and lanky with toothy grins.

"Where you goin' to sleep, Jane?" asked one of

the boys and the others all hooted good-humouredly.

"This is Peter's mother, Mrs Molloy," Jane said quickly.

There was a brief awkward pause before one of the girls offered to make me a cup of coffee.

I shook my head making some excuse even though I'd have liked to stay awhile. To rest myself here where the taped music in the background was reminiscent of Tristram Long and his fiddle, and anything was possible so long as it was fun.

"Mrs Molloy, would you know what's wrong with this sauce?" asked another girl who was at the cooker stirring something in a pot.

It was an old-fashioned cooker, almost as decrepit as the one I used to struggle over in our Rosepark House days. The top, between the rings, was encrusted with grease and when the girl stepped back the oven door, which she had been holding shut with her knee, creaked open. The saucepan contained a mess of whitish lumps and golden rivulets.

"The milk's sour," I said.

"Oh shit!" The girl scowled, then in a quick movement tipped everything into a bin beside the old stone sink.

"Who's going to go for takeaway?" she called over her shoulder and a friendly argument immediately broke out.

And so I left Jane to settle into the easy-going muddle of her friends' house and came back to Bella Vista.

My girls had started a picnic in the garden. It

wasn't actually raining but the evening had grown cold and windy, tearing rose blossoms off the bush beside the hall-door. I sat on the garden seat, shivering, and told them about Jane's new arrangement while they munched cheese and egg sandwiches.

They seemed to know all about it.

"Her mother's raging," said Anne cockily.

Then, although there was no connection, Beth started talking about a boy of her own age whose body had been taken out of the river. The chill had got into my bones. I moved away from their chatter and speculation. I hoped that Jane was going to be all right. I hoped that they were all going to be all right in spite of the terrible things that happened. Life seemed as fragile as the petals fluttering from the old rosebush.

24th May: A significant development in our neighbourhood has been the arrival of new owners in the house across the road from our front gate. It is a thirties house which was until recently inhabited by a reclusive woman. Her days were spent working in her magnificent garden. I only ever saw her in church wearing, winter and summer, year in and year out, a green anorak and cavalry twill trousers.

Once she caught up with me as I walked along the road with Marie, Beth and Anne and said, "They remind me of my gels—in England—during the war." I looked into her weather-beaten face with its red gash of lipstick and struggled for something sociable to say but she had forged on ahead. Her final disappearance was just as abrupt.

An ambulance at the gate one day, and a FOR SALE sign put up by Alan immediately afterwards. Clive met the new owners when he inspected the house on their behalf.

Their name is Daly. He is an Irishman and his wife, Sophia, is Greek. Last night they gave a house-warming party. Everyone in the neighbourhood was invited. Sophia Daly is petite, glamorous, a great cook. Long tables held selections of rainbow-coloured dainties. Andrew Daly mixed lethal cocktails with a heavy hand. Everyone quickly got drunk and hilarious. It was Andrew's birthday. He was thirty years old, the big three O. Decorations gave a carnival atmosphere. I felt older than I wanted to be. I wished we could turn back the clock. I wished we hadn't married so young. I wished I could rewind my life as it if was a tape. I'd had enough to drink to make it seem like a reasonable proposition.

It seemed so long since I'd been at a party! I couldn't always live the way I had lived over the past months, in a knot, eating my heart out over the cruelty of Peter's death.

"Don't push me around." I heard Ruth's voice out in the hall. Turning, I saw her enter with Alan behind her.

I didn't greet them. I was here to enjoy myself. I was in no mood for Ruth and her troubles as I wondered what Andrew Daly used as the base for his special pink punch cocktail.

"Please, Alan!" I heard her voice. She sounded tearful.

I couldn't avoid seeing him pinch her arm. I was forced into remembering how he had been on that Sunday afternoon. I was looking into a cold yawning hole and Ruth lay at the bottom with a dark destroyed look on her face. The party was just a facade, we had no business here.

"Leave her alone," I said sharply.

He looked sullen then stepped towards me, caught my arm and twisted the skin between his hands so that it burned. In spite of the cocktails I'd drunk I could smell the whiskey on his breath.

"Shut up or I'll make you squeal again," he said and I had a glimpse of Ruth's terror-stricken existence. I wanted to run away and hide but his grip was too strong for me to wriggle free.

"OK, sweetie, how about another of these?"

Andrew Daly was beside us, all aftershave and hair mousse, another tumbler of his pink concoction in his hand.

"You two know each other?" he smiled. He could have advertised toothpaste to good effect.

"Too long. Back in the bad old days she used to be a good fuck, pardon my French, now she's turned into a right bitch," said Alan loudly.

The people near us had stopped talking. The Dalys had invited everybody in the neighbourhood and so it was a mixed bunch of young and old, butterfly glasses, teased hair, blue rinses, jeans, dark suits, mini skirts and pussycat bows. I watched as they merged into a collage of modern suburbia.

"How about Paris. Remember that time in Paris?" Alan prodded.

"Oh, Paris," Andrew Daly picked up the name like a crow grabbing a breadcrumb. "Great place. Sophia and I just love it. Do you enjoy Paris,

Dixie—Mrs Molloy?"

I saw by his expression that he was terrified that a row was about to start.

"Sure," I said. "It's terrific. The Champs Élysées and all that."

"I remember you in that big old wooden bed and squatting on the bidet beside the fireplace in that dump behind the Galeries Lafayette," Alan snorted. "God, you were mad for it! I always knew Clive was only half a man. Couldn't give you what you wanted. Am I right?"

I heard a titter. I stole a glance towards Ruth. She was watching with her fist screwed up against her lips. I perceived that Clive was standing beside her.

"I don't know what you're getting at," I managed haughtily. Then, I hiccuped.

Piped music suddenly swelled through the room masking my discomfort. Sophia had tactfully turned up the volume of the speakers. People turned to talk to each other too loudly and too fast. The house began to hum like a beehive.

I helped myself to a savoury from a passing tray and crammed it into my mouth. It was covered with some sort of burning peppery sauce. I took a swig from my glass which made me splutter as Clive moved in saying, "You've drunk too much of that stuff." He was having a plain soda water himself.

My palate was on fire and tears sprang to my eyes. It was all so unjust, so unfair.

"You might think of Ruth before starting a scene," he said coldly.

The flames I had swallowed turned into a

140

raging furnace. "You're as thick as the wall." I said. "You can't even see what he does to her. He rapes her, rapes her, I'm telling you. Don't think that it's because you're sexy that she fancies you. It's always because she wants to get away from him, nothing else. Alan's right about that. You're not the answer to a maiden's prayer by a long shot, you never were. You can't even hold a candle to Brendan Collins."

I suppose if you want to say something unforgivable to your husband or your partner you might as well say it in front of as many people as possible. No matter how atrociously you behave there will always be one or two in a large crowd who will sympathise and see themselves as kindred spirits.

No thunderbolt struck me down on the thick cream carpet, instead Sophia was by my side. "It's Andrew's mixtures, I'm afraid that they trigger people off," she explained with a little laugh. Then she was pressing my arm and leading me off to another room where some people were dying to meet me.

"What has Brendan Collins got that I haven't got?" joked a tall man whom I'd never seen before. Then seeing that I was embarrassed – for my crassness had shocked me back into sobriety – he amended his question to "Has Brendan been around lately?"

I shook my head. "He's gone to Mayo."

"To hell or to Connaught?"

The tall man scrutinised me then shot out his hand grinning, "I'm Harry Mercer—I know you—you're Clive's wife."

"Oh please," I said, "don't rub it in."

Suddenly life was liveable again.

"What we both want," said Harry Mercer, "is some good strong coffee." He steered me towards the Dalys' brightly redecorated kitchen.

A procession of people sauntered in and out as Harry and I sat at a round pine table chatting over pottery mugs. There was no sign of Clive or the Whites.

"I know what happened to Peter," was one of the first things that Harry said. It seemed that he had a son the same age who had been in Peter's class in school. "He's in Australia now," Harry added and, after a pause, "and his mother's in England—permanently."

Without the least sign of awkwardness he explained the circumstances. He was a builder, that was how he knew Clive. It was he who had done the renovations for the Dalys, that was why he was at the party. He had returned to Ireland ten years ago after a long stint as a contractor in London. His wife was English. She had come over with him and stuck it out for as long as she could, then she'd gone back. It was a usual thing, Harry said, over here was a queer place for a woman from outside to come to.

I listened while admiring the spotlighting system in the Dalys' ceiling and Sophia's collection of exotic house plants which thrived in every possible shelf and cubby hole. It was a relief just to sit and let somebody talk. It was restful to be in such pleasant surroundings. The spat with Clive was something that had happened in a bad dream, it faded in my mind.

When Sophia came in and murmured that Clive wanted to leave I nodded but made no move. A while later I was dancing in the Dalys' living-room. Harry's arms felt like home and when he rested his cheek against my hair I moved my face around until my lips smiled against his. After a moment he pushed me back from him and began to execute a complicated solo routine which quickly turned into a party piece and excluded me.

I joined the watchers while he twirled on flashing feet, twisting his hands over his head. Then Sophia pranced forward and together they began to dance in the Greek style, circling and stamping and marking each other's movements. As I watched I began to feel second-rate, gritty and as jealous as a teenager. Here I was, a woman with grown children, and yet, I had to clutch the back of a chair to restrain myself from pushing Sophia out of the way and reclaiming Harry's attention.

Andrew Daly stood nearby, looking pleased. He began to clap to the music and others copied him. Nobody was taking any notice of me. I took a deep breath, pulled myself out of the musical vortex with the gyrating couple at its centre, tiptoed across the hall and let myself out into the night air. Nobody noticed my departure.

The walk up our driveway was dark and every snap of a twig seemed like a lurking strangler. The house itself was in darkness but the hot water had been left switched on. I ran a bath and soaked in it until I felt unwound and virtuous. When I crept into our room Clive was snoring heavily. I told myself that he obviously didn't care what happened to me except when it affected his own plans.

# Chapter Ten

3rd June: Jane's baby will soon be born. I think wildly of having a child myself; something to fill the empty space at the centre of my being. I'm almost forty. Forty-plus mothers are all the rage. But who will father it?

Clive has barely spoken to me since the party in Dalys'. When he looks my way his expression is grim. He goes to bed at ten o'clock or else stays out until all hours. I have no idea where he has been or what he is thinking about.

I wrote a regulation thank-you note to the Dalys and sent Anne off to push it through their letter-box. That is the nearest I have come to making contact with them. I met Harry Mercer by chance in a city chemist's shop while I was optimistically buying myself suntan lotion.

"Are you expecting hot weather?" he asked in his good-humoured voice. His manner was such a contrast to Clive's that I wanted to place my palm against his warm smooth cheek. Dark tendrils of hair curled at the open neck of his sports shirt. He was off to play golf. I looked down at the counter and saw through the glass top a display of the newly available cutely named condoms. Because of Harry they made me blush like a schoolgirl. I knew he was staring at them too and grinning.

"See you round, Dixie." He gave my neck a little squeeze as he rested his hand on my shoulders.

I nodded awkwardly and ran. When I got home I began to think again about having a baby. Madness. I went upstairs and into Peter's bedroom. I felt full of futile regrets, sorry that I'd ever cleared out the big wooden press in the corner of its jumble of old school books and comics and all the worn-out jeans and jumpers. The paraphernalia of youth. It was Clive who'd made me get rid of everything, Clive who'd told me it was morbid to hold onto things that were of no value whatsoever. Harry Mercer would have let me keep anything I wanted to, I felt sure of that. Harry would put my peace of mind at the top of the list.

The central heating radiator had been turned off in the room; that was Clive's idea too. "No point in firing money away in these hard times." I walked over and twirled the black knob at the side. My son's room wasn't going to be kept like a chilly morgue. I looked out at the garden. The lawn was full of flat brown toadstools, so big that I could see them from upstairs. Maybe I should put some in Clive's portion of stew at dinner-time. Maybe...Maybe...Maybe I'd eat some myself and then return to curl up on the stripped mattress in this dark room and lapse easily into forgetfulness.

"Aunt Dixie?" The door pushed open. I turned

and saw Jane. She was hot-faced and heavy-eyed.

"Mrs Connors let me in," she said.

Circles of sweat stretched under the armpits of her pink T-shirt. She wore it tucked into a pair of track suit bottoms. The elastic waist came up under her breasts and her belly was a huge bulge. It was clear that the baby had moved down.

"Don't I look awful!" she sighed. Then she said in a brighter voice, "Do you know that Monsignor Patrick is outside – with Uncle Clive?"

"Fantastic," I said bitterly. "Just the person."

"Aunt Dixie, can I just tell you something?" Jane sat down on the end of the bed. "The one thing I hope about this baby is that it helps to make things happier again. I mean, more like they used to be. Like when Mama and Dada used to go off on holidays with you and you came home with lovely presents. Remember that little music box with the ballerina? And the jackets that time you went to Morocco? And holidays in Kilkee. Maybe we could all go and visit there after the baby is born – even for a weekend. How about that?"

Her eyes were too bright. She looked feverish.

"Jane," I said, "I'll have to go down and check on the Monsignor. I wasn't expecting him. I've nothing in to feed him with. Though why I should bother to provide anything for him God only knows. He has no business showing up without advance notice. He must think I've nothing better to do all day than loll around on lace cushions waiting for the likes of him."

"I'll help," Jane offered. "What'll you give him?"

"Wormburgers," I said casting a wistful glance at the toadstools outside.

Considering what happened later we prepared a much better spread for the Monsignor than he deserved. I defrosted some prawns and made a mayonnaise. Jane brought in some lettuce from the garden. Beth showed up and concocted a curried rice salad. Anne arrived and between them they set the dining-room table while I went upstairs and changed into nun-like navy and a prim white blouse.

During the course of our meal it transpired that the Monsignor was actually here because Clive had invited him without telling me. Even so I was caught unprepared for what came next.

"I think you've been a wonderful wife and mother, Dixie," Clive announced pompously after supper. He and Monsignor Patrick and I had retired, for reasons that seemed vague to me, to the drawing-room.

I immediately felt uneasy and puzzled.

Monsignor Patrick was staring with pursed lips into his brandy and soda. Suddenly he lifted his head and looked at me with what I supposed was meant to be a judicious and penetrating gaze.

"I'm afraid, Dixie, that this is going to be painful," he began then he prissily took a sip of the sparkling golden liquid.

"I want it put on record that I've tried to find an easier alternative," Clive said stupidly.

"I don't know what you're talking about. I don't even know why you're here." I addressed myself to Monsignor Patrick.

"All in due course, Dixie. All in due course. You

must know that I've both your best interests in mind. I've already told Clive that he can rely on me to help in every way I can."

My dormant dislike for him flared. "What's all this about? It sounds like an awful load of rubbish."

"My poor girl." He shook his head with unctuous sympathy.

At that moment the evening sun shone in the window right into my face, dazzling me so that he and Clive were darkened into shadowy figures speaking from inside a cavern.

"I'll make sure that you have enough money to live on," said Clive's voice.

"We must appreciate how the courts of the Church always try to act with the fullest possible degree of compassion and understanding," said Monsignor Patrick.

"In our case we were both unfortunately much too young," added Clive.

"I'm not excusing myself, I've been old-fashioned at times. The modern-day attitude to an unwed mother is in many ways more Christian. That young Jane. Her career will be in no way damaged. I must accuse myself of putting undue influence on Clive at the time of your marriage." Monsignor Patrick sounded full of self-satisfaction.

I felt as if I was being slowly set in concrete. It was just as well. Otherwise I'd have given way to my impulse to claw his hypocritical face as I gradually realised what was happening. I was being tricked, they wanted to blind me, as they had blinded themselves, with false logic. Clive and Monsignor Patrick had joined forces against me.

Church rules were being twisted so that Clive could wriggle out between the bars.

"Nowadays, of course, we'd refuse to perform the marriage ceremony until after the child was born. That way there can be no question of undue pressure, if you understand me," said Monsignor Patrick.

There was no need for him to fill in the gaps.

"Believe me," Clive said imploringly, "I've tried. Especially since Peter was killed. I hate to do this, Dixie."

"In some cases a Church annulment is the truest confirmation of our own flawed humanity and a sincere act of humility," prodded Monsignor Patrick's cunning old voice. He continued, "Of course, Dixie, you have been wonderful in many ways. I often say that a medal should be struck for all our Irish mothers."

If it had been anybody but the Monsignor I might not have reacted so hastily. I might, just might, have tried counting to ten instead of jumping to my feet so that the sun was no longer shining in my eyes.

"I don't get it," I said. "How long have you been hatching this up, Clive – or, was it your idea, Monsignor? I bet it was you, you old crook. You've always turned up your nose at me because of Peter. Well, how about Clive and his carry-on with Ruth White? You know about that, don't you? You know that Danny, poor little Danny, is their love-child? Have you fixed all that up as well? And Alan – how have you squared him off? Am I the only poor eejit being shut out in the cold?"

"Dixie," Monsignor Patrick lay back like an old

black sack full of nastiness in my best armchair. "Dixie, I know it hurts, I know it won't be easy. But with the help of God we can all carry our burdens. This is a painful decision for everybody. Don't let us make it more distressing by saying things that may well lead to even more regrets later on."

Black and white lights flashed in my head. "One thing I won't regret is telling you the true facts." The words flew from my lips. "Peter was my child," I screamed, "Clive had no hand, act or part in him. No, I'm not claiming a virgin birth. I'm not that daft. But it was another man – not Clive. I just used you, Clive. You just came in handy."

"Stop – Dixie!" Clive buried his face in his hands. His shoulders heaved. He seemed completely shattered.

"Well, well," Monsignor Patrick scrutinised me with an impassive face.

I glared back at him.

He blinked, then gave the tiniest of nods.

I turned towards the empty fireplace and rested my arm on the mantelpiece. So that was what people meant when they said someone had scored an own goal. I have never been a sports fan but I knew that there was only one thing left for me to do. I forced my legs to carry me steadily out into the hall without looking back and took care to close the door softly on the silence within.

12th June: The scene: Bella Vista's kitchen. A patch of sunshine that spread across the table top and lit up my gold cigarette packet. I have started to smoke again. Early afternoon and there were already several butts in the glass ashtray. The radio was on. A drug addict was being interviewed. "I need two hundred pound a day to feed my habit," he said, "I have to rob it." I imagined him creeping up behind Peter with a knife in his hand for the sake of petty cash. I switched the radio off and went back to scrutinising the situations vacant column in the paper. What I'd actually like to be is a hired killer. What I find is: Administrative Assistant, Senior Bar Person, Young Person, Young Person, Young...I gave up. Anyhow, I'd have been astonished to find a job for which I could apply. I switched to the travel column: London, France, Lourdes, Spain, Canaries, Rome.

Monsignor Patrick went to Rome the day after he visited us. I'd peeped into Clive's personal diary while I was making his bed. "Uncle Patrick. Vatican. Annulment. Immature?" I'd suppressed an urge to scrawl "shithead" across the page.

I felt the walls of the kitchen closing in on me. They moved tighter and tighter so that I could hardly breathe, then they burst apart leaving me bare-assed and terrified under the open sky. I began to shake. The house was giving me the jitters. I had to get out.

I hurried upstairs and looked out a fresh blouse and skirt, applied blusher, eyeliner, lipstick, pulled a comb through my hair. I was getting careless, letting myself go.

In spite of our estrangement, Clive and I were still sharing a bedroom. The fact irritated me. It made me reluctant to linger at the dressing-table. At bedtime I hurried into my nightie without delaying to apply cold cream, hand cream or anything else. In the morning my toilet was scrappy and haphazard. But I was staying here, I wasn't giving an inch. I decided that when I got back from town I'd start shifting Clive's stuff into the small spare room where everything, back as far as his mother's old sewing machine, had been stored for donkey's years.

I didn't care what the girls thought. They were going to know the whole story soon enough. Perfume squirted from the atomiser as viciously as snake's venom. I made a few final touches to my face and discovered that in spite of everything I looked amazingly well.

I ran out of the house. Just to be in the fresh air was good. I feasted my eyes on the garden and felt certain that Clive wasn't going to get his way. I'd survived hard times before. I'd get through this patch. Besides if my marriage was going to be broken up I wanted to do it in my own way, when I felt the time was right. Or did I want to stay with Clive until death etc.? Yes and no. I couldn't say. I wasn't together enough to be sure and I feared for the girls as well as myself.

I switched on the engine, put the car in gear and accelerated down the drive too fast, much too fast, just as Clive's car came streaking up towards the house as if he thought the place was burning down. I saw his face for an instant like something glanced through a soap bubble, or a fish coming to the surface of a lake. The mouth was a gaping circle. The eyes protruded. I'm sure my own expression mirrored his as we caught sight of each other in that moment of suspended time that went on and on and on, happening over and over in slow motion.

Then it was a world full of crunching metal, the snap of twigs, the hiss of breaking glass. Shadows and light flickered in quick alternation. My left hand scrabbled uselessly at the controls, my right one was wrenched in a half circle by the steering wheel. For three seconds I thought I was dead. We were both dead. I was plunging through undergrowth, the underworld, being swallowed up by the earth. There was an enormous sensation of regret. I had never meant it to happen like this.

14th June: A python had swallowed me up to the waist. I tried to move my legs but they were held fast in its hot dry gullet. I felt like Hans Andersen's little mermaid. Even so I managed to smile. The girls had come into the hospital to tell me about Jane's baby boy.

Anne, Bridget and Beth competed with superlatives. "Fabulous," "fantastic," "really excellent."

"Jane thinks he looks like Peter," said Anne. The three of them eyed me cautiously.

"Good," I said. It hurt when I nodded my head. I didn't know what sort of painkillers I was on, but, except for my legs, I seemed to be made of cotton wool.

"Daddy got his own car going this morning," said Beth.

"What's my one like?" I asked nervously.

Anne giggled, "All squashed. It's lucky you didn't get killed."

"Hard to kill a bad thing." I drifted off into a

sudden doze against the background of their voices. They'd been very good. They'd brought me chocolates and flowers and in the middle of all the panic Jane's baby had been born. I napped for a while, sluggish pain-filled dreams. When I woke up Clive was there saying, "You were driving like a lunatic."

I wasn't, I was just the person in the smaller car. Tears seeped from under my eyelids as a nurse materialised all bustle and efficiency.

She simpered flirtatiously at Clive. "Your husband's gorgeous," she said in a stage whisper as she leant down to smooth my pillows. In fact, Clive looked haggard. He had a sticking plaster across the back of his hand. "Go away, Clive," I muttered hoarsely as the nurse squeaked around the room in her rubbery shoes. I wanted to think about Jane's baby. Could it really be Peter's? How freakish it was that men who are clinically dead can still be fathers. No wonder they need so many things, armies, corporations, hierarchies, to keep them latched on to the world. First Tristram, now Peter. "So it's a boy," I said, sighing. I didn't know if that made it worse or better. My mind was only functioning in spurts.

"I brought you a paper." Clive placed a rolled-up *Irish Independent* on my blanket then made a helpless gesture with his hands.

Suddenly I wanted to see the baby. I had a hunger to see it. I had a bittersweet taste in my mouth. Tears began to flow again. "I want to go home," I said. The nurse had left us alone.

"There's no rush." Clive looked unhappy. "There's no rush about anything, Dixie. According to Uncle Patrick this business may take ages." He was trying to sound matter of fact but he couldn't keep the quaver out of his voice. "They're very slow about annulments."

"Have you and Ruth made any plans?" I asked stupidly.

His face became set in stone. "That's for her to decide."

"...and Alan," I offered weakly.

"As soon as you're on your feet I'm going away for a while," he said abruptly.

"Where to?" I felt a stir of curiosity.

"To look for work for one thing," said Clive. He walked to the end of the bed. I was too sore to lift my head. He seemed very far away. I wished that I was in a public ward instead of this room where there was no refuge from Clive moaning about the harsh realities.

"This is all going to cost money. Everything costs money," he said. He sounded resentful and mean.

"It's your idea," I retorted weakly.

"It wasn't me who caused that bloody car crash," he burst out. "One car written off."

"I suppose you care more about the car than me," I said.

"And there's no question of getting you a replacement."

I turned and looked at the wall. If I counted slowly back from one hundred he'd be gone by the time I'd finished.

"Dixie," he intruded on my attempts to calm myself. "I still have to get you to clarify what you told Uncle Patrick about some other man making you pregnant. Was that true?"

"It's a bit late to go into that now," I said.

"I'd agree if it wasn't for the fact that you destroyed my life by laying it at my door. Who was he, Dixie? Where is he now?"

It wasn't fair. I was so full of drugs that I couldn't stop myself from crying. "Dead," I sobbed. "Leave me be."

I could hear Clive's hoarse breathing. "You're a mystery to me, Dixie. I don't know why you had to blame me."

"It was too difficult. I couldn't help it," I moaned. Then I pressed my face against my pillow waiting for him to say something else, but he tiptoed away.

Soon somebody else was standing beside the bed. I turned round painfully and found it was Harry Mercer with a sheaf of pinky gold gladioli cradled in his arms.

"I was going to make it red roses but then they seemed corny," he grinned.

I just lay there, looking, not even able to smile, as he blotted out the utter emptiness of zero.

# Chapter Eleven

7th August: I've been home for more than a
month. I arrived to a full house. Marie, Beth, Anne
plus Jane and baby Oliver. And, of course, in the
background, Clive.

The lease was up in the place Jane had moved
into with her student friends. The others had all
gone abroad for the summer, to work. Jane came
to us instead of to Evergreen. Danny had
developed chickenpox, or measles, or some
mysterious virus which was highly contagious.
That, anyway, was the official excuse; but I don't
know.

Jane was a little at a loss with Oliver and
complained incessantly about her figure. She had,
she said, turned into a female mammoth. She
couldn't get into a pair of jeans, the buttons of her
blouse kept popping open. I persuaded her to
persevere with breast-feeding and to be patient
about her waistline. My own daughters hovered in
the background as I spoke in calm, practical tones.
Meanwhile, I couldn't take my eyes off Oliver. He
was, in fact, a miniature replica of my son.

But the breast-feeding was not a success. Jane's supply of milk was too spasmodic and she was eating junk food and forgetting to take plenty of liquids. I had an ache in my own breasts from the car crash and sometimes it felt as if they might start to ooze when the baby cried.

"Oh please, how will I teach him to drink from a bottle," Jane wailed after a sleepless night.

"I'll teach you how," I said.

Then, this morning, Ruth called in. I was shocked by her appearance, her lanky hair and pale face. But her manner was subdued and equable. She'd been meaning to come in, she didn't know where the time had gone, and so on. In the sitting-room she sat staring at the glass of sherry I'd poured for her without drinking it. She had hardly glanced at the infant.

I sat with her for a while but could think of no words to fill the spaces between us. She was so inattentive and vague that it didn't even seem possible to ask about Danny. After about fifteen minutes she took a sip from her sherry glass, stood up and smoothed her skirt, then tiptoed out of the room. A few seconds later we saw her passing across the garden.

There was a brief silence before Jane said nervously, "Well, it was better than a big row."

"Why a row?" asked Marie who was perched on the arm of a chair.

Jane pulled a face. "She's very straight-laced. She's never going to accept that I actually didn't mind being pregnant. She thinks it's a sin."

"She's probably just tired with Danny sick and all that," I said.

After lunch I went shopping for baby formula, bottles and other necessities. I travelled in on the bus and several people whom I didn't recognise came up to ask kind questions about my own accident and about Jane. I murmured awkward inadequate responses. I had obviously become an object of local curiosity. I decided I would take a taxi home.

It was my first day to venture into the city like this and after doing several errands I grew confused and silly. I was almost sorry I hadn't humbled myself and asked Clive to bring me to town.

Clive: Our life together seems to be fixed in that moment when we peered aghast through our separate windscreens. Any second now it is all going to shatter. Lucky we were both wearing safety belts, lucky that it was two of my ribs that broke and not my neck. I repeat these obvious facts several times a day.

"Exhibit A," Clive said pointing to my car as he drove me home from the hospital. The battered chassis had been towed to a garage on the Ennis Road. I peered out at it in painful bewilderment. I hadn't the energy to argue about whose fault it had been. I was reluctant to even look at Clive's face in case it turned back into the shrieking mask that was imprinted on my mind.

"Look, right now, if I had my way, you and Ruth could set up tomorrow as man and wife but it's just not possible," I'd said in a moment of frantic appeasement.

"Don't start talking about something you know nothing at all about," he'd said.

I thought of the Sunday I'd followed them out the country and of the savage aftermath between Ruth and Alan. It was as if a curse had been laid on us all since then. People who've been cursed seldom escape their destiny.

"I'll do anything," I said. "Anything within reason."

Clive remained silent.

These days I'm so preoccupied with Jane, the baby, domestic matters, that I haven't had time to brood.

I had even put Harry Mercer's visit, bearing flowers, to the back of my mind until he appeared today in front of a flower stall in the shopping mall as I struggled along with a clutch of plastic bags.

"Hi there!" He blocked my path and bent to kiss my cheek. Behind him more gladioli, roses, carnations, tiger lilies, luxuriated among trailing vines and white delicate sprays.

I felt weak at the knees as I said, "Who's the lucky lady this time?"

"One guess."

He bounded away from me and with a flash of white cuffs and gold watch completed a quick transaction with the stall-holder. A single red rose was tucked into the bag containing nappies and baby powder.

"You're looking very dressed up," I said, awkward as a teenager.

He winked, put a finger to his lips, then looped my various packages around the fingers of his left hand and put his right arm around my waist.

"Let's run away," he said. "Are you game?"

"I can't. I have a grandson now," I answered.

He laughed. "That's great! That's the stuff. And here I was worried because you looked so lonesome but you're not lonesome at all."

I'd forgotten how warm his brown eyes were. He gave a thumbs up sign to the flower stall woman and I saw her move towards a bucket of perfect, velvety pink carnations. She had a roll of cellophane in her hand.

"If you haven't a car I'll run you home," he announced. His manner was pleased and matter-of-fact. I couldn't imagine anyone ever saying no to him about anything.

I allowed myself to scrutinise him as we drove towards Bella Vista. He had what my mother used to call an open face. His mouth was generous, his nose straight, his dark eyes wide-spaced. Handsome, handsomer than Clive ever was. I could see calluses on his hard-worked hands. I bet he'd rather starve than work in an office. But his suit sleeves rippled like silk against his arms. I noticed for the first time the silver glint in his hair. He was probably older than he looked. Fifty? Fifty-four?

I expected him to just drop me at the hall-door and drive away. Instead he was on the doorstep before I was, holding my bags, obviously waiting to be invited in.

"Aren't you busy? Don't you have to get back to work?" I asked tentatively.

"I've worked enough for one day. I've been at a meeting all morning, buying myself a new hotel," he said comfortably.

"For what?" I asked, surprised.

162

"A sideline. Sophia Daly is going to come out and supervise the dining-room."

I felt an unreasonable pang of jealousy as I turned the key in the door and led him inside.

The girls and the baby were in the sitting-room watching an old Marx Brothers film on TV. Bridget White was there as well. She and Anne were sitting cross-legged on cushions, playing an infantile game of Beggar my Neighbour and shrieking at the comic parts of the picture.

Harry promptly sat himself down in a chair and clasped his hands across his stomach. Introductions were out of the question but he seemed perfectly at home. I dithered on the threshold, contemplating switching off the set, then decided to go and make some coffee instead.

August 25th: Today Jane and myself went into the city with Oliver. Jane wanted to pick up some forms in connection with allowances for her child. She also wanted to make some enquiries about college courses. It was one of those days when I found myself seriously handicapped by not having a car.

A dark silence exists between Evergreen and Bella Vista now. Alan and Ruth have made no contact with us for days. Jane doesn't seem to notice and I'm just as happy to keep out of their way. Therefore, it came as a shock to turn a corner and literally bump into Alan walking along with Harry Mercer.

"Well! So we meet again!" boomed Harry. He was bursting with good humour and energy.

I found I immediately clutched Jane's arm in what was intended to be a gesture of mutual support. The baby, whom she was carrying in a little padded sling, squirmed and began to wail.

Alan scowled in discomfort. "Look, Harry, call up to the office later. Then we can talk." He spoke quickly then loomed over Oliver for a few seconds like a hawk. My hands clenched. I wanted to protest but there was no need for in a second he was gone.

Harry Mercer had missed nothing. "I suppose it's hard for a man like Alan to discover suddenly that he's a grandfather," he said. "What age is he anyway? Forty? Forty-two?"

"Twenty-one," said Jane boldly.

Harry chuckled. "I like you, Jane White," he said. "You just don't give a damn."

Jane gave a small laugh. "Not really!"

He was dressed today in an anorak over an open-neck shirt of mossy coloured checks. He looked comfortable and relaxed. "Junior's getting big, Jane," he said stroking the top of Oliver's head with a strong sure finger.

Then he stepped back, thrust his hands into his anorak pockets, jingled some money and said, "Well, what can I do for you two beautiful women?"

Jane folded her arms around Oliver and asked, "What were you doing with Dada?"

"Ah," Harry said teasingly, "I don't think I could possibly tell you that."

"Go on," said Jane, "why not?"

He turned quickly towards me and said, "This is your son's baby, isn't it? The poor boy who was killed in Dublin. I bet it means a lot to have him continued in the flesh, so to speak."

I nodded and said awkwardly, "It's difficult to talk about."

Once again Harry's physical presence affected me greatly. I wanted to rest my head against his chest. I wanted to have him take care of me.

"Aunt Dixie, we've loads to do," Jane broke in. "We've to pick up Anne's birthday cake on top of everything."

"Oh, you're having a birthday. Isn't that a pity now," said Harry, "just when I was going to ask you if you'd like to take a run down to the coast. I'm heading off to Lahinch this afternoon. I could have picked you up on the way." He addressed his remarks to me.

I found I was sick with disappointment. I wanted to cancel Anne's birthday tea on the spot.

"Another time I'd love to." I tried hard to sound nonchalant.

Harry nodded gravely. "I won't forget." When he clasped my upper arm my cheeks burned with pleasure and I had a mad impulse to beg him to come to Anne's birthday tea and forget about Lahinch, except that a refusal would have broken me.

Jane had already gone to stand at the traffic lights.

"He's a funny fish, isn't he, Aunt Dixie?" she said when I joined her.

"Look, Jane, you're grown-up now, you have a child. Don't you think it's time to cut out the 'aunt' bit?" I spoke sharply.

"OK, I'm sorry, Aunt...I mean Dixie. I mean he's nice and all that but don't you think he's a little bit...well, he seems to push himself in.

Talking about Peter and everything." Jane
frowned, her gaze fixed on the middle distance.

"Come on before the little green man
disappears," I said stepping into the roadway. I
found I had no wish to discuss Harry Mercer with
Jane.

4th September: Harry walked very close to me, as
close as a lover, as we made our way across Kilkee's
pale strand. I breathed deeply, filling my lungs
with his closeness. The season was over; there
were very few people about.

It was more than a year since I'd visited here.
"I've always loved this place," I said. Behind us
was the green slope of George's Head, ahead of us
the grey flat expanses of rock around the pollock
holes.

"I bet you're glad you came so." Harry
squeezed my shoulders.

I nodded.

"Going to have a swim right away?"

"Yep."

I knew I was wrong. I knew I was wicked. This
was how I'd felt on those afternoons in Tristram's
shop. This was what I'd been looking for when I'd
taken up with Brendan Collins. I felt wet and
lascivious and excited because this was going to be
the real thing.

I dropped my belongings smack in the centre
of the strand. "I hope you brought swimming
trunks," I said smiling. From the second, only two
hours ago, that I'd picked up the phone and heard
Harry's voice I'd felt like a kid let out of school.

Harry grinned. "I'm just a culchie. I can't

swim."

"That's cheating!" I'd had a wish in my heart to run across the strand with him, to go plunging together into the stinging waves.

"You go ahead, Dixie. I'm going to stand here and mind your stuff."

"It won't need much minding," I said.

There was nobody at all around except a clutch of women sitting on rugs with a few tiny children digging sandcastles near them plus two small boys fishing in the little river. I became all thumbs unfastening my clothes while Harry watched. At one stage I said, "I wish you'd go away. You're making me awkward."

"Go on, you like having me here," he said as I slipped off my brassiere and hesitated a moment before pulling up my swimsuit top.

"Wow! Not bad—not bad for a grandmother." Harry was laughing at me. I made a pretence of kicking sand at him then I stood in my plain black suit trying to act as if I wasn't posing, wasn't excited by him scrutinising me. I wished he would touch my arm again, touch my breasts, move closer still.

"You'd better run for it before I make a disgrace of myself," he said. I was glad of the gruff note in his voice and the way his eyes glistened. Then he gave my bottom a smart smack and launched me out over the sand towards the ocean.

I hunched up at the water's edge, the way I always did, shocked by its coldness. Then I gingerly forced myself into the swirling waters wondering why I had come, what I was doing there. I should be at home setting my house in order. I should be attempting to have a serious discussion with Clive.

This morning I had dusted down his exercise bicycle. It hadn't been used for months. The situation between us was in a similar state of stony indifference and neglect. Clive never spends a second more than he has to in the house. Whenever he looks at me his expression grows mulish.

Forget it. I was with Harry. I took a deep breath and lunged out into the water and pointed myself in the direction of the rocks. When I got to them I'd have a short rest and swim back. I'm a poor swimmer but it wasn't far. Anyway, I'd swum in this area so often in previous years that I believed that I could touch bottom any time I wanted to.

I planned to stay in the water for a little while with Harry watching me, then I would return and emerge like a goddess from the sea. It seemed important that I should come out of the waves and walk towards him, a creature arriving from another element. It was the way I wanted the prelude to whatever was going to happen between us to be played. I wanted to turn myself into a magical being, a dream woman, an ivory statue come to life. The stuff of ordinary existence lay coiled on the sand around my watch and bracelet. I wanted to be a butterfly coming out of the chrysalis, a snake shedding its skin.

But it had been a cold summer. The water had never properly warmed. I seemed to be pushing my way through an ice pack and getting nowhere. Then I saw that the sky was clouding over with darker clouds rolling in from the west. I was a little tired. I put a leg down to touch bottom and found nothing there.

Sometimes storms and heavy tides can make the contours of the beach change. I was swimming over a big hole, how big I couldn't say. I began to dog-paddle round in widening circles but no matter where I tried I was still out of my depth and the ocean's swell had increased alarmingly.

My vision of mermaid-cum-goddess was doused by the first shock wave. I was held in a dark place, seashells roaring in my ears.

I was in danger of being submerged in an instant. Why had the beach been so empty? Was there some sinister reason we hadn't heard about? A stitch in my side was worsening as I manoeuvred myself again to face the shore. I could see Harry and the blob which was my belongings. I couldn't tell whether he was watching or not but he was clearly not involved in my distress.

The sun had come out again briefly. It etched the hotels and the amusement park and turned the cake shop window into a glinting rectangle. It would be shining into the eyes of anybody looking in this direction. All they would see were dark shadows over the water. I moaned as another foamy wave splashed over my head. My legs were still managing to function but my breathing was going to bits. It was my own fault. My ribs had barely healed after the car crash.

Once again I saw the houses as the water see-sawed down and then they disappeared. I was turning into one huge shiver. My arms and legs were flapping like a human windmill. I saw myself as in a mirror, gasping the way fishes gasp when landed. My mouth awry, my eyes popping out.

I thought momentarily of Tristram. Merely a flash. Tristram behind his shop counter taking a pencil from behind his ear to add up a long tot. The sun had vanished again. The sky was the colour of the carbon paper in those old-fashioned cash books.

Tristram's music, funeral music, nearer my God to thee. Oh Jesus save me and I'll never sin again!

"I didn't see you, Dixie. I wasn't looking. Good girl, are you all right now? Is she coming round?"

The roaring tumult in my ears gradually faded away and I could hear Harry's voice. I felt puzzled and when I tried to lift my head I felt sick. Sand lodged disgustingly between my teeth as my guts spewed out onto the ground. My stomach was ripped open.

"Are you her husband?" asked a youth with wild red hair and freckles. His body was beaded with water and rivulets ran down his legs from his swimming trunks.

"A friend," said Harry.

The young man bent down towards me. "You'll be all right, Missis. It's got bad around that part. A few people have had bad frights." He grinned.

"He's the one who got to you. Saved your life." Harry sounded impressed.

"I thought it was an octopus," I tried weakly to joke. All I had been conscious of was some enormous threshing being with countless feelers.

"What we're going to do is go someplace and get ourselves ossified," Harry proposed after my rescuer had been thanked again and refused an invitation to join us for a celebratory drink.

I couldn't even nod my head. I felt as if an iron bar was clamped under my chin while a sledgehammer pounded in the small of my back. My hands hurt when I pressed them gingerly against the wet sand.

"I want to go home." I got up painfully and stood facing Harry, unable to look at him.

"Sure," he said, "maybe it's the best thing to do." He put an arm around me and said, "You're OK. Don't worry. I'll get you back in no time."

In fact I'd changed my mind. I wanted to stay here, be with him, finish the day as planned. I had a lump in my throat.

He led me to the car and settled me in. We had hardly left the town before I began to shiver and couldn't stop. My teeth chattered. I was in a state of shock.

I remember Harry pulling up outside a roadside pub and bringing me out a baby Power. He fed it to me as if I was a baby. Alcohol trickled from the sides of my mouth. I hiccuped, but after several sips I felt better and was able to finish the rest myself.

"Good girl. Good woman," Harry kept repeating.

Roses gently bloomed in my cheeks and skin changed back from fish scales into human flesh. A hot coal burned comfortingly in the centre of my chest. I was filled with gratitude.

"Thank you, Harry. Oh, thank you," I repeated as we headed on towards Ennis. I wanted to pull his hand from the steering wheel and smother it with kisses.

"For what?"

"Everything...all this." I made a vague gesture.

Then suddenly the comic aspect of our outing struck me and made me giggly and when I giggled I hiccuped. Harry kept his attention fixed on the road.

"I thought we'd be you know what by now." The thick way I said the words set me giggling worse than ever.

"What?"

"Loversh—Oh God!" He could have had me there and then if he'd stopped the car at the approach to the Ennis roundabout.

This time it was Harry who laughed.

"Would you tell me what it's like to be legally divorced?" I felt proud at articulating such a difficult sentence correctly.

The car slowed considerably. Harry's mouth was suddenly clamped tight shut but the whiskey had made me persistent.

"Come on, Harry, I'm curious. I want to know what it's like to be divorced. I mean, is it easier or harder."

I saw the warning in his sidelong glance but I pressed on, "Please. It's important to me." I didn't realise how hurt I'd be by his reply.

"Look," he said, "I don't care to discuss it. I've nothing against divorce in principle but Madge and I are still married."

"Madge!" She even had a name. I don't know why I should feel surprised. But hearing it made her tangible, as if she was an intrusive presence sitting somewhere behind my left shoulder. "Great," I said, "thanks. You've been a terrific help." I felt a huge sense of disappointment and lay sadly back in my seat looking out at the road towards Limerick. A whole raw area seemed to have opened up between us. We barely knew each other; it shouldn't have mattered so much.

We hardly spoke for the rest of the journey until we were close to Bella Vista.

Then Harry sighed and said, "You know, Dixie, I think you and I met each other at the wrong time."

I nodded.

"You're still a lovely woman," he added. Then, as we reached the top of the driveway and Beth, wearing a sunny yellow shirt, came wheeling her bicycle round the side of the house, "And you've got lovely daughters and a lovely home."

"I wish that boy hadn't been on the beach. I wish I'd been washed out to sea and drowned," I burst out shaken by a tumult of mixed feelings.

"Hush." Harry put his hand across my mouth. "That's a desperate thing to say. God forgive you, Dixie. You didn't mean it."

But I had meant it. My wickedness has always known no bounds. We said a brief goodbye and I climbed out of the car and headed for the front door and the pots and pans and explanations.

# Chapter Twelve

16th September: "I'm going to the Middle East for five years," Clive announced this morning. "I thought I'd better tell you before I signed the contract." He could have been talking about going out to buy a newspaper.

I was still in bed, recumbent against my pillows. Clive was all spruced up and wearing his office suit. It put me at a disadvantage. It seemed as if I was merely a layabout slut doing nothing while he struggled to carry the world on his shoulders. He stood with his mouth curved in a static smile, waiting for my reaction.

"It's a question of necessity," he said after I'd failed to comment.

"How's that? I don't know what you mean."

His expression changed. He scowled into space. "I think you should trot up and talk to Brendan Collins's successor," he said nastily.

"But..."

"Seriously. I mean it, Dixie. You have no idea of the cash situation at all. You think it grows on trees."

"How can I know anything," I wailed. "You never discuss anything with me. For instance you hadn't the manners to discuss this stupid annulment business before trotting off to your bloody uncle."

"I'd no idea that Monsignor Patrick would bring up the matter like that," Clive said stiffly. "He took me by surprise as well as you the night he came to tea but he's thinking of our best interests. He feels that it's important it doesn't drag on for years, for everyone's sake."

"If I believed that I'd believe anything," I said bitterly. "And I suppose the Monsignor has advised you to go abroad as well. And anyway," I thumped the sheet, "has anything more happened about this annulment thing or am I only going to be told after it's all tied up?"

"Don't be stupid. And as for going out to this job, there isn't any alternative I'm afraid," Clive said sighing.

"None!" I spoke mockingly.

"Unless," he paused, "well, Alan is selling up his house."

"Evergreen!" My attention was immediately diverted.

"So it seems. He'll be getting a good price. That Harry Mercer fellow has made him an offer he couldn't refuse, or so the story goes."

"Harry Mercer!" I squawked.

"For God's sake, Dixie, don't go broadcasting that around the city. Alan won't want it getting about until the deal is through."

I could only stare and mumble as Clive began to pace up and down the carpet. A sharp pain had developed in my side. "What's going to happen to all the children?" I said. "What's going to happen to Jane and Oliver?"

"Don't depress me further, Dixie," Clive said gloomily. "Anyway this Middle Eastern business will mean you can hang on here for as long as I'm away. I've made up my mind to go. It will give us all a breathing space."

"And Ruth?" I asked.

He jumped as if I'd conjured up a ghost. "That's another matter. Ruth's not well. Anyway it's none of your business." He had a shifty look about him as he scurried out of the room.

Left alone I contemplated the turn of events. About Harry Mercer! I didn't believe it. It was a trick, a falsehood. And Clive, abandoning all of us. How would Ruth feel? Although I didn't think that they saw much of each other nowadays. I resolutely put the lid back on Ruth. I had enough on my plate. Men were all bastards. They expected us to settle for anything they chose to dream up. I thought of the cold damp hard-working slog in Rosepark House. Then I saw Ruth stuck on the side of the road, with Danny, in a caravan. I could do nothing to help her. She had made her own bed. I began to feel so nervous that I wanted to curl up under the blankets but I forced myself out onto the floor.

Clive couldn't be all that hard up; business wasn't that bad. I never read financial pages but surely architects didn't go bankrupt. And Harry Mercer! He couldn't be buying Evergreen. I shied away from the thought. It was something Clive had made up to torment me with, he'd heard something, suspected something. Although, after all, what was there to suspect?

When I was dressed I opened Clive's wardrobe and worked my way feverishly through his suit pockets, especially the secret inside ones. If he was going to spy on me I'd have to arm myself for the defence. Anyway, if we weren't having normal marital relations he shouldn't expect me to live like a nun. Although, I was indeed living an uncomfortably chaste existence, wasn't I? I put my hand into the small pocket near the waistband of a pair of linen trousers and found a packet of contraceptives.

I grinned at it, feeling victorious, but my mood quickly changed. I was being cheap and sneaky. The contraceptives meant nothing. Clive had taken these trousers with him when he went away with Ruth after Christmas. I put them back and opened the window wide to air the room.

None of it mattered. Life was sad, sad. I heard the crunch of footsteps on the garden path and Jane's voice cooing at Oliver. I wanted to rush out and tell her to be careful, tell her not to walk into a trap. It was so easy when you were young to think things could right themselves of their own accord, to believe that there would always be another chance.

I went back to the idea of Harry Mercer as owner of Evergreen. I supposed if that came about his English wife would come back and live there too. "I'm still married," he'd said in the car.

Slowly I became aware of a persistent sound which turned out to be the telephone ringing beside Clive's bed. Maybe it was Harry himself; if so I could ask him. "You might have told me," I'd say, "you might have put me in the picture." But it wasn't Harry. It was the nursing home where my mother exists in her own lost world.

17th September: Today I had to travel to Dublin because the nursing home contacted me about my mother. My mother was a disappointed woman. Her tongue and thoughts perpetually picked over the particulars of the bad hand that life had dealt her. My father's lack of success in his job, his failure to give her a bigger house, more money, expensive clothes, a good holiday, a son. "I never wanted a daughter," she told me frequently when I was small. "I don't like little girls. They're sly."

She was a pale scrawny woman with horn-rimmed spectacles and iron-grey hair. My father was fat and pasty and wore similar spectacles. When I discovered the biological facts of life, I initially dismissed them as amazing nonsense. The thought of my parents indulging in such carry-on was beyond the limits of belief.

"Of course they do it to each other. They'd have to or you wouldn't have been born," crowed my best friend, a bold-faced girl called Josephine.

When I eventually allowed myself to believe her, I felt aggrieved. How dare they impose themselves on me as parents. I turned the dismay and disappointment they beamed in my direction back on them like a cruel spotlight. I was a quiet child, earning my mother's description "sly." But I wasn't sly, I suffered from a paralysing inability to communicate normally with the outside world. Then I stumbled into Tristram's orbit and he taught me what my body was all about.

Poor Tristram. I realise now that all he probably wanted was a little diversion to brighten the long hours minding his shop that always smelt claustrophobically of streaky bacon. Instead he got me, hurricane Dixie.

When the fact that I was pregnant hit me I was terrified. I'd met Clive and dated him once or twice, but he was even less sexually experienced than I was. Something that wasn't unusual, especially for a Monsignor's nephew, at the beginning of the seventies. In those days even married people argued fiercely about the evils of contraception.

I took the train, which was practically empty. I had a table and four seats to myself. I stared out of the window at hillocky fields, black-faced sheep, a fine red-brick house basking behind a row of trees. It was a magnificent afternoon. I wasn't looking forward to visiting my mother. I find it frightening to sit with someone who is merely a shell of flesh and bone. Brain sickness frightens me and I have been a neglectful daughter. But she has been well provided for financially. The sale of the house she despised realised far more than expected, thanks to a shopping complex finding it essential to their development. Clive supervised the investment of her money. It has been enough to keep her.

When I reached Dublin I got a taxi straight to the nursing home. I was received by the sister in charge in a room with a drab carpet and walls painted a bad shade of brown.

Although it was sunny outside the room was

gloomily lit by a central fitting that resembled a nest of steel serpents. A portrait of a gentleman in a wig sneered at us from over the fireplace. He was a dark-eyed handsome rogue who looked as if he'd enjoy burning a few peasants.

"Your mother never lost her faith. She was clutching her rosary beads when they carried her out to the ambulance," the sister said.

"What do you plan to do now?" she asked after some more platitudes.

I didn't know. I had only received the phone call yesterday, saying that my mother had taken a bad turn and was being moved into a general hospital.

"I'll have to wait and see what the situation is."

I could see my answer displeased the nurse. "It's not usual to hold rooms, we have a long waiting list," she said.

"It's just that I'll have to consult my husband," I offered.

"It's not fitting that you should expect other people to take on your rightful responsibilities," said the sister brusquely. I suspected that she wanted to order me to collect the few belongings of my mother's and take them away.

"Please," I said in a panic, "I need time. I haven't been to the hospital yet."

"You haven't been here very much, Mrs Molloy." The nurse was a fat rubbery woman. I felt that if you hit her it would be like hitting a punch-ball.

"What could I have done? What was the use?"

"You're her daughter." The eyes in the rubbery face were black shiny glass.

I wanted to defend myself. I wanted to say she'd never given me much tender loving care. I hadn't been what she'd wanted at all.

"We can't wait indefinitely for you to figure things out, Mrs Molloy. If you'd been visiting regularly you'd have seen this coming," said sister is an icy voice.

I nodded and, feeling bruised, picked up my bag and overnight case and headed for the door.

20th September: It seems my mother has had a mild stroke but her life...if you can call it a life...is in no immediate danger. I've had several days of drifting around Dublin in between useless vigils in the hospital. My mother, naturally, doesn't recognise me. Her hair is cropped in a way that she never wore it and fans out in flimsy white feathers. Most of the time her eyes are closed and her face, although peaky, looks calm. I'm told that she's not in pain although sometimes she whimpers softly.

I can't stay in the hospital all the time. It is too oppressive. Yesterday I took a bus across the city to where I grew up. As I approached my destination dread and tension took hold of me. I was going to be met by my own past. Clive would be there, young and guilty, his eyes gleaming with lust. The sound of Tristram Long's violin would thread its way along the narrow street, my mother would be putting out slices of corned beef on lettuce leaves for our tea.

When I got there I felt completely at a loss. The past had gone down the drain. Nothing struck a spark of recognition. It was all bustle and shoppers and glassed-in arcades full of greenery. I'd had no business coming here. I might as well have gone to the moon. I couldn't even figure out where our house, or Tristram's shop, had been located.

I had left Jane in charge in Bella Vista and I hoped that she was coping. It was my intention to take the evening train down and spend at least a day at home. I came back to the centre of the city and went to a shop selling baby clothes. When Peter was small I never had enough money for luxuries.

I splurged on dungarees with teddy bears and clowns appliquéd, a stack of poster-bright tiny jumpers, a minuscule blue denim jacket just because IMAGINE A WORLD OF PLEASURE had been embroidered across its back in lime-green letters. The shop was part of an inner city development. There was still time to kill so I went to look at a big place nearby which specialised in second-hand clothes. I had no intention of buying anything, it was just that I had read about it in a magazine. When I went in I found that the ground floor was completely given over to women's garments. The first thing that struck me was the battered air that emanated from a rack of overcoats. They were all of good quality and heavy cloth but there was a sag about their shoulders, a droop to their hems, that spoke of failed hopes. I fingered the sleeve of a navy one. It had a full skirt and a belt. There was still years of wear left in it so long as you didn't want to cut a dash. My mother used to have a coat like that, I thought automatically.

"It'd be a sin to throw it out." I dropped the sleeve as if I'd been stung although I had only imagined the words.

Turning round I was faced with a row of blocky skirts. I ran a hand down one and felt the bottom that shaped it. I shivered. The skirts were the same, too good to throw out, as were the badly ironed blouses in stiff cotton, the stocking stitch jumpers, ribbed cardigans and wire baskets full of felt hats. The handbags. I recognised instantly that if I opened one of those handbags I'd smell my mother's cache of peppermint sweets. This was where the ghosts had gathered after being ousted from their suburban haunts. These were the garments my mother and her counterparts had worn as they trudged through a world filled with ingratitude and ungodliness. These were the leavings of apathetic women.

The night-dresses puzzled me. I couldn't understand how they could possibly have made their way here. Night-dresses like these didn't flaunt themselves for strangers to finger. No, they tucked themselves modestly in heart-shaped cases fashioned from satin and lace. Night-dresses belonged in the dark unless, of course...I suddenly had a bad taste in my mouth. That blue nylon with a white neck frill was an exact replica of the one my mother was wearing today. These were corpse garments, genuine ghost substances. Any minute now they'd reach out and grab me. Taking hold of myself I blundered into the street and came face to face with Harry Mercer.

In my excited frame of mind it seemed that fate had placed him there.

"Ah, the glamorous Mrs Molloy," he said.

"Meets that gorgeous hunk, Harry Mercer," I

bounced back. Behind me I felt the sinister stuff in the shop change into harmless leaves shed casually from the tree of life.

"I've just been spooked," I said lightly putting my hand in his and offering my cheek for a kiss.

He just stood there, looking at my face. "I thought you'd be in Limerick," he said. "I'm taking it for granted you've heard about the fire."

# Chapter Thirteen

9th October: I'm back in Dublin again, in a hotel room, on my own. My mother's condition remains unchanged and I find it restful to sit staring at her vacant face. No questions, no explanations.

At least, nobody was killed in the fire. That's the best I can say, but Evergreen is gone.

I took a lift back to Limerick with Harry Mercer that day only half-believing him. He was gentle with me but emphatic. "Listen, sweetheart, those old houses can be tinder boxes. Something goes wrong and whoosh!"

And the cause? Nobody was quite sure. Danny had been up at cockcrow cooking his own breakfast, but you couldn't swear to it. Who'd ever expect a kid to start making chips at six a.m.?

"I don't want to be the one to say it," said Harry, "but those deep fat fryers are lethal. At least the kid didn't get burned. Ran out into the garden and left the door open behind him and that fanned the flames, you see. Good thing his brother happened to smell the smoke and got the rest of them up and out in time."

When I got home I found Clive, Alan and Ruth, Jane and the baby, Danny and Beth and Anne all assembled in our front room. Ruth looked ill and thin as a rake. When she saw me she picked up a napkin that was lying across her lap and began to cry into it. All the others were eating a haphazard meal.

"Beth and I got this ready," Anne said jumping up to hug me. Everybody else seemed too bewildered to take note of my sudden arrival. The deep freeze had obviously been plundered. Plates of smoked salmon, trout and almond casserole and foil containers of chicken curry were ranged on the sideboard.

"Are you OK, Dixie?" Clive asked out of nowhere.

I nodded.

"Isn't it awful?" said Jane tearfully. She had Oliver pressed against a yellow sunburst on a red sweatshirt. Her hair was loose and wild. She looked worn-out.

"Well, you've heard the good news," said Alan heavily. Then, all at once, everyone was on a talking high. This had happened, that happened, this was the way it was. The fire brigade had taken ages. It started in a pile of newspapers on the kitchen windowsill, the whole neighbourhood had turned out to look. Duffy's circus was nothing in comparison. Water everywhere, and a fool of a newspaper reporter. The smell of smoke. A bush fire. The Towering Inferno.

"It was an accident," Danny's voice piped up over and over. "It was an accident."

"You're the accident. You've been one bloody

accident from start to finish." Alan sounded hoarse. His words descended on us like a pall. Ruth's weeping intensified and Clive went over and stroked her hair. Danny bent his head. His shoulders shook but he made no sound.

"I'm going in to look for myself," I said. Nobody made any further comment and I let myself out into the evening air. I walked down our drive which was damp and autumny and turned in Evergreen's gate. The air was acrid and ruined walls rose blackly in the dusky light. I got a shock when Alan came up behind me and stood too close for comfort.

"What do you think of that?" he hissed and I could smell whiskey on his breath.

"Who let you out?" I grumbled sourly as if I was speaking to a dog.

"Jesus Christ! Is that all you have to say? My house gone. The lovely house I sweated blood to buy. The house I'd just managed to sell."

"Your house. Your house, I love that. The den where you could beat up your wife and kids."

"I never laid a hand on a child in my life though I could strangle Danny this minute."

"I know what a brute you could be. I saw you with Ruth."

"Did you now. And so you've come in here to gloat. Is that it?"

"I'm sad about the house. I'm sorry for Ruth and the kids."

"And I don't count." His voice grew whingey. "When I think what I've put up with over the years ... from Ruth, from your husband, from that brat I've brought up as my own son, big soft eejit that I am. I should take out a gun and shoot the lot of you. And the place was sold, contract drawn up and everything. Sold. Harry Mercer was due to sign on the dotted line the day it happened. The cat was in the bag. Have you any notion at all how hard it is to get a client for a house that size?"

I was shocked into silence at the mention of Harry.

"Have you no pity for me at all?" said Alan.

The long journey from Dublin, the upset of my mother's sickness, my own distress and confusion had left me too tired to be frightened of him. "I don't care what happens to you, you deserve it. I've seen you terrorise your wife. I've seen you rape her, you brute," I said recklessly.

"I swear, Dixie, you've always been asking for it." He had grabbed me before I could stir and I was feebly kicking his shins.

We struggled, panting in the darkness. I felt the roughness of his unshaven chin against my cheek. My throat contracted as if I was choking and when I tried to scream I sounded more like a cheeping chaffinch.

I felt every ounce of his bulky animal force pressing on me and struggled fiercely to keep my balance. Luckily, he must have had a good deal to drink and he was even more tired than I was.

We were standing on the gravel sweep in front of the house. All sorts of household objects were piled everywhere. Alan stumbled against something and lost his footing. As he did I was able to pull free. I reached out for the nearest solid object and found an ornamental doorstop that consisted of a brass claw with a long handle. For

188

years it had been used to keep the inner door of Evergreen's hall propped open.

As Alan scrambled upright I whammed it hard between his legs. If I'd had time to raise it over our heads I'd have smashed in his skull. I was seized by a wild glee as he crumpled to the ground. I wasn't hurt. Alan was. Then, grunting, he got to his feet and groaning, sat down on the edge of an overturned table. I backed away and something soft wrapped itself around my ankle. It was a piece of silky clothing. I began to grow nervous. "Are you all right?" I asked tentatively.

He snarled and growled, then said, "Dixie, you were always bad news. You're a frigid bitch." It was all he could manage. I waited, as unimpressed by his big wet sobs as a statue is by the rain.

I moved away but when I reached the gate I was driven to turn back and yell, "Don't come in to us tonight. Ruth's welcome, but you're not."

I went back into my own house and nobody asked where I'd been, or why I was so dishevelled, or where Alan had disappeared to. They were all too preoccupied with their own problems.

15th October: Bella Vista is a menagerie with Ruth, Jane, baby Oliver, Jim, Bridget and Danny plus our own gang. Tessa White and Marie are absent because they, thankfully, are on teacher training courses. Even so the house is bursting at the seams.

There's no sign of Alan and Harry hasn't phoned. Why should he?

Ruth drifts around in her own never-never land and Clive is out most of the time. He has a backlog of appointments because of the fire. He still intends leaving for the Middle East. Maybe Harry has gone abroad on business; it seems to be the usual thing at the moment.

"Is this all a desperate nuisance, Dixie?" Jane asked me today. She was upstairs in Peter's room changing Oliver's nappy. It seems only hours ago that she and Peter were sitting on the carpet here playing cards.

"It's worse than a nuisance," I said tiredly.

My life was stretched to snapping point between my mother's sick bed and the confusion here. Downstairs the radio was playing pop music at a brain-battering pitch. I kept turning it off because I thought wildly that Harry might ring and I wouldn't hear the phone. But the racket was always switched on again within seconds. It seemed that the younger ones couldn't function without it going full blast. And Ruth was becoming more of a problem. She floated around the place as if she couldn't see us or else shut herself away in one of the rooms. At meal times she ate nothing. "I'm getting seriously worried about your mother," I said.

"Mama? I suppose she's upset. We're all wrecked by what happened." Dressed in a woolly red jumper and matching knee socks Jane looked about ten years old and completely carefree.

"It must be much worse for her," I said although I didn't altogether believe this.

Jane flopped limply against a chest-of-drawers with Oliver propped on her outstretched thighs. "You should have been here with the fire brigade arrived," she said. "She was laughing her head off. She was quite mad."

"Was Alan around?"

"Dada? Of course. Dada was in bits. Everyone except Mama was crying and shouting. For a while we couldn't find Danny. He'd hidden in the shrubbery. For a while we thought he was still inside. He was terrified because he thought he'd be put in jail."

"Poor Danny. It must have been a nightmare."

"He's safe now. Dixie, I need your help."

"My help?" I saw she was only half-interested in our discussion.

Her face pinkened. "I'm going away. With Sandy, my professor. He's been in touch. He read about the fire in the paper. He wants me to go and live with him. You don't mind, I hope."

"How can I mind?" I smiled and shrugged. I wanted to go away someplace myself. I wanted someone to be kind to me and kiss me better.

"Are you sure it's a good idea? You've got to consider Oliver as well as yourself," was all I could think of in the way of admonishment.

"Sure as can be." She was nonchalant as she pressed shut the studs on the little blue trousers I'd bought him. She picked him up and shook him and rubbed her nose against his. "Course I am," she said, "course I am. Say bye bye to Granny now." She tucked Oliver into the crook of her arm and waggled one of his little pink mitts. She reminded me of myself, as a child, playing house. When the game grew boring you just dumped it and turned to hopscotch or forfeits.

Jane laughed. "Don't look so shocked! I'm not going just yet. Not until next week or the week after." Then her brother Jim barged in and announced that there was a Harry somebody downstairs wanting to see me.

He'd just been passing, he said. And it crossed his mind that I might like an afternoon out to cheer me up. I only made a half-hearted attempt at refusing him. I left it to him to surprise me with a destination but I recognised the lake the minute we arrived.

"I've often been here," I said. This was where Clive and I had come in an attempt at reconciliation after Peter was killed. I wished he'd chosen someplace else.

"Done my own share of courting here in my day." Harry faced me and turned my coat collar up around my neck. It was very cold; the sky was a grey blanket. Even so my heart was lighter than it had been for ages.

"Were they all as nice as me?"

He pressed his cold nose into my cheek. "How nice are you, Dixie? Whoa there, what's the hurry?" he asked as I pulled him towards me.

To tell the truth I could hardly keep my hands off him. I was one step away from bliss. But I played along. "Clive's leaving to go and work in the Middle East," I offered.

"So you'll be all on your own." He caught my hand and led me over to where excavations were in progress. A large area was cordoned off by post and wire fencing. A round wooden structure was half built in the centre. "I remember having a picnic, a whole crowd of us right in that spot." He shook his head. "Jeez, where does life go? I'm getting old."

I pinched a yellow flower from a gorse bush

and rolled it to a powder between my finger and thumb.

"Do you want to sleep with me?" I asked, then felt terrified in case he answered "no."

He pulled me towards him and gave me a bear hug, rubbing his chin on the top of my head.

"I can't get you out of my mind, you witch," he said. "I've been mad about you ever since I met you in Dalys'. You know that too."

I closed my eyes and leaned against him, not sure that he was telling the truth. Then I took a deep breath and decided to be brave. "That day in Kilkee, when I nearly drowned, right? Coming home you said something about your wife…"

"My wife," he echoed. "It's hard to explain." He stopped. His breathing remained unhurried.

I waited, all ears, my right hand clutching at his coat. The rustle of leaves broke harshly on the air followed by the sound of dogs barking. I turned round and saw a hare burst through the hedge of a field down nearer the lake. A pack of beagle hounds followed close behind her. I saw the fright in the hare's popping eyes as it streaked past us then veered left and headed up the hill where Clive had sat with his sketch book. The dogs followed in close pursuit. I knew stories of witches turning into hunted animals. I believed that hares when dying gave a shriek that chilled the blood of anyone who heard it. I detest blood sports. Our moment had been spoiled. I put my hands over my ears and began to scream. All around was confusion. Harry was laughing at me as he helped me towards the car.

"It's only a sport. There's worse ways of passing

the time," he said when we were driving away.

"It's horrible," I moaned. I didn't want to think of what had just happened. I felt smeared by blood and guts and lumps of quivering fur.

"You'd be foolish to take it too seriously," Harry said. There was an undertone to his words that made me afraid he found me idiotic.

"Take me home," I whispered. "I've got a headache."

I wanted him to protest and argue, to suggest that we go to a hotel for a meal or a drink, to tell me that the evening hadn't even begun. But he just nodded soberly and said, "OK. If that's what you want."

19th October: About Ruth yesterday. But how to write about Ruth is the problem. I'm finding it very difficult to say anything about my doppelganger; Clive's lady friend, the mother of Clive's son. I've coped by treating her as part of the furniture and now she is definitely part of it. An awkward object in the wrong place.

It would be better if Clive was still interested in her, I think, but these days she just seems to make him sad. She talks to him in whispers and he fills himself a double scotch and drains it too fast before answering her with a false heartiness. I'm trying to avoid getting caught between them.

What is to be done about Evergreen is uppermost in our minds. Even Clive's plans for going abroad come second. "I'll be here for a while yet," he said the other day in answer to some hesitant query of Ruth's. Our own girls have absorbed the fact of the fire and are now reacting with fits of nostalgic weeping and unhappy faces. Ruth's children are all wan and devastated, drifting off like poor derelicts with borrowed books and sports gear. Danny has nightmares that wake him screaming at the dark. Jane is the least affected. She has her own life to think about. Her professor is supposed to be due any day. The only bright spot is that since our tussle Alan has vanished from the domestic scene entirely as only a man can.

I feel secretly victorious about this, but we can't give his family house room for ever. I've been trying to poke Clive into contacting him and making him fix something but Clive just looks more sorrowful than ever and says, "What's the rush! Give it a week or two. Remember if it wasn't for Danny they'd still have the house." The twist of bitterness around his mouth stops me from pressing the point.

And so I have Ruth. She came into the kitchen yesterday but instead of shuffling her feet the way she does nowadays she was energetic and quick. Mrs Connors and I had just been having an argument. Mrs Connors wanted more money because of all the extra work. I wanted her to work more hours if she got more pay. Mrs Connors claimed that she'd miss the one and only convenient bus home if she stayed a second after three-thirty. Ruth entered and marched across the freshly washed tiles. Her rubber soles left a slimy trail in their wake which Mrs Connors attacked, grumbling, with a J-cloth.

Ruth looked down at her with an expression of amazement and then she looked at me. "I have to go in next door," she said. "I'd like you to come too." Her voice was official and bossy, very different from the meek evasive way she speaks most of the time.

Her brisk approach startled me.

"I don't think I could stand going in on my own but I think I should take a look. I've been talking to one of the workmen. He thinks the place is being sold for sites. Do you believe that, Dixie? Anyway it doesn't matter. Alan can do any sort of deal that he wants to so long as I never have to live with him again. It's time to move on, isn't it, Dixie? We can't just sit here watching our lives trickle away. Your so-called husband says I can stay with you until I know what I want to do. But that's not good enough. I'll have to organise something."

I felt relieved. I ignored the fact that Ruth's eyes were unnaturally bright and her manner a bit disjointed. This was better than having her silent and apathetic. However, I wanted to get her away from Mrs Connors who was standing close to us, damp cloth in hand, her nostrils distended with curiosity.

"Come on," I said, "let's go and investigate the situation."

The grounds of Evergreen were all litter and confusion. We picked our way past piles of rubble. Ruth's quick pace turned into a manic trot as she galloped from spot to spot in a frenzy of recognition. Blackened pots, tablecloths, a cracked mirror, suitcases, bags, chests, a stuffed animal's head, Jim's aquarium, an out-dated first communion dress, some plants tumbled out of ornamental pots. She picked items up at random and let them drop. Soon we found ourselves round by the side where the master bedroom was. It was furthest away from the kitchen and the least damaged, but the window had been left wide open and a tail of a curtain twisted out across the sill.

"You remember what happened me in this room, Dixie." Ruth's cold viciousness took me unawares. "I knew it wouldn't be destroyed. No such luck."

Her manner was compelling. I found myself copying her as she clambered across the flower-bed and looked inside. The cold and damp pressed like a blanket against our faces. Chairs were upturned on the bed. A plethora of photographs curling at the edges were scattered about on the carpet.

"Look." Ruth pointed to where an old portrait of her hung over a chest of drawers. Alan had commissioned it from a local artist just after we'd met them. I had forgotten about it and the party at which it was unveiled, a wild night with lots of singing and drink. I peered in for a closer look, realising how very beautiful Ruth had been at the time. How gold her hair was, how alluring her eyes. Then there was a loud crack and I watched as the portrait slithered to the ground.

"I should have done that years ago," Ruth said in my ear. The damage had been done by a rock she had picked up from the stone border near our feet. She glared as she wiped her hand against the front of her jacket.

She wants to frighten me, I thought, she wants

to make everything melodramatic. I'd have to try and calm her down.

"It's your fault that it's too late, much too late," Ruth said.

"Is that what you brought me in for?" I tried to sound reasonable.

"That!...and that," she pointed at the damaged canvas. Her laugh was as sharp as a squabbling crow. "I hate the person I was then. I was a confused brainless dope. And I met all the wrong sort. I met you."

"You were gorgeous," I said sincerely.

"That's shit!" She did a turn-around and jumped back onto the path. "The whole thing was shitty and so were you, Dixie. How come you acted so cheap, letting Alan have you when you didn't even love him? For God's sake, you couldn't even have liked him. He's disgusting. He's gross. He always was."

"Why did you marry him, so? I don't remember him being so bad...at first."

She frowned at the grass. "He was my fate. He came along. My parents liked him. But it was all wrong and you helped him."

"Ruth, I have this weird feeling that you've forgotten that it was you who fell in love with my husband. What was I supposed to do...play gooseberry while the two of you acted out love's old sweet song?"

"But Clive and I didn't start it, Dixie. It was you and Alan in Paris. Bang, bang, bang. A public fireworks display. Clive and I were attracted all right but we wouldn't have gone to bed together if you two hadn't set the fashion."

"This is foolish," I said. "You're overwrought. We've had enough upset without making false recriminations about what happened years ago."

"I'm not talking about years ago. I'm talking about what's still going on. You couldn't wait to get into bed with Alan but that wasn't as bad as what you did last winter, leaving me with him that Sunday."

"Come on," I felt defensive, "that was between you and him."

"Listen," Ruth stepped closer to me, "you're going to hear this. Stop ignoring me. Stop acting the innocent when it all goes back to you playing games with Alan. Because that's all any of it is to you, Dixie, a game."

"Peter," I blurted out but just saying his name hurt so much that I couldn't go on.

Ruth took no notice. She was in her own space, talking from her own shadows. "I'm dead, Dixie, thanks to you. I'm trying to make you understand. I'm dead. That Sunday with Alan was the end of me and you let him do it. Why? Was it because you've no heart at all? Do you know what happened after you left me that day? For a start you just disappeared. I couldn't believe it! I kept thinking you'd gone for help or for a doctor or something and that you were going to come back. I was lying on the bed. That's where you'd put me and all the ice had melted. I hadn't even the strength to get under the blankets and it was freezing. I began to think then that maybe you'd contacted the hospital and they were sending out an ambulance because I felt as if I'd started bleeding from everywhere. Everywhere. I thought that if they didn't hurry up I'd be dead before they arrived and then I stopped caring about that. I imagined how sorry you were going to be. I especially liked the thought of you being sorry, Dixie. Then I thought that if they just came in time to give me an injection so that I could sleep for about a week I might be able to start living again and maybe it wouldn't be so bad and that it would be better than dying. I'd been with Clive earlier and I was afraid that maybe I was really a sinful person and it would be better if I didn't die for a while. I said an act of contrition and tried to make myself repent for all the good times with Clive. I said "mea culpa" over and over. I thought I'd try going to daily Mass. I was probably feverish but I was certain you'd come back. I was going to ask you to bring me a cup of Bovril and some toast. And I wanted a warm nightie from the hot-press and a pair of panties and some sanitary towels. I hoped that you'd arrive before any of the children did.

My head was sore and when the door opened I didn't turn my head. I just whispered 'hello.' I heard you tiptoeing across the carpet and you reminded me of a creature making little furry noises. Then you picked up my hand and kissed it and I couldn't believe it. It wasn't you, it was a man, it was Clive! I didn't know whether to be ashamed or glad, a bit of both I suppose, because I'd especially asked you not to tell Clive."

Ruth rubbed her face distractedly. "And then he kissed my other hand and my throat, and, of course I realised that it wasn't Clive at all. How could it be? It was Alan. He must have just taken a shower. He was reeking of that aftershave he uses. I suppose he thinks it makes him irresistible. He'd believe anything. Always splashing himself with the stuff as if that would make him less of a beast. Are you with me?"

I nodded reluctantly.

She smacked her forehead. "Of course he didn't stop there, not Alan. My lawful husband, connubial rights, all that rubbish. I even tried to put him off by saying you were coming back but he laughed at me. And I cursed. I cursed all of us, but he didn't care."

A magpie fluttered down beside us on the grass.

"One for sorrow," Ruth said. She was shaking. Her voice had grown trembly again. "And then when I saw it was useless, Dixie, you never would come and stop him, I just died. And he didn't care. He just still went on and did, you know, everything. As if I was dirt, or an animal or a zombie, as if I wasn't one big mass of soreness, as if he'd never laid a hand on me. I just gave up and let him. There was nothing else I could do, but ever since then nothing matters. I couldn't even let Clive touch me when we went on holidays. It's all just unreal. Sometimes I blame you and I want to hate you, but most of the time I'm too dried up inside."

"I'm sorry, Ruth, I'm truly sorry," I said, but it was no good.

# Chapter Fourteen

22nd October: After Ruth's outburst I found myself growing more watchful in her presence. I noted how Clive behaved, how he skirted her chair carefully as if it was an enemy's tent pitched in his sitting-room. At meal times he jumped up and left the table the minute he had finished eating. Whenever Ruth spoke, which was seldom, he flinched as if a pin had been stuck in his arm. In fact he was acting the way he'd acted towards me years ago when his affair with Ruth began. He looked perpetually dejected.

There was also the question of household expenses. Ruth was contributing nothing. I'd even had to hand out cash to Jim and Danny for haircuts. And Mrs Connor's grumbling had increased in volume because of the stacks of dirty clothes. ("What you need, Mrs Molloy, is a full-time laundress.") What I needed, I felt, was a dirty weekend in the London Ritz with Harry Mercer. The Whites were going to need new winter coats and shoes. I was keeping count. Alan would have to cough up. Wherever he was hanging out these days he would have to be contacted and I reluctantly realised that the only person who was motivated to do so was myself.

I'd also grown defensive about Ruth's allegations that I'd abandoned her to Alan's brutality. I knew she was being irrational but even so she had filled me with guilty regrets. Of course I should have done more for her that Sunday. If I'd tried I could surely have restrained Alan. Used violence myself with Ruth backing me up? Attacked him with a lavatory brush? Called the guards? Why hadn't I? I was my own severest critic.

There was only one thing for it, seek out Alan and force him to help solve the problem of Ruth and the children. I dressed carefully and soberly, as if I was going to visit Mother. It was a relief to get out of Bella Vista with its uneasy adults and mopey children.

"We've got things to discuss, Alan," I said.

I'd found him lunching in the bar of a hotel near his office. It was a basement bar with dark wood, dim lights and low visibility. It was only by standing close to him that I could be certain of his identity.

"Where did you come out of?" he blustered not bothering to hide his obvious disgust at my arrival.

I felt equally turned-off. Ruth was right about his aftershave. It repelled me, but I had a mission to carry out.

"I took in your Jane and the baby but I don't see why I should be landed with the problem of your entire family." I sat up on the vacant stool beside his.

Alan swivelled round to face me. "What's the boul' Clive doin'? Isn't he the one who should be looking after it? The way I see it, it's his problem more than mine."

"Would madam like to see a menu?" A barman held out a printed sheet.

I shook my head.

"Bring her a gin and tonic, lots of ice," Alan ordered.

"There's clothes and haircuts," I said, "and food."

"You know how that fire started, you know it was the little bugger's fault. Pity he didn't burn as well."

"You're sick," I said angrily.

"He shouldn't have been born in the first place. How come that moron, Clive, didn't use a condom? Too holy, I suppose. Never heard of spermicidal jellies or anything else. I'll tell you, Dixie, I was never one shouting for abortion, by and large killing innocent children isn't on, but if it was to happen all over again Ruth'd find herself in a London clinic before she could say who's the father."

"You beast." I was breaking out in a cold sweat.

"Don't give me that crap. There's too many unwanted people in the world as it is. Right! Look at Africa, look at India." His voice grew louder. "Don't tell me you've never felt it'd be better for some people if they were taken care of carefully and hygienically. Just put quietly out of the way, you know, not tortured or used for research. Not concentration camp stuff. Babies that are going to fuck everything up by being born, old folks that there's no hope for. I hope to God someone pulls out my plug if I ever go gaga. There'll be no hard feelings. I want to die compos mentis."

I wanted to put my hands over my ears. My mother came to mind; her unnecessary existence, her decomposing brain cells, her ancient hands clutching at her bed sheet, the fact that she could be that way for one, two, five years. Nobody could say. If she'd been left unattended after her heart attack it would all be over for her by now, over for me as well.

"Shut up," I said harshly. "You're only trying to square your conscience. The way you've treated Ruth has been awful and that's the real problem."

"Go away, Dixie. That subject is closed." Alan turned and putting his elbows on the counter addressed the bottles and bar mirrors. "If you see Harry Mercer on your way out you can tell him I'm down here."

I found myself seized by a determination to impose my will on his, to let him see that he couldn't call the tune as easily as that.

"You can't just walk away from it," I said. "I'm not going to let you."

He was silent for a minute then he spoke, "For fuck's sake, Dixie, I don't know what you want from me but you've got one hell of a nerve coming after me like this. I'll do something about Ruth when I'm straightened out. In the meantime you can show her the door if you want to. I wouldn't blame you. She'll manage. She'll find somebody else to latch on to. She's as cute as they come."

"Is that why you raped her?"

He swung back to face me, breathing heavily, his feet swinging against the stool legs. "Don't you ever try saying that again, you stupid bitch. It didn't happen. She's not worth raping – neither are you."

"Is that so!" I shouted. I didn't give a damn about the shadowy figures stirring in the background of the bar. "Remember that day in Lisdoonvarna when I had to beat you off with a poker," I yelled.

There was a pause in which I thought that he was going to hit me, in which I dared him to hit me. Instead he smirked and pulled a wad of notes out of an inside pocket. He peeled off a few and held them out.

"Take the cash, Dixie, and scram. You're boring me. Was it Clive who sent you in? I believe his practice is nearly on the rocks."

I snatched the money and dashed it to the ground. If he wanted it back he could grovel for it in the dark.

He swayed a little on his seat. His manner grew more sneering and spiteful. He shook his head as if amazed and said, "I don't know in the name of God what I ever saw in you. I must have been in a bad way when I let you coax me into your bed."

My untouched gin and tonic was on the counter. The ice had melted. "I hadn't even the strength to get under the blankets and it was freezing." I could hear Ruth's voice. Her weakness was my strength. Fire coursed through me. It let me reach for my neglected drink. The glass burned

206

in my hand. I leaned towards Alan, flame spurting from my pupils. He looked surprised; he even puckered his lips as if he thought I was about to kiss him. My free hand tugged at the front of his shirt. There was a tearing sound and then I dashed the contents of the tumbler in his face.

I was ablaze as I watched him splutter and rock like Humpty Dumpty. I replaced the glass and, turning, bumped smack into a man's tweed jacket.

"Well, well, Dixie, you're in fighting form," said Harry Mercer's voice. Then he gently pushed me aside and said, "Sorry I'm late, Alan. I got held up. Looks like you could do with the loan of a hankie – or a shirt." He beamed at us both.

I ran for it. Outside the daylight took me by surprise. It sparkled with diamond hardness making my eyes water. The fire had left me and I felt as if all the blood had been drained from my body. I wasn't brave any longer, I was merely embarrassed. I'd made an asshole of myself for nothing.

25th October: After my outburst to Alan I returned home feeling bad. Harry Mercer telephoned me later that evening.

"I hate myself," I said.

"Why don't we go someplace where I can cheer you up?"

"Would you trust me to behave myself in public?"

"If you can stand it so can I."

He was laughing at me. I had a million family matters to attend to. "Some other time—maybe." I hung up. I was going to be brisk and sensible. I was middle-aged and almost menopausal. I didn't need a man; especially one with a wife. But I must keep busy, not lie around on sofas like Ruth, behaving as if the world owed me a living.

From time to time Ruth rouses herself to pick on one of her family. Yesterday she reduced Jane to tears by accusing her of "lewd behaviour" when Jane announced that she was planning to move out and stay with a friend in Dublin. It was all very messy with Ruth growing animated and Jane hysterical. Jane told me about it and I put my arms around her and said, as if I believed it possible, "I'll handle your mother. You get yourself sorted out."

Later I sought Ruth out and said I thought it a good idea for Jane to go off and make a life for herself.

"What sort of life?" Ruth asked warily.

"A future," I said.

"Future?" Ruth appeared to mull over the word.

"She can't hang around here indefinitely," I said.

"I'd prefer to have nothing more to do with her. She's cheap and she's a liar." Ruth's lips formed a thin line that reminded me of my mother.

Today Jane asked me if it would be possible for her to have Peter's drawing instruments and text books. All her own stuff was ruined by the fire. She was suddenly busy and full of secret plans.

As for the younger ones: the girls and Jim, being much of an age, have formed themselves into a protective mass of adolescence full of code words such as "peef" meaning "pre-fire." Danny, I notice, makes it his business to keep away from all of them as much as possible. Oliver, bless him, lies on a patchwork quilt gurgling and burping and waving his little fists. "He's the image of Peter," I say to Jane.

Jane shakes her head. "Maybe," she says. "I hope so."

Monsignor Patrick turned up this morning, his first contact since the fire. "God's will is hard to fathom," he intoned.

"That's right," I said. "Thanks very much, I'll tell the Whites to pass on that piece of information to the insurance company."

"You're very sharp today, Dixie," he said, looking lugubrious. We were standing on the doorstep and I had no intention of inviting him inside.

When he had reluctantly climbed back into his car and driven off I returned indoors. I needed a few moments' privacy and headed for the study. It has become a dumping ground for the crates and boxes of relics and baubles that have been salvaged from Evergreen. Nobody has had the initiative, yet, to start sorting through the stuff. Except, perhaps, Jane looking out stuff to take away with her.

It turned out that I didn't have the room to myself. Danny was there before me. I failed to notice him at first because he was crouching beside the locked door that leads to the unused rooms at the back. It was a stuffy undefined smell that caught my attention. I had moved around the piled up debris and stood beside Clive's exercise bike wondering if I should give it a try. It might energise me, help me to think more clearly—then I saw the child.

He was kneeling with his back to me, his eye plugged to the keyhole. At first, when I spoke, he remained motionless. "Danny!" I shook his shoulder. He scrambled to his feet and stood pressed against the wooden panels, pasty-faced and shaking. It struck me how skinny he had grown, weedy in fact, and he had violet shadows under his eyes. His jumper had a roughed-up look and his grey school slacks were the worse for wear. It was lunch-time and he must have just come in from school.

"Why aren't you in the kitchen? Mrs Connors has burgers and mash ready." I spoke sternly.

He peered up into my face as if he was prepared to be sentenced for some crime. His lips were very tightly closed and his nostrils distended.

"What on earth are you up to? There's nothing in there. All you'll get is a cold in your eye." I kept my tone light, wishing that he didn't look so orphaned.

His expression grew sulky and he poked the edge of the carpet with his shoe. "I saw Dada. He was walking around."

"Come on, Danny, tell me another one." I kept my voice even.

"You look, then you'll see," he said but didn't budge.

"I don't have to. I know he couldn't be in there." I was benign and maternal.

"It's not fair. Everyone thinks I'm making things up. They thought I was making up the fire." Danny was not crying but his voice sounded as if he had a sponge in his mouth. "I couldn't get them out of bed to come and see. I didn't run out of the house until I had to. I banged and banged on all the doors and nobody came and the smoke got so bad that I had to just run and leave it or I'd have been burned to death too."

"OK, OK," I said comfortingly. "Let me take a peep."

I reached out a hand but he moved away from me and stumbled against something which clattered across the floor and shattered. "It's not my fault," he hissed like a little wild cat.

Our eyes rested on the mess of broken glass, spilled matches and the half-smoked cigarette. I bent down and picked it up. The tip was still glowing.

I should have given him hell, I should have walloped him, told Ruth, told Clive, had him punished severely. I should have chased him when, with a flying leap he cleared a box of water-logged books and dashed out of the room, but my heart failed me.

Instead I knelt down and put my own eye to the keyhole and saw what I expected to see – a long empty passageway. Then I got a dustpan and brush and cleaned up the mess.

28th October: Today Jane's professor arrived to collect her. I walked slap into him at the top of our driveway as I trudged back from our local grocery shop. He was a pleasant, untidy-looking character of almost my own age with a pot belly and prematurely white hair. At first I had no idea of who he was.

It was a cool grey afternoon brightened by russet tinges in the shrubberies and golden leaves carpeting the wild area between our house and Evergreen. As more leaves fall, the deserted house shows itself in blacker lines through the branches.

Before her friend and I could introduce ourselves Jane hailed me. "Dixie. Hey! I hope you don't mind me leaving in such a rush, but honestly I have to! This is Sandy – the professor I've told you about." She reminded me of a volcano erupting. Jackets, books, boots, scarves, Peter's drawing materials, tin boxes flowed from her grasp into the boot of a red Ford Escort; and baby blankets, a furry dog.

"Where's the baby? What are you doing with Oliver?"

Jane blinked and came to a sudden stop. "Taking him, of course. Sandy has found us a brilliant place. Don't worry. I've left the address on the kitchen pegboard." She was out of breath.

So this was how it was done. Easy as falling off a log. Just go.

"Don't worry." She shook her head at me and grinned.

"Oh, Jane—" It was all happening too quickly for me. I was at a loss.

"I'll look after them both. Don't worry." Sandy was beside her beaming toothily. I guessed that he had put on his ill-fitting brown suit as a gesture towards conventionality. It only pointed up the oddness, on such a cold day, of his bare feet in their monkish sandals and the decrepit state of his cream polo-neck. His frosty hair hung in a straggle of curls crying out for a scissors. He could have been Jane's father, except when he smiled and his dimples showed.

"She's a sweet girl. I'll appreciate her, I promise," he said.

Jane excused herself and hurried back into the house.

I began to feel tense. Sandy's eyes had a wicked green gleam that reminded me of Brendan Collins. It was a bit like encountering a ghost, although Brendan was still existing comfortably in County Mayo. Opening gambits froze on my lips while crows cawed mockingly in the copper beech.

"I hope you're not vexed," he said.

I didn't know how to respond. He was different from what I had imagined. Not a bit professorial, or even reliable.

"Jane's very young," I said, feeling inadequate.

He nodded. "Yep. I feel comfortable with young women. The age difference doesn't bother me. Of course, I know it's a bit hard for some people to accept but Jane and I will manage fine." He was still dimpling at me.

I found it annoying. "And your wife?" I asked tartly.

Sandy raised his eyebrows a fraction. "We're separated at the moment. I can't see us getting back together." He tried on a woebegone little boy face.

When Jane reappeared with Oliver on one arm and a duffel bag slung over her shoulder I wanted to catch her and hold her captive, but what had I to offer in exchange?

"I'll be in Dublin in a few days' time," I said

213

desperately. I was overdue a visit to my mother.

"I left the address." Jane was bouncy and jubilant. "I haven't said goodbye to Mama. Maybe you'll explain." She managed to look contrite for half a second.

When they had driven off the place was blanketed in silence but not for long.

"Dixie. Dixie!" Ruth's voice shrilled threateningly from the porch.

As I moved towards her I found myself wishing that it was I and not Jane who had driven away and that I too had an open road to the future instead of eternally having to hack through the thicket thrown up by the past.

# Chapter Fifteen

29th October: "We have to get Ruth out of the house," Clive said harshly over our morning cornflakes. "I've too much on my plate as it is. I can't cope with this any longer. You'll have to back me up, Dixie." He looked unhappy. It served him right. He'd brought the latest bit of trouble with Ruth down on his own head.

Perversely I jumped to her defence, shouting, "Don't be such a complete bastard. I can't possibly ask her to go. She depends on us, she's really in a desperate state. All you had to do was leave her alone. I warned you she was in a bad mood, but we can't dump her. You do owe her more than that, Clive. Do you hear me?"

"The woman needs treatment. Look!" Clive jumped to his feet, planked his left one on a stool and rolled up his trouser leg. His wounded shinbone was a mixture of plum and purple with yellow streaks. Blood oozed from a deep scar at its centre. "I can't imagine what it would be like if I hadn't been strong enough to hold her off. Supposing it had been one of the children—or you?"

"She did it because she's still in love with you," I said sombrely.

"Christ!" Clive put his foot back on the floor and let his trouser leg fall. "What am I going to do?"

"Well, don't come to me for sympathy," I said. Yesterday, after Jane and her professor had driven off, I'd had a hard time with Ruth myself. She'd acted like a woman possessed, cursing and ranting and calling Jane names. Then she'd lain down on the sitting-room carpet and screamed.

"Don't be frightened. She's suffering from shock," I'd said to Jim, Anne and Bridget who had come racing in from the kitchen. "Honestly. It's delayed reaction. People are often this way after an accident or something like the fire. Leave her with me. She'll be all right."

And I had managed to talk her down. Eventually, I even got her to stand up and comb her hair and admit she was being a goose. "I'm all right now," she had repeated several times, settling herself quietly in a chair. After an hour or so of peace she had announced that she was going to go and lie down.

"Don't go near her," I'd warned Clive when he'd said he wanted to wish her goodnight.

He paid no attention. It was something that he felt he ought to do. He had been drinking before he came home and was in a mildly maudlin mood. I had been aware of him opening her door and a few minutes later there had been a fierce racket and Ruth's voice screaming. It seemed that she accused him of being her enemy and coming in to spy on her. Clive had moved towards her

216

with some idea of giving her an embrace. Then he had been attacked with an antique flat iron, one of a set that are ranged in the tiled fireplace as a reminder of older times. It seemed to me that he had been asking for it.

"Look at it this way; it's just as well she hadn't a gun," I said as Clive hobbled experimentally on his injured leg.

He looked at me, wild-eyed. "Exactly! That's why we'd better see that she gets some sort of help."

"We can't do anything without Alan. We're properly stuck now that he's removed himself from the scene. He'll have to be contacted." I felt my face reddening as I spoke. I was still embarrassed about the incident in the hotel bar.

"I don't know that Alan's the answer. This is more a woman's job. You should make enquiries, Dixie. You'd know where to ask."

"Ask what?"

"About finding someplace where she could go. One of those hostels, or shelters, or something. A place that takes kids."

"Her kids! Danny? He's your child."

"Please, Dixie, we've got to be rational about all this."

I was shocked. "Rational! What's rational about betraying an unhappy woman?"

He stared at me. "I'll never make you out," he said.

"I'm not going to be the one who crucifies Ruth."

"Now you're being melodramatic."

"Clive," I said, "you know she doesn't bear

217

you, of all people, ill-will."

"Ha! Ha! Ha!" his manner became sardonic. "You can't be so dumb that you don't know that this was the last straw." He went on to explain that he was on the verge of bankruptcy. His practice was finished. The whole bleeding country was finished. We could expect the bailiffs to come hammering at the hall-door if things didn't improve fast. Ruth and Alan were the lucky ones, in fact. Their house would sell more easily in its dilapidated state. Demolishing it would be that much easier. It would cost a fortune to knock down Bella Vista and there'd be no insurance claim. He wished that Danny would set fire to Bella Vista. He'd even buy him a box of matches. Ha! Ha! again.

And, while he worried himself stupid, all I could waste my time on was Ruth, and Jane, and any damn person that came to the door. Besides which, there was the annulment. That would have to be hurried up. And it was going to cost money, and he didn't suppose that I was going to be in a position to contribute a brass farthing. Ha! bloody Ha! once more.

In the meantime there was just one little thing I just might do. I might ask my new friend Harry Mercer to consider buying this place at a price favourable to Clive. He'd still be getting a bargain. But the trouble with these fellows who'd made their pile in England was that they were tough customers to deal with.

"Ah, so it's Harry Mercer that's the trouble." I pounced on the name. My blood was up. I'd fight fire with fire.

"Alan showed him the back part the other day. It seems that it fits in with his overall scheme. A connecting area between both our sites. Covered walk, car bays, that sort of thing."

I thought of Danny in the study, insisting that he had seen Alan through the keyhole. I should have been wise enough to believe him.

"I have no connection with Harry Mercer, but it seems that you've been bringing Alan and him around the place without even letting me know." I felt as if I had been dipped in ice. Even the tips of my ears tingled.

"It's business," Clive said shortly.

I felt a flash of pure venom. "So my opinion doesn't count?"

"Let's try and be a little bit constructive. Let's at least make our minds up about Ruth," said Clive coldly.

The lull that descended seemed to come from an outside force. Maybe it was caused by Ruth herself who had suddenly appeared in the doorway wearing a scraggy yellow candlewick dressing gown which made her skin turn the colour of a tallow candle.

She didn't say a word, just looked at us for a few seconds then turned and glided away. Before we could resume the back door had burst open and Mrs Connors charged in bursting out of her tweed coat, her face set in grumpy morning lines. Clive was gone with a quick nod and I was left to listen to Mrs Connors's gloomy thoughts for the day.

30th October: This morning, just as I finished

painting my face, the telephone rang. It was Jane to say that Oliver was as cross as a weasel. He hadn't stopped crying since they'd left Limerick. Indeed, I could hear his wails in the background.

"You should take him to a doctor," I said.

"I already have. But I don't think it's going to be any use. The doctor wouldn't give me anything for him."

"Maybe it was the car journey."

"Sandy says that it's him. That he and the baby give each other bad vibes." Jane's voice sounded clogged with weariness and suppressed tears. "I'll never be able to study."

I grew exasperated and asked, "What do you expect me to do? Clive and I have enough on our plates as it is."

Our financial troubles, the annulment, Ruth, my mother. All around me time bombs ticked towards explosion time.

"And Sandy expects me to do all the cooking and everything," she wailed. "He wants Irish stew tonight and there isn't even a place I could get to to shop for it. There isn't a supermarket within miles. I've run out of nappies for Oliver. And he went up to Ella, that's his wife, last night and didn't come home until about three. When he's here he spends all his time reading other students' papers and complaining about Oliver. He's not a bit pleasant. He's snappy and mean. He doesn't think I should go to lectures although I've got all that sorted out. He says there's no way I'll be able to get someone to mind a baby that bawls all the time but I know it's because he doesn't want to pay for it. I'm sorry, Dixie. I'm sorry..." Jane's voice was swamped by crying. She recovered herself enough to say, "I was thinking that if you spoke to Dada he might let me have some cash for the time being so I could get myself fixed up properly."

"You've really walked yourself into it," I said. I was in no mood for playing Mary Poppins. And yet, she'd been Peter's girl. Surely I owed it to her for Peter's sake. I thought of us all clustered behind the hearse on that miserable morning. Jane's sobbing was an echo from that unbearable day.

"Jane, I'll do what I can," I said at last, "but don't expect a miracle."

I decided to act quickly. I finished dressing with care, twisting my hair into a tight business-like coil, putting on more eye shadow and rouge and selecting lacy black tights to go with a violet two-piece that I seldom wore because it had cost so much. Ruth's door was still closed as I crossed the landing. She seldom appeared before midday.

I phoned Alan's office, asked to speak to him without giving my name and hung up before he came on the line. Next I called a taxi and headed for town.

I would weather this out for Peter's sake. He wouldn't have wanted his friend Jane to be hurt. Sandy was one of those secret dictators who can make a girl's life a misery. I shouldn't have allowed Jane to leave with him, I should have been able to see past those dimples.

In Alan's office I brushed aside his receptionist's attempts to hold me back and marched straight into his inner sanctum. It was eleven thirty a.m. Alan sat at his desk. Under the fluorescent light his scalp shone pinkly through his pale fuzz of hair. He would soon be completely bald. In compensation, perhaps, he had grown a small bristly moustache. All it did was make him look more like a pig.

"I'm here about Jane," I said briskly over the heads of two men who sat facing him.

"Dixie!" He blinked up at me.

"And her baby. That man she went off with isn't taking care of them properly."

"Well now, she should have thought of that before she left." Alan held his gold pen as if he was about to sign a form. His desk was covered with papers.

The pinstriped pair who had been huddled in front of him straightened up and swivelled around in my direction. I realised that they were Clive and Harry Mercer.

"Get out, Dixie. You shouldn't be here," Clive ordered curtly, as if trying to shame me.

"Hold on now, hold on." Harry Mercer jumped to his feet and clasped my hand between both of his. "It's only a bit of business, nothing that can't wait. Anyway you've arrived in the nick of time to save my skin. These two boyos are trying to hold me up to ransom." He glowed with good humour and virility. Just being touched by him made me feel appreciated, happier, more in control.

"The dotted line can wait," he said over his shoulder while Clive stared at us, gnashing his teeth.

Why did I have to arrive just then? Clive has been tearing his hair out. It was stupid, stupid. Anyway it's not my problem, Jane isn't my daughter. Jane is old enough to fend for herself. And it wasn't any old dotted line. It was Bella Vista that lay on Alan's desk. Plans, contracts, solicitors' documents, reams of red tape, facts and figures.

Clive arrived home at tea-time, livid. "Now we're all up the Swanee! You really blew it, didn't you. You gave him a chance to wriggle off the hook. There's no hope of him offering a decent price now. We'll end up worse off than the tinkers. I wanted to do my best for you before heading off but feck that. You can go and live in a tent."

I thought of Peter and Jane and their brief summer idyll last year. "There's worse things than tents," I said. "A house can be a bloody jail."

"You're a nut. I gave you the best house in the city and you threw it in my face."

"All I ever wanted..." I took a deep breath.

"Go on..." Clive looked dangerous.

I saw Tristram, thin as a brush handle, stepping up his narrow stairs ahead of me. I saw his dilapidated shop with living quarters. The boards had a special sort of creak, like a treasure chest being opened. Because of the dry goods kept in the back room there was always a musty, sugary smell, like a Turkish bazaar. Tristram's body was pale and relentless, his nipples the colour of acid drops. When he held me close his ribs felt as if they would crack through his skin. His heart thumped like a dog's tail beating against a carpet. I put out my hand to touch him and he turned to smoke.

The palms of my hands were moist. "I don't want another row, Clive," I said.

"This isn't a row, this is the bitter truth." His face had a cold glassed-in look. "The money has dried up all over the place. Our only hope is to shift the house for the best price possible and invest the cash as well as we can. It wouldn't be so bad if the bank was more co-operative. Brendan Collins was decent enough but his successor is worse than Scrooge."

"I believe you, I believe you," I said. "But what can I do?"

"You could work on Harry Mercer for one." Clive threw the remark out like a gauntlet. "A few blandishments from you wouldn't go astray. Any fool could see that he fancies you."

It would have been laughable if it wasn't so appalling. But no – it wasn't funny or dreadful. It was absurd. I felt helpless. "Do you think I'm going to seduce him for you?" I said.

"It wouldn't be the first time you've tricked a man."

"Come off it." I looked at Clive, half-expecting him to sprout horns.

"And Mrs Connors has to go. Pay her off on Friday." He snapped his fingers.

"And the girls...What'll I do about them? Bring them up to the Saturday market and sell them off as slaves?"

"The girls." Clive's voice thickened with emotion. "I'm so sick of this. You know bloody well they've got to get a fair deal. I wouldn't give a damn what happened if it wasn't for them so don't try to pin that one on me, Dixie. I'm at my wits' end trying to work out something that will give them some sort of chance." Tears started into his eyes. "I love them," he said simply. "I loved Peter. You should never have told me, you bitch. How do you think I felt finding out that he wasn't mine, that it was all a fake? It took all the good out of everything, all those years of them growing up, all those years feeling such a heel about Ruth, all the times I was hard on him because he couldn't think of anything but music. I thought it was only an act, but I suppose it was his nature. Who was his father anyway—some fellow singing in a pub or something?" His voice grew brutal. "The first man you managed to coax to stay around while you opened your legs for him?"

I should have been furious, I should have been hurt to the core. But Clive and I have gone beyond hurting each other. What I felt was a tug of sympathy, of bonding, of a mutual wish to disentangle ourselves once and for all from the whole miserable mess.

"I'll tell you anything you want to know, Clive," I said evenly. "And Peter's father was quite old. But he didn't go to pubs, he lived near our house, he was called Tim Long. But before I go on I just want to find out if you're serious about Harry Mercer."

"Oh, for God's sake, Dixie—forget it. What can you do? I swear I don't want you to come to any harm."

"I hear you," I said giving a shiver of pleasure as Harry Mercer breathed down my neck.

1st November: I bought the local paper on a whim and while rifling through the pages turned up the property section. The photograph of Bella Vista jumped out at me. "Elegant gentleman's residence," "a most desirable property," "magnificent Georgian mansion," "a showpiece dwelling." I arrived home half-expecting to find a string of potential buyers already on the driveway but there wasn't a soul to be seen.

It was a very windy day and the porch was full of leaves. I got a brush and swept them into the flower-bed, then entered the silent house and made myself coffee and spread the paper on the dining-room table for a closer look. It was the mid-term break. Anne, Bridget, Danny and Beth dashed in as I bent over the newsprint. I tried to shield the page from them to give myself time to digest it but their eyes spotted the photograph at once and they fell on the sale notice with whoops and shouts and a babble of comment.

A few seconds later Ruth shuffled in. She looked bloodless and exhausted. Her slacks and jumper were old and baggy and her hair hung in rat's tails.

"How about coffee?" I offered.

She shook her head and moved to the table and studied the paper. Then she looked up at me, her expression communicating nothing. "I think I'd like a gin and tonic," she said.

"Why not. I'll even have one with you." I found myself being falsely hearty.

The drink was kept over in a built-in cupboard in the study. I went to get it and Ruth followed me carrying two glass tumblers.

"Do you approve, Dixie?" she asked as I poured our drinks.

"Do you mean about selling the house?" My hand shook and I spilled some drink.

"I suppose it's that smooth Harry Mercer. He's very plausible," Ruth said. She took the gin bottle from my grasp and added some more to our glasses.

I remained silent.

"Property developers!" Ruth gave a little sneer. "They're worse than auctioneers. Nobody likes them."

"Ruth, I know things have been bad for you," I said. "I'm sorry. But maybe it'll be better when we all get away from each other—get out of each other's pockets. I know Clive feels that way. He feels guilty about you on top of everything," I said sincerely.

"I wanted to poison him while we were in the Canaries. Did he ever tell you that? I'm sure he guessed. I tried to set a trap. I'd bought stuff in a chemists to mix in. It wasn't strong enough, it only made him violently sick. It wasn't fatal."

"Stop talking nonsense, Ruth," I said sternly. "Anyway no Spanish chemist would ever give you a dangerous substance without a prescription. Remember the time we went to Majorca and I got gastritis?"

"You're wrong. It was easy. I pretended it was for fleas. The island had been infested by them. Everybody was buying the stuff."

I struggled to dismiss her talk as rubbish. But I saw Clive pale and haggard, suffering severe stomach cramps, miserable after his winter holiday.

"It was the only thing. He kept trying to fuck me," Ruth said in a monotonous voice.

I wasn't able for her revelations. There are some doors that should be kept locked.

"I've always tried not to get caught between you and Clive," I said helplessly.

"What you mean is you've never wanted to help anyone except yourself," she said sourly.

"You're under stress, Ruth," I said. "You should see the doctor, have a proper check-up."

"That's what I mean. You don't want to know. Neither do the doctors. All they can think of is prescribing tranquillisers. Most of them are frauds as well." She finished off her drink in one long swallow. Rain had started to batter against the windowpanes. I waited nervously for what she was going to say next.

But suddenly her manner changed. She looked around the room with a speculative expression. "All that stuff seems as if it belongs to ghosts." She pointed at the heaped boxes from Evergreen. Then she said wistfully, "Oh, Dixie, I used to love it so much in here. I always felt so safe and happy. I was sure that things were going to be fine."

The confusion in the room, the scraps and souvenirs and rubbish, made a fitting scenario for the two of us. It was like standing in a battlefield after the war was over.

Unexpectedly, Ruth grinned. "You and Clive gave some great parties. This room brings it all back," she said.

For a second I saw the golden siren who had entwined herself around Clive on this very spot. Her mouth grew moist, her eyes shone. Then she was seized by a fit of coughing and the impression quickly faded and she was her nervous, despondent, badly groomed, reclusive present-day self again.

# Chapter Sixteen

2nd November: "This is the master bedroom," I said to Harry Mercer. We were finishing a tour of the house. He had arrived on the doorstep uninvited, taking me off my guard. It was four o'clock in the afternoon and a glorious November day.

"Which bed is yours?"

"I don't see that that matters," I gasped, feeling bothered and embarrassed. He stroked my cheek with a finger and I began to babble, "It's not as if you'll be living here. I don't suppose it'll even be a bedroom when you've finished with the place. What are you planning—offices? Luxury flats? Even if it's flats you wouldn't leave the room like this. It's too big. It would have to be divided up."

"It's a tragedy to see these big family houses go," Harry said. "If you and I slept in this room, Dixie, I can promise you it wouldn't be in twin beds. And I'd never sell up. I'd give you a dozen kids to keep the place filled." I noticed how a gold tooth gave his smile a wicked gleam.

I turned away from him towards the garden so

that he wouldn't see me blush. I was frightened of the power he had to beguile me. Outside, Jim and Danny and Bridget and Anne were playing an aimless game of tennis. Boys vs. girls.

Clive was away. He had gone to Dublin by train to have lunch with Monsignor Patrick. There were fresh developments in our annulment case, some points to be clarified. Clive had wanted me to travel up with him and I had refused. It seemed to me a futile exercise. I would only be giving Monsignor Patrick another opportunity to be smug.

Harry was saying, "Of course I'll have to come back again with a man to check the essentials. I always believe in making a deal with my eyes open. Nothing wrong with your essentials though, Dixie."

"There was a cock pheasant out there in the garden last year," I said hurriedly, inconsequentially, to change the subject.

"Was there indeed?" Harry ran a probing finger the length of my spine and I shuddered. This was fate. I sensed him zeroing in on me, then his mouth was hungry on the back of my neck.

We couldn't behave like this with the children playing outside. I tried to resist as he pulled me round to face him and pressed me close. I felt him growing huge against me, my head was full of birds singing in a rainstorm. "Come on," he was saying, "come on, Dixie."

My own heart was thumping in my ears. It seemed a lifetime since I'd had good sex. I wished that I'd never known what it was like. "Not here." I found I was sobbing. "Not here. We can't,

Harry."

"You're a funny one. And you're mad for it, you want it as much as I do."

There was a note in his voice that made me feel he was playing with me, mocking my hunger. Unnerved, I began to cry and struggle. Immediately he let me go. We faced each other, breathing heavily. I could hear the cries in the garden like an advancing horde. I saw the door open that previous time and Peter's hurt, bewildered face looking at me with Brendan Collins. "Not here, Harry. I just couldn't here. Not with the children around, I'd feel too crowded."

He cocked his head on one side, saying, "Lock the door."

"It doesn't have a lock," I said ruefully; "we'd be more private up in the railway station."

Suddenly he was shrewd-eyed, composed, holding me at arm's length. "Where, Dixie? You name it." He spoke urgently then his gaze grew smoky. "Don't think you can keep me on a string."

My nonchalance was only a posture as I said, "You fancy yourself, don't you? You think every woman is ready to fall into your arms."

"Dixie, Dixie, I didn't think you were the blow hot, blow cold sort. I thought you'd some spirit. I thought you were sincere."

It was so unfair that a tear slid down my cheek. Another one followed unchecked and another as if I was a Victorian miss in some domestic drama.

"God save us, what's this at all? We can't have waterworks, they'll spoil your looks."

"I'm worn-out."

As he pulled me close to him and I rested my head against his shoulder I felt as fragile as a wren's egg.

He stroked my hair and kissed the top of my head, but this time like a Dutch Uncle instead of a lover. "You're wrecked," he said. "I should leave you alone."

I had to clench my hands so tightly that my nails dug into my palms to keep myself from chasing him as he went out the door. Then I looked at my untidy self in the dressing-table mirror, the unflattering pink blouse with a missing button, the wild hair. I was getting as unkempt as Ruth. And lines were etching themselves around my eyes, and an unpleasant red spot flared on my left cheekbone. I looked disgusting. I'd made a complete fool of myself. No wonder Harry thought I was there for the asking. I mopped my face with a tissue, put on some make-up and changed my slacks for a black skirt with a slit up the back and my crumpled blouse for emerald-green angora.

The tennis had ended and down in the kitchen the kids were preparing a snack. I watched as Jim loaded a plate with several slices of corned beef, two beefburgers and some mashed potato which had been left over from lunch-time. "It's just a snack, Aunt Dixie," he said apologetically. He had grown huge. He was much taller than Alan. They had all grown immensely. The kitchen was full of a noisy, hungry, sweaty mass of teenagers. There were only four of them but it sounded and felt like forty. They made me, in my green jumper, feel as flimsy and used up as last Sunday's paper.

And they were having fun. Jim and Beth tussling for the mayonnaise jar were having fun. And I was in the way. I would have been better off still locked in Harry's embrace.

I left the young ones stuffing themselves and headed for the front part of the house. As I crossed the hall the phone rang.

"Just giving you a buzz to see if you're still talking to me," said Harry. He was using his car phone. After he'd left me he'd driven the complete circle of the road several times. He had finally come to the conclusion that he was stone mad but he had to see me again at any price. "I'm your slave, Dixie," he said. "I've the car parked just inside Evergreen's gate."

My heart kept doing flip-flops as he spoke. Finally I hung up and crept like a thief to the cubby-hole in the back hall where we hung our coats. I snatched an anorak and dragged it on with eager fingers. "You're a rosy jewel, Dixie. You're solid gold. You're a deep one. You have me tormented." Harry's meaningless blandishments and his urgent coaxing, "Only for a minute. We'll just go for a little drive," sang in my ears.

I hurried out into the garden. It was growing dark but in spite of this, to my dazzled eyes, the grass seemed to have a green and luminous shine. Heavy scents rose from the damp earth. I felt purged of all my apprehensions and hesitancies. It was only as I pulled open the door of the Mercedes and glimpsed Harry's expression as he leaned across with his hand outstretched that doubts began to niggle.

Maybe Clive had somehow set this up. "You

could work on Harry Mercer," he'd said. I felt a touch of sourness even before Harry switched on the engine.

3rd November: As soon as he touched me I melted. But now I'm furious. I'm afraid that I'm a victim of one vast hypocrisy, a great deception, treachery. I think that all Harry wanted was a bit of easy sex.

We went from Evergreen's garden to a recently renovated hotel outside the city and ate duck and salmon in its small elegant restaurant. I found it difficult to make trivial conversation against a background of rosy wallpaper and bright chandeliers. All I could do was stare at Harry, memorising the cleft in his chin, the amazing length of his eyelashes. I felt myself expanding like a flower in a hothouse.

"Dixie, you're a dangerous woman," he said winking at me over a glass of red wine. I had to sit on my hands to keep myself from reaching across the table for him. Instead I slipped off a shoe and caressed his ankle with a silken foot.

"Dangerous altogether," he repeated while my head roared with suppressed passion. He shook his head as my foot reached his knee. "Brendan Collins was right when he warned me to look out."

The remark rocked me to the core. I felt cheated. "You've been talking to Brendan Collins? How come?"

Harry paused, registering astonishment at my anxiety as much as bewilderment about how to reply. "There's nothing fishy about it. Brendan

and I are pals from way back. I haven't been all
my life in England. The pair of us used to share
digs. Holy God, he gave me my first ever loan to
buy machinery. He's a jewel of a man, one of the
best."

"You met him and talked about me." Feeling
betrayed, I slipped my foot back into its shoe.

"Not lately. Don't look like that! It's not as if
he isn't fond of you. He was very fond of you."

"I can't say I return the compliment. There
wasn't much to be fond of. He always had a big
mouth. It was the biggest thing about him," I said
crudely.

"No need to get upset. There's no law against
having a little bit on the side, if there was we'd all
be in jail," said Harry good-humouredly.

His attitude made me feel very vulnerable.
"When did you last see him?" I was forced to ask.

"Come on, Dixie, eat up your lovely fish before
it spoils," Harry answered. Suddenly he leaned
forward and said with a rough lecherousness,
"Finish that off and we'll go upstairs so I can fuck
you stupid. I want something better than I got in
the Merc."

I felt embarrassed. "Don't be in such a rush," I
managed to say.

"I'm sure and certain you want it as much as I
do. What went on in the car proves it."

I didn't want to be reminded about the two of
us threshing about on the back seat of Harry's car
in Evergreen's grounds. It unnerved me, making
me fumble and drop my fork onto the floor.

A waiter immediately appeared to pick it up.
After he'd replaced it with a fresh one he

continued to hover within earshot. We had already caused a mild flutter at the reception desk by booking a room for the night. There had been a loaded silence when we said that we would bring in our bags after we'd eaten. "If Madam wants to freshen up there's a ladies room on the first right," said a girl with a blond chignon and immaculate nails. The ghost of her smile mocked me as I stared at my tousled reflection and realised that I had no lipstick with me.

"I can't remember when I last had it off with a woman in the back of a car," grinned Harry.

I closed my eyes. I didn't want to see the waiter's knowing face. "What do you want?" I murmured. There was no point in fighting back.

"What do you think, you bold girl?" His voice was amused and confident.

I opened my eyes and turned away from him. The restaurant tables were very close together. An elderly couple nearby, with pale pierrot faces, were listening to and watching us with enthralled expressions. When he caught my eye the man took a pocket handkerchief from his dark suit and mopped his forehead. I felt the wall, the glasses, the lights, the purple daisies in the window bays, the dessert trolley, closing in on me like the trappings of war. I felt the waiter's suppressed laughter and Harry's deceit. God knows what sort of stories he and Brendan had swapped about me. I jumped up and raced for the exit, spilling over my wine as I went.

"I say, what terribly odd behaviour," the ageing pierrot announced to his wife in my wake.

I was a wreck as I stumbled along the dark road

away from the hotel. A breeze had blown up and there had been a heavy shower of rain. When I splashed into a large puddle I was tempted to turn and go back to the hotel. A car was approaching and I stuck out my thumb for a lift. If it didn't stop I'd go back. I'd rather let Harry humiliate me in public than end up as a mangled road accident statistic. As the car passed me it slowed down and jerked to a halt. The passenger door swung open. I hurried towards it steeling myself for a catechism about my personal history. Or maybe I'd be driven up a mountainside and raped. Would Harry give a damn if I was?

"Good girl, yourself," said the fat farmer at the wheel. He was a plump, pleasant, compulsive talker who had no interest whatsoever in my reasons for being on the road alone on a dark November evening. What concerned him were the two bags of seed waiting for him at the city railway station. And the lateness of the train, the state of the country, the uncertain weather, the price of cattle, the bad harvest, the Minister for Agriculture, the increase in robberies in rural areas and the possibility that Saint Patrick hadn't really banished all the snakes from Ireland.

I slumped in the corner of my seat pulling my light wool wrap tighter over my green jumper. My high-heeled shoes were soaked through. I felt like a seabird who had been caught in an oil spill. I was sticky everywhere.

We reached the railway station and I left the farmer to hunt for his bags of seed. I hailed a taxi to Bella Vista. When we arrived there I hurried in to get money to pay the driver. As I collected it I registered the fact that Jane, as well as Ruth, was in the sitting-room.

"I'm back, Dixie," said Jane unnecessarily.

Danny was slouched on a chair reading a *Beano*. My own family seemed to have vanished.

I ran out and paid the taxi-driver. As I came back in again Anne hurried down the stairs. She stopped a few steps from the bottom and announced melodramatically, "Grandmother is dead. The message just came."

Almost simultaneously Jane put her head around the sitting-room door and said urgently, "Dixie, Harry Mercer phoned. He wanted to know if you'd got home all right."

5th November: Yesterday Clive and myself met up with our daughters in the hospital foyer. Monsignor Patrick arrived on our heels protesting that the least he could do was officiate at my mother's obsequies. I went through the ceremonies with a feeling of unreality. I stared in incomprehension as Mother was plucked from the shadows of her final years and placed centre stage in a wooden box.

After she had been buried in the grave beside my father, Monsignor Patrick came with us to a Dublin hotel for a family meal. The girls all had dark circles under their eyes and wept easily. The only person besides ourselves at the funeral Mass had been a woman with blond permed hair and a dark coat. When she approached me as the coffin was being placed in the hearse I discovered that she was a nun from the nursing home. Her sole purpose in being there seemed to be to ask me to collect my mother's few belongings as quickly as possible.

"Or would you rather if we gave them to some charitable organisation?" she suggested chirpily.

I recalled the second-hand clothes shop with its dismal winceyette night-dresses outside which I'd met Harry Mercer. I would be along before nightfall to collect everything, I said and was rewarded with a precise handshake and a nod.

"So where are the Whites today?" Monsignor Patrick asked in the hotel, a large Scotch in his hand and plate of roast beef and vegetables in front of him.

Nobody answered.

"It wasn't a bit creepy and Bridget told me it would be," Anne said. "I'd have been scared to kiss her, though. Bridget says your mouth can stick to a dead person because of the cold. Like frostbite." Then she looked devastated and wailed, "I kept thinking about Peter."

"Bridget is a silly little idiot and so are you," Marie burst out. Then it was too much for everyone and the girls and I started crying. Clive and Monsignor Patrick made an attempt at normal conversation and eventually we all calmed down a little. Anne and Marie even began to argue because Anne claimed that Marie was bossing her.

"Oh stop it," I scolded. I was glad that the conversation did not return to the Whites. With things as they stood there was no question of Ruth being at Mother's funeral—or Alan. I wondered what was happening in Bella Vista. I wondered if Harry had tried to contact me again.

Next thing Anne, in spite of warning looks from me, addressed herself breezily to Monsignor

Patrick. "Jane left her new man and came back with the baby. He's a dote. I'm delighted."

"Please God she will settle down and be a good mother to the child," he said with shameful hypocrisy.

I looked at my gin and tonic, a little embarrassed, and said, "Eat up your dinner, Anne."

"When will Grandmother's name be put on the tombstone?" asked Marie in an inadequate attempt at civilised conversation.

I shook my head. "I don't know. Soon. When I can manage it."

Beth said loudly, "I bet Grandfather's pleased to have her there with him." Beth had dressed herself with care. Her short, newly spiked hair was her only non-black adornment.

Clive roused himself to interject, "You look like something from a horror movie, Beth...a stand-in for Mrs Dracula, but you don't have to be so morbid."

Beth looked crushed but said defiantly, "Well wouldn't you want Mummy with you? I mean married people, they belong together."

"The Church teaches that there are NO marriages in Heaven," said Monsignor Patrick coldly.

"Anyway, I'm leaving instructions to have myself cremated," Clive said, clinching the matter.

"So that's that." I shrugged wishing I could take off the jacket of my black costume and cool down but I knew that the chiffon blouse underneath was indecently transparent. There was an uneasy silence. I saw Anne roll a piece of bread into pellets and flick them at Beth. I needed to go to the ladies room. To reach it I had to walk through the hotel bar.

It was a quiet hour for business and the only person there was a man who seemed to be alone. As I made my way back to the dining-room he turned and looked at me. "Dixie... I don't believe it!" He swayed on his stool and it took me a minute to recognise Brendan Collins.

"Come here. Sit down. Prove that you're real." He tried to ease himself from the stool then gave up.

"I can't stay," I said uneasily.

"Have a drink. What's the harm? I'm bombed myself."

"Maybe later," I told him feeling scared that an awkward situation was going to develop.

"I'll take it as an insult if you don't." He set his lips in a mean line.

"I can't. I'm with Clive and the girls. It's my mother. She was buried this morning."

"Oh Jesus, Dixie." In an attempt at gallantry he half fell off the stool.

I caught him as he slipped to the ground. He threw his arms around me in tipsy commiseration. He was wearing a scratchy sports coat in loud green and orange checks. I guessed that Peggy must have chosen it. He put his face so close to mine that the red veins in his bloodshot eyes were as clear as motorways on a road map. He had been drinking, heavily. County Mayo clearly did not agree with him.

"Missed you, Dixie. Missed you real bad. Give us a kiss."

242

His breath came in sour wistful gusts as he pressed his nose against my cheek. I screamed and tried to squirm out of his grasp as his lips slobbered against my face. It served me right, I thought remorsefully. How could I ever have let him near me? He caught the back of my head in a strong grip and forced my face round so that he could kiss me on the lips. But I was still able to see, out of the corner of my eye, Monsignor Patrick striding pompously in our direction.

## Chapter Seventeen

6th November: This morning I was downstairs at nine a.m. It wasn't my first trip. I had been prowling around the house all night. The sky was silvery blue and a bird cheeped lonesomely in the copper beech. I opened the hall-door and looked at the straggly winter flower-beds full of tangled stems and seedpods. The macracarpas had been trimmed and looked ragged and miserable. Wind clattered through a palm tree. It all spelt desolation.

I went back into the living-room and tried to read yesterday's paper but even Mother's death notice seemed incomprehensible. I imagined the headlines we could have been faced with in today's tabloids.

WOMAN ATTACKS INTRUDER. PROPERTY DEVELOPER SLAUGHTERED BY DISTRAUGHT HOUSE GUEST. HOUSE BUYER DEALT FATAL BLOW BY FAMILY FRIEND.

Our arrival home had been a horrific sequel to the debacle with Brendan Collins. After Monsignor Patrick surprised us in the bar Brendan refused to climb quietly back up onto his bar-stool.

Oblivious to my dark looks and sharp tone he shambled after me to the dining-room where he shook hands with Clive and the girls, mumbling about being sorry for their trouble.

When the Monsignor returned from the gents', Brendan, his voice gravelly with emotion and liquor, said that he'd never forgotten the day the Monsignor met up with us while we were eating oysters in Moran's.

"You came to our rescue. We were nearly stranded," he said. "Not that there was any harm in it, mind. Just Dixie and myself, old friends, having a bite to eat. Everything purely platonic, mind. Celibate as a bishop myself."

The occasion of my mother's funeral had been turned into a farce. Furious, I gathered up my bag and scarf and pushed my way out into the street. Our journey home was punctuated by terse spiteful exchanges between Clive and myself while the girls chattered happily behind us.

"Tell me something, Dixie. How did everything get into such a muddle?" Clive suddenly demanded as we waited in a traffic jam in Castletroy. His voice had softened.

"I don't know." I felt weepy. I supposed that we were in the throes of early mid-life crisis. It was all the fault of our age.

"Maybe things will improve when we get things sorted out between us," Clive said in a low voice. "We can always be friends. There doesn't have to be any vendetta stuff."

The silence from the back seat made me apprehensive that the girls were listening in until I glanced over my shoulder and saw that all three had fallen asleep like ladies-in-waiting in a tale of enchantment.

My daughters, I loved them, I thought. I loved every hair on their heads. "Couldn't we try again?" I managed a half-laugh. "After all, we survived Rosepark House."

Clive pushed out his lower lip, furrowed his brow and said nothing.

At Bella Vista the squad car did not immediately alarm us. I clearly remember thinking, "I hope it's not some more depressing red tape about Peter." Darkness had fallen and the front room lights were on. As we drove up the yellow blind pulled back and Jane's face flattened itself against the window for a second.

The girls woke as Clive switched off the engine and there was a stir of groans and grumbles. Alan coming out to meet us was a puzzlement. "I'm feeling sick," wailed Beth who is always a bad traveller and she rushed inside. Seconds later she was out again gasping that there were police everywhere.

Some instinct made me clap my hands over my ears and I watched Alan and Clive mouthing sentences at each other. They both scowled, then Clive turned and caught my wrist and pulled my hand away so that I could hear.

I wish I had drowned that day in Kilkee because I'd be out of this tangle.

"Ruth thought it was a burglar," Clive said, his breath coming in short tight gasps as if he was going to have a heart attack. "She was taking precautions. I wouldn't blame her with the stuff you hear about nowadays."

Alan and Clive, all our children and myself were in the front room. It was late, eleven thirty or twelve. Harry Mercer had been viciously attacked by Ruth under mysterious circumstances. She was suffering from shock and had been taken to the hospital. I went over to stir up a flame in the fire and it was only when I'd rooted around for the poker that I remembered it had been taken away by the guards.

"What possessed her?" said Alan and I thought how old he looked and how his hair was a horrible colour with all that yellowy-grey, like nicotine stains.

"He might pull through. I hope to God he does," Clive said meaning Harry Mercer.

Alan stood up. "Even if he does the sale will be gone up the Swanee."

"Has his wife been contacted?" I asked nervously.

Clive turned on me. "What wife? There's no wife that I ever heard of."

"I think her name's Madge."

Clive and Alan looked each other.

"First I ever heard of her. Thought he had a harem of rich madams," snorted Alan.

"He certainly doesn't have a house. He lives all the time in hotels," amplified Clive.

I felt confused. The very first time I met him Harry had introduced the topic of his wife.

"She's English. She lived with him for a while over here but she didn't like it. They have a son. He's in Australia," I said. It sounded unlikely when

I thought about it.

"It sounds as if you two were very pally," Alan sneered.

"There's all kinds of gossip about him," said Clive.

"He's not averse to a romp with the women," said Alan.

"I'll bet he didn't rape them," I said.

"You should know." Alan's face turned puce.

For a moment the atmosphere was very nasty. We teetered on the brink of mutual destruction. Then we became aware that we had our children sitting around the room as tired and confused as we were.

"Whatever Ruth did you're the person responsible," I said to Alan.

"Is that a fact now? From the story the kids gave me it sounds as if something very peculiar was going on."

"Aunt Dixie," said Danny as I walked over the sideboard to steady myself, "is Mama going to go to jail?"

I wanted to comfort him. I wanted to say that I hoped not. I explained as best I could that there had been an accident, his mother had had a bad fright. She'd been taken into hospital for observation, just like Mr Mercer, but he mustn't worry about it.

So much for yesterday. The telephone rang at six o'clock this morning. Before I'd picked it up I feared that Harry was dead but my imagination was running away with me. Harry wasn't dead although I nearly had a seizure because my heart was pounding so hard. I almost swooned with relief before going into Clive and whispering, "Alan just called. Harry Mercer is going to be all right." I felt very happy. Whatever had happened in our absence would all be easily explained.

Clive grunted and pulled a blanket over his head while I returned to the sitting-room. In the morning light I noticed things. Shards of a broken vase that Ruth had knocked off the mantelpiece, a crack in a mirror, a tear in our expensive embossed wallpaper that could have been made by somebody wielding a heavy implement. But Harry was alive. I felt that there should be a six-piece jazz band playing behind banks of roses and carnations.

I cooked a breakfast. A big gelatinous pot of porridge that nobody except myself wanted. I had the sort of hunger I hadn't had for years. In those early days of the foursome my eating habits were a joke. "Miss Piggy, yum, yum." Alan tickled me to the verge of hysterics when he caught me munching dinner rolls in bed. I think it was a false hunger created by my precarious joie-de-vivre. This morning I ate three plates of porridge in a solitary ritual feast.

"Are you OK, Mum? I can stay home for the day if you're not." Marie burst into my happy distraction as I gloated over my empty plate. She was heading back to her new teaching job in County Cork.

"I'm fine, sweetheart. Just building myself up." I gestured at my empty bowl.

Marie looked worried. "You must be whacked. You've had a rotten few days."

"Look after yourself, don't worry about me," I said.

"Just call if you want me to come back. It's only a few hours away. Promise."

She was making me nervous, rubbing the gloss off my euphoria. I pointed at the kitchen clock and said, "If you don't hurry you'll miss your bus."

8th November: This morning I hurried out our gateway just as Andrew Daly was driving away from his house. I had spent a great deal of time in front of my mirror, dressing up. I hadn't met Andrew since the night of his house-warming party. However, he immediately stopped his car and flashed his lights offering me a lift.

"Where to?" he asked watching me closely as I got in.

"Town. Anywhere. I don't care." I hoped he didn't notice my discomposure. I knew that I was ridiculously over-dressed for the hour of the day and the weather. Décolleté blouse under green velvet suit, mock croc high-heels and a ton of jewellery.

"Going someplace special?" Andrew eyed me as if I was a tart.

"Visiting."

He gave the sort of wolf whistle I hadn't heard since I was a kid. Tristram used to do it to tease me.

"I'm in a hurry." I stared straight ahead at the road.

"Yup. Sorry." He put his foot on the accelerator. "How's Ruth, your neighbour, ex-neighbour. I mean is she all right now?" he asked.

"She's been having a hard time," I said hoping

I sounded enigmatic. "You should bring her over to see Sophia. She loves company." It was clear that he hadn't heard about last night's business with Harry.

"I find it a nuisance not having a car," I said to change the subject.

"Heard you wrote the last one off. You'll just have to get Clive to buy you a new one," he said full of cheer.

It wasn't until he had pulled up in O'Connell Street to let me out that I asked the question burning in my brain. "Tell me something about Harry Mercer," I challenged. "Does he actually have a wife or is it just something he tells people?" My head began to spin. If what Andrew said proved that Harry had been fooling me I wouldn't go to the hospital.

"Old Harry!" My heart missed a beat. Andrew quirked an eyebrow. "Sometimes I think he has and sometimes I think he hasn't. That's Harry for you."

"Right," I said dully, closing the door with a sense of anticlimax. I'd have to make my own mind up, wouldn't I! What did it matter anyway? Maybe he'd invented Madge to save us both from each other. She'd been a safety valve to keep things from getting out of hand between us.

9th November: I have been suffering from bouts of delusion about Harry Mercer. The scales fell from my eyes when I walked into his hospital room and found Jane sitting beside his bed. I could have been invisible as I stood in the doorway watching them. Then, Jane lifted her head and focused on me and immediately asked if I'd baby-sit for the weekend so that she and Harry could go off together and stay for a couple of nights in a Connemara hotel.

I felt utterly stymied. I refused to accept the fact that she could be serious. Then Harry said, "Well, isn't this nice. Two of my girlfriends have come to see me." And turning to Jane he said, "My darling, you didn't tell me to expect Dixie." Propped up against white pillows, with a large plaster on his forehead and his hair tousled he looked amazingly young.

"Doesn't he look great, Dixie?" Jane gave a sudden smile.

"Where's your baby?" I asked her.

"One of the girls from the house I stayed in before he was born is keeping him for the day. She's moved. She's living in town."

"Have a grape," said Harry. "Jane brought them."

"No thanks." I felt shrivelled with hurt and embarrassment. The gifts I had brought, flowers, spy thrillers, liqueur chocolates, brandy and a packet of smoked salmon, turned to dust in my arms.

"Hey, hey - what's all this?" Harry said with an amused nod in their direction. "Christmas isn't until next month."

"I was just telling Harry how good you were, how generous," said Jane. "I was telling him that if it hadn't been for you I'd never had made it through the past year. I'd never have found myself."

"Found me is what she really means," said

Harry taking Jane's hand and brushing it against his lips.

My scalp prickled as if my hair was standing on end. Maybe it was. I felt frightened as well as tricked. "What's been going on?" I asked. "What brings you here, Jane? Is it something to do with last night? What got into Ruth? I still don't know what happened."

"It was our fault," said Jane and Harry in unison.

"Mine more than hers. I'm the biggest and boldest," said Harry touching his bandages gently. "I deserved to get clocked."

"No. It was my fault for bringing you upstairs," said Jane. She was suddenly embarrassed, sending me sidelong glances as she fiddled with a loose thread on her canary-coloured jumper.

I stared at them blankly. "What were you doing upstairs?"

Harry guffawed, then groaned. "Come on, Dixie, love. What do grown-ups usually go upstairs for if it's not to have a pee?"

"We went into your room because we thought it would be more private. That was very wrong," said Jane, "and Mama heard us. That's what the row was all about. You know how she's been. Oh Dixie," tears rolled down her face, "I'd have told you when you arrived but I couldn't say anything in front of the younger ones. Only Marie knew, nobody else. But they mustn't do anything cruel to Mama. Please, I'd feel so guilty. I know she didn't mean it. She thought it was robbers. She was really very brave, creeping upstairs like that with the poker."

I felt helpless and out of my depth. Jane and Harry, a barb pierced my heart. And yet, I remembered my own girlhood, my assignations with Tristram, the subterfuge and excuses, the fear of prying questions. I suppose you can't behave any other way when you're young and silly.

I remembered the cold torpid smell of the linoleum on Tristram Long's stairs and how it used to fill my nostrils like an exotic perfume with promises of passion. Maybe Jane felt the same way leading Harry into my room. Maybe the brazenness of it turned her on. I'd never for a second suspected that she and Harry had even looked at each other, but I couldn't shame myself by protesting.

"No hard feelings, Dixie?" said Harry as if he could read my mind.

I shook my head, not trusting myself to answer. I turned away from Harry and concentrated on Jane. "You're old enough to decide who you want to associate with, although I'd expect to be asked before you made use of my room," I said not bothering to keep the coldness out of my voice. "No wonder you scared the wits out of Ruth. She hasn't been well. This won't improve her state of mind. She's already at risk. And she's a danger to other people too. Harry could have been murdered. Look at the way she attacked Clive. And she tried to poison his food."

"Dixie, Mama doesn't even cook these days," Jane said impatiently.

"No. But will you believe me if I say she's been known to put flea powder in Clive's dinners?"

Harry and Jane burst out laughing

254

simultaneously. Then Jane mopped her eyes and apologised for their awfulness, saying that they didn't mean it but that after all the tension she was ready to crack-up herself.

Not you, baby, I thought, looking at the way she peeped lovingly at Harry and snuggled her hand in the crook of his neck in a gesture that was both girlish and wanton.

As soon as I'd left the hospital I began to think of hundreds of things that I could have done or said. When I reached Bella Vista I went straight to our bedroom. By that time I hated myself for being so craven. I should have screamed at them, I should have been abusive. Harry Mercer was a sneak, a molester, a pervert, a cheat. I threw myself face downward on my bed but then I imagined two bodies writhing beneath me. They began to coil around me like snakes. Or maybe they had done it on the carpet, over there in front of the wardrobe so that they could watch themselves in the mirror. I wouldn't have just gone for Harry if I'd found them, I'd have murdered them both. I could actually sniff Harry in the room. Maybe that's how he got his kicks, setting one woman up against another. If there was such a person as Madge she had my sympathy.

How could Jane ever cope with a man like Harry on equal terms? She was too young for him. Young people nowadays believed that a slice of any pie in the sky was theirs for the asking. They expected everything to be easy. Easy come, easy go. I could tell her it seldom worked out that way. I remembered Brendan's plump body pressing against mine, both of us greedy in our nakedness. And then the door opened.

I screamed. This was how Peter had found us. But Peter was dead; it was Danny standing there, wearing his grey school pullover.

"Aunt Dixie," he said apprehensively, "Mrs Connors isn't downstairs and there's nothing to eat for dinner."

10th November: I'm calmer today. I've managed to be civil to Jane, I've even said that I'll consider minding Oliver for her. I brought her up to see Ruth in the psychiatric wing of the other hospital in the city.

Ruth had a pale drowned look as if she had been held face down in water for too long. It was because of the heavy medication. I touched her arm and it felt soft and limp as a cuddly toy's. She didn't want to talk, she just wanted to keep on sleeping.

Around tea-time Monsignor Patrick showed up with a manila envelope full of documents. Clive and I sat with him in the drawing-room and had a long and tedious discussion. I let Clive make all the decisions. I didn't care any more.

"I'm sure, Dixie, you have a wide circle of friends who will stand by you," said Monsignor Patrick. I heard the dislike in his voice and knew he was thinking of Brendan Collins.

"Sure," I said jauntily. "Thousands."

After he left Clive talked to me about his new job. A firm offer had finally come through from the international company he had been negotiating with. "I'll see that you and the girls are all right, Dixie," he said but I still refused to show interest.

"Ruth's the person you should say this to," I said balefully.

"That's all over." He shook his head and I was prepared to bet that he'd never said that to Ruth directly. He looked too uneasy.

"And there's Danny. What about him? You'd better sort things out with Alan."

"I've got to earn a living. That's more than you've ever had to do. I can't take care of everything." He sounded defensive.

"I've looked after the kids and fetched and carried. Sometimes I think I've looked after everyone in the world."

"Especially Dixie Molloy!"

"It won't be "Molloy" much longer. That's a relief. If I didn't look after myself nobody else would. I don't even have a car and where are the girls and I going to live?"

"You'll be able to use my car," said Clive, "and the house question will sort itself out. Don't be so negative."

I got up and walked out to the kitchen and attacked an accumulation of dirty dishes before the quarrel became more serious. Scraping congealed brown masses off white dinner plates and rinsing them under a stream of hot water I swore that I would get by. I went to work on a sackload of cutlery. From now on I would live minute by minute, knife by fork. Stainless steel flashed through my fingers like sprats.

"Bugger Jane," I thought viciously. She could have had whoever she wanted. Look at the way she took up with her professor. I felt a rush of affinity with Sandy's wife, two-timed by a student with baby. I'd like to see Harry Mercer changing nappies. Maybe he'd get his wife, if she existed, involved; set up a ménage à trois.

When I'd finished it was an effort to pull myself upstairs holding onto the banisters. Clive was already in bed. As I put my head on the pillow I knew that this was how Ruth must feel. My cheek bones ached as if from a sharp blow and a searing pain bored right up through me, blistering my vagina and sending scalding spears of pain straight up into my skull.

I fell into a deep sleep but was shaken awake shivering and sweating. Barely an hour had passed. As I lay staring into the dark I knew that on the other side of the city Ruth was lying in her limp doll posture, and she wasn't asleep either. She was too busy blaming me, wishing the worst on me, dragging me down and down and down to join her.

# Chapter Eighteen

12th November: This has been the longest year of my life. The person I was twelve months ago is caught in another world, the place that existed before everything exploded in my face. It is the same for Ruth. Only now and again do I get a flash of something that reminds me of the pair of innocents we were. Perhaps more naive than innocent, thinking that women of our background and upbringing could buck the system and make it work to our advantage.

I feel now that Ruth was the wise one, the one who saw to the heart of things. It was she who saw the danger in our old, comfortable, laissez-faire existence. I was the one who thought that a fool's paradise could last indefinitely. And then I think otherwise, that all the trouble was caused by Alan's brutality and we've all been victims of his monstrous behaviour. But anyway I can't think of setting things to rights. We're almost forty and you can't change much at forty. The earth has revolved too often. You get dizzy if you think too hard. I found that out when I called a secretarial college about doing a refresher course.

"Is it for yourself or a young person?" asked the girl on the switchboard.

"Myself," I said. "I'm planning to go back to work." Once I'd said it I quite liked the idea. The clack of typewriters, shorthand notebooks, cosy chats over coffee, myself playing sympathetic agony aunt to girls like my own daughters. "I'm mature and responsible," I added, "but I probably need a few tips before I start seriously looking around."

"You mean you want to update your skills. Can you tell me which type of computers you have worked with, and word processors, fax, etc.?" I hated the pert voice as it continued rattling off a list of technical gobbledygook. It all sounded like a dialect from a new planet. There was no point in saying anything that would reveal my ignorance. I hung up.

It was almost a relief to take charge of Oliver while Jane headed off with Harry, although Clive was appalled.

"What are you trying to prove?" he asked as I heated a bottle between peeling and chopping vegetables for a stew.

"Nothing," I said. "I just decided to do Jane a favour."

"Where's she gone?" he asked.

"Off with a friend."

"Male or female?"

"Harry Mercer."

"And you let her!" He looked ready to collapse.

"She's not my daughter," I said, "and besides she's an adult."

"I can't make you out," said Clive. "My mind boggles."

I ignored him, put the casserole in the oven, tested the milk on my inner wrist, and scooped Oliver out of his playpen.

It hadn't occurred to me to worry about Alan making a fuss. I was too busy to give him much thought. Ruth was the person on my mind. They were too overcrowded in the hospital to hold onto her. They had already contacted me to say that what she needed most was rest in friendly surroundings. It looked as if I was going to have to carry on as caretaker mother. There were things that would have to be clarified, but as far as I knew nothing definite had been arranged.

I was alone in the kitchen when Alan arrived. Oliver had drunk his bottle and been put into his cot. I was skimming through the day's paper when he came in silently and touched my back. It was so unexpected that I toppled over my mug of coffee. Then I turned and saw the implacable set of his jaw.

He caught the left side of my face between his finger and thumb and squeezed hard. I closed my eyes and promised myself that if he hurt me badly I'd see that he went to jail. He let go and stepped back. Both doors of the kitchen were closed and it felt very hot.

"I could break your neck," he said.

I attempted a laugh. "Me! What have I done?"

"Screw that." He took the overturned coffee mug from the table and dashed it onto the tiles.

"Cut that out, Alan," I said firmly, hiding my fear.

"I felt there was something fishy about you being so interested in Harry Mercer," he said. "You did it to spite me. Him and her. That shifty hoor is sleeping with Jane and it was you that set it up. I'll have him run out of the country."

He grabbed my right arm and twisted it behind me and forced me to my feet so that I was pulled against the frosty whiteness of his shirt.

"Get out," I said, "get out, get out, get out."

"I blame you. I could murder you." His breath was hot on my face.

I could see a carving knife on the kitchen table but there was no way I could reach it if I managed to break free. The playpen was in the way. I said nothing, hoping that by ignoring him I could make him let me go.

"You stupid bag." His eyes glittered.

"The kids will be in from school any minute." My voice seemed to come from a great distance.

"Don't pull that one. They won't be in for hours." It was true.

Terror gripped me. I knew what was going to happen. A wave of blackness swept over me as he twisted his hands into my hair and tugged. "One thing I'm sure of, you'll never feel like having sex with anyone again by the time I'm finished," he said.

I was surprised how bouncy the rubber tiles on our kitchen floor felt as my body collapsed. They seemed to undulate like the base of a bouncing castle at a child's birthday party. And the walls were swaying too and the ceiling scudded in all directions like clouds before a whirlwind. I saw the carving knife on the kitchen table and knew Alan must have seen it too. I dreaded the moment when he'd take it in his hand. I thought of my flesh bursting open, of the blood and pain. I prayed that something would happen to prevent him from using it. And then I began to feel that it would be better if he did.

14th November: This afternoon I lay on the bed that used to be Peter's. Jane sleeps in it now with Oliver's cot nearby. Jane is still away with Harry, the baby is my jailer keeping me imprisoned in the house. My body still hurts in hidden places from the bashing that Alan gave me. When I move suddenly my flesh stings as if it has been wrapped in barbed wire. But when anyone asks me what happened I fob them off, saying that it was a silly accident.

They don't press me too hard. The feeling is one of general relief that Ruth was stopped before she committed the ultimate horror. Alan was lucky that she failed to strike a mortal blow.

I'd had no idea that she had arrived with Alan. He must have forgotten about her too in the heat of the moment. Suddenly, as he and I struggled like alleycats on the kitchen floor and I discovered how brutal and wicked he could be, she materialised.

"The knife!" Was that what I croaked as I shuddered waiting for my next humiliation at Alan's hands? She crouched over us like a panther, eyes narrowed, taking it all in. Our eyes met, hers and mine, and for a moment everything between us was crystal clear. I watched as she lifted her arm, the knife angled at its target and then as she lunged I screamed and turned my head and waited, wincing, for Alan to change into a gurgling helpless mass. I remembered the knife coming down like lightning, like the wrath of God. I was in the ocean again, drowning, Alan a millstone around my neck.

But in that instant the doorbell shrilled, shocking me back to full awareness. Alan lifted his body and groaned. Ruth stood, the knife still in her hand, a deathly glaze on her face.

"Look at yourself, Dixie." Her voice was wooden.

I stood up painfully and tugged at my ripped blouse. I couldn't move because I was hobbled by my tights and knickers around my ankles. My skirt was a crumpled ball on the floor. I felt whorish and degraded by my nakedness. As the doorbell shrilled again I rearranged my soiled and tattered clothing as best I could.

Alan had managed to get to his feet and was lurching around the kitchen cursing and displaying his shirt sleeve and the dark patch spreading up near the shoulder.

"What have you got to say about that?" He shook his fist at Ruth and she backed away from him and dropped the knife beside the playpen.

I should never have answered the door. It would have been safer to allow whoever it was to go away. As I walked across the hall Alan was behind me, his hand in the small of my back, his wounded arm held out from his body. "She's getting worse but I'll fix her. Have you been putting her up to this?" he said tersely. If there was any justice, I thought, she'd have plunged the knife in hard enough to kill him.

If it had been anybody other than Monsignor Patrick on the doorstep I'm sure that things would have worked out differently. I would have been able to tell my version of the story; somebody would have listened.

However, the fact was that Alan, in spite of his wound, was much more composed and collected than I was. My wits had deserted me. It seemed inevitable that Monsignor Patrick should address his enquiries to Alan.

"Of course it's the children we must think of first in these unhappy situations," said Monsignor Patrick making little gestures with downturned palms as if he was patting the heads of invisible first communicants. "Mother Church has entrusted the children, born or unborn, to our charge." We were in the drawing-room waiting for the doctor.

"Women don't count, I suppose." I couldn't resist the interruption.

"All human souls are equal in God's sight, that is the mystery," said Monsignor Patrick suavely. "And that's why we must get the best possible care for poor Ruth."

I turned to look at Ruth. She had fallen asleep after a bout of weeping and now lay on the green velvet couch behind us.

"How exactly did it come about that she attacked you, Dixie? It would be beneficial perhaps if we could ascertain exactly what triggered off this unfortunate outburst," said Monsignor Patrick.

I wanted to tell the facts. I would have cut off my right arm if it could have made them see the truth. I was being indecently assaulted by Alan. Alan was a rapist. But that wasn't what I said.

"The knife," I said, "the knife was on the table."

"The knife." They tossed the words to each other in echoing assurances. "The knife was on the table."

Alan looked at me, saw what a fool I was. "Thank God I was there," he said. "A cut on the arm is a small price to pay."

"That damn knife," I said feeling the sharp points of a thousand twisting in my guts.

There was a crunching sound as the doctor's car pulled up outside on the gravel. Clive hurried to get to the door before any of the children reached it. We wanted to keep them out of this.

"I feel God directed me here this afternoon," Monsignor Patrick announced solemnly to Alan and myself. "A woman in Ruth's state of mind is a person possessed. Such people have the strength of..." He paused.

"The devil," Alan said it for him.

I sat stiffened into paralysed frustration.

The doctor was a brisk matter-of-fact man who seemed utterly unfazed by the fact that a woman like Ruth should have started making unprovoked attacks on men.

"How well did you know her?" he asked Clive after he'd finished dressing Alan's wound. Clive was displaying his injured shin which had developed a minor infection.

"Ruth thought the world of him," said Alan,

acting as spokesperson for everyone.

I glanced across at Ruth who had woken up and was looking dazedly at us all. When she caught my eye she registered no emotion. I wanted to go and sit beside her, cuddle her, comfort her, tell her how sorry I was, tell her it was going to be all right, but I did nothing.

Meanwhile, the men had merged into a solid block of concerned brotherhood.

"I must check her tranquillisers. Some pills can have an adverse effect in certain cases," the doctor said.

I wanted to spit. I wanted Ruth to spit. I wanted to tell them all to go to hell. But I had been badly frightened. If Ruth had shown any signs of wanting my help, if she hadn't sat there as if carved of stone it would have been possible for me to be a heroine. Instead I asked if I could make anybody a cup of tea.

In the kitchen, waiting for the kettle to boil, I found myself standing contemplatively with a packet of rat poison in my hand. It would be more efficacious than Ruth's flea powder. But my hands began to shake and I knew that I would be scared to use it. The moment passed.

"It's all right, Dixie. Don't bother with that. They've taken Ruth away. They thought it best to do it while you were out of the room," said Clive, coming in from the dining-room.

All day today I have lived with my betrayal.

21st November: A week has passed. What have I got to say?

I've been so busy minding all the kids,

explaining to them that Ruth is going to be all
right, pretending that by Christmas everything
should be normal, that I can't think straight. But
I've put on a convincing act. Jane, back from
Connemara, didn't seem to realise that any crisis
had taken place. She assumed that Ruth had just
had a mild relapse.

"Are you in love with Harry?" I asked her
today. I was lying down and she'd brought me a
cup of tea.

She pulled a face. "Oh, I don't know. Maybe,
maybe not." She sat down at the foot of the bed.
"I haven't thought about it. Anyway, I'll be
annihilated if I don't go back to college. I do want
to go back and get my degree. That'll take a while.
I don't know how Harry'd feel."

Oh, I know she's young and flighty. I
swallowed hard. "Will you be able to manage? It
won't be easy with Oliver," I warned.

"When you were my age I bet you didn't mind
life being hard," she said with a little pout.

"Don't think I don't understand," I said falsely.
"When I was your age I'd had Peter and we'd just
moved down here."

"You see! The only way I can find out if I can
manage it is to go ahead and try."

"Make sure you don't bite off more than you
can chew."

She scowled. "You sound like Dada. But it's my
life. I can do whatever I like."

"All right. Tell me about Connemara. Was the
hotel nice? Were there many there? It's a popular
spot. Did Harry know it well?" Against my will I
was hungry for details of Harry.

"The bed was great. I slept like a stone. I suppose it was because I hadn't to think about night feeds. Oh, and there was about an acre of marble in the foyer."

"Nothing else?"

Jane looked puzzled but anxious to please. "What else is there?"

"Well, what's Harry like in bed?" I felt a fool for asking.

Jane turned a furious red. "I don't think you should ask me that. Anyway, why do you want to know?" She sounded shocked. "You don't expect me to start talking about it." Then she giggled, "He snored and he wore awful pyjamas. But why does it matter?"

"Because I have doubts about Harry Mercer. Serious doubts."

"What kind?" Jane didn't sound convinced.

"He's too smooth."

"He likes you." Jane considered me carefully.

"Is he passionate?"

"You fancy him yourself, don't you?" Jane's voice lifted. "Well, he doesn't belong to me; you can have him if you want to. He's nearer your age than mine."

"That's very teenagish," I said.

"If I'm teenagish you're old-fashioned. You and Uncle Clive and Mama and Dada. I know the four of you had some sort of scene. Mama hated it. She was always very upset when she got back from those holiday trips you all went off on. I suppose it had something to do with you and Dada. But it always seemed like something out of an old black and white movie you'd see on TV. Parties,

269

romantic music, very sentimental."

"You've got it all wrong, Jane," I said sharply.

"Well, I know Dada used to like you," Jane said defensively. "And anyway it's your business. I don't see why it should have mattered so long as you were all happy."

"We weren't happy," I said sadly. "I don't think that any of us knows what happiness is." I threw back the sheets and jumped out onto the floor so fast that I was attacked by vertigo.

"That's the way it looked to us anyway. Children notice things and you all seemed like you could have anything you wanted. It was nice," Jane said as if her mind was made up. "The things that happen to me are just ordinary," she said. "They could happen to anybody."

I dressed and went outside. I could hear the drone of heavy machinery in Evergreen's grounds. The property had been sold to a consortium who are building an office block. Harry was out of the running. That meant there was no question of him buying Bella Vista.

I stared at the winter hedges wondering about him, wondering if Jane thought me a cantankerous jealous woman. Or maybe she found me comical. Maybe I was comical. I began to shake with silent laughter. All the things that had happened to me were jokes of fate. Maybe, I thought wildly, it was Tristram Long who was doing it. Maybe he was up there with God, both of them sitting on golden thrones behind the clouds, splitting their sides at my desperate antics.

My heart quickened as I heard a car turning in the driveway. This was how the princess felt when

she heard the thundering hooves of the prince's
white charger. But I was being ludicrous. When
the car came into view I saw it was only
Monsignor Patrick's. I did myself a favour by
immediately inventing ten sure-fire reasons for
getting myself off the premises.

# Chapter Nineteen

24th November: Beth, Anne and the young Whites closet themselves in front of the television after school. It seems impossible to get them to stir. I'm hoarse from shouting at them to start sorting and packing their belongings. Alan has rented a house. Jim, Bridget and Danny are moving in with him. It is supposed to happen tomorrow.

"Why can't we wait until Mama is well?" suggested Danny from where he lay, propped on his elbow, still wearing his school clothes.

"Go and change," I said automatically. Ruth is going to need treatment for a long time to come. I know I'll never have the courage to go and visit her. Cowardice is my maiden name. My own nerves jangle when I think of her.

"Have you gone in to see her?" I challenged Clive.

He didn't reply.

I hurried around the house. Mrs Connors has left us and everything is half-finished. I'll never get organised if the house is sold. I'm caught in a cul-de-sac. I need someone to take me by the hand and lead me away. I have no energy. If I had a car things would be a bit easier.

I think of how, a year ago, I was capable, in my perversity, of spying on Ruth and Clive and then Peter was murdered. I've stopped caring about anything. Indifference wraps me in a grey blanket. This is why I don't argue when the children ignore my demands.

I called into Alan's office this morning. There were arrangements to be made about keys and tea chests. We avoided looking directly at each other. I felt very agitated and anxious. Every time he made a sudden movement I jumped.

"Ruth sends me complaints every day," he frowned at me.

"She has plenty to complain about," I said.

"She never knew when she was well off," he said brusquely.

"You've never heard my side of it," he complained when I sneered. "I gave her a good home. You should have seen the dump she came out of," he went on when I refused to be drawn.

"I was with her when her mother died. It seemed all right," I said.

"Did you meet the notorious uncle?" he said with a leering undertone to his voice. "The child molester. He was some beaut."

I didn't believe him. Anyhow, if there was something dark in Ruth's background I didn't want to know. I knew too much about her sorrows already. I grabbed the things I needed and walked angrily out of his office.

In Bella Vista all the boxes of Evergreen salvage had to be gone through, decisions made about what to keep and what to throw away. I forced myself to switch off the television set in the middle of an Australian soap.

"Oh, that man called," Anne announced in the shocked silence.

"What man?"

"Mr Mercer."

"You're lying," I said.

"Mummy!" she wailed. "He told me to tell you he wanted to say goodbye."

I didn't believe her and yet I couldn't be sure.

"When's Mama going to be here?" asked Danny, keeping up his usual refrain.

"Shut up, Danny." Jim scuffed the edge of the hearth rug with his Doc Martens, his face hot and angry. "I don't want to go to that place Dad has. It's a kip. It's all Danny's fault that Evergreen was burned. He should be made pay. He should be in jail."

"Where are Jane and Oliver going to stay?" asked Bridget diffidently.

"Don't ask." I felt helpless. It wasn't their fault. I wanted things to be OK for them. I was doing the best I could.

And then, this evening, our children had a big row with the Whites. One of them threw a glass of something over another one. Who did it was never made clear, but the hostile reactions showed the state of tension they were all in. Then Clive arrived home in a jubilant mood. He had been made a good offer for the house and his contract in the Middle East had been sorted out. They expected him before Christmas.

"Christmas!" the girls howled.

"The Muslims don't celebrate the Nativity," Clive said smugly, and to me, "Now we'll all have to get cracking."

30th November: Ruth showed up. I'd always felt that she would. She arrived as I was coming from the bathroom after washing my hair. She looked like a burnt-out wreck but she claimed that the hospital had allowed her leave. She wouldn't give me exact details. It had something to do with closures and cutbacks. The usual thing nowadays.

An hour beforehand I had seen Jane and Oliver off the premises. Jane departed looking very gypsyish. Her hair was tied up in a red chiffon scarf and she wore a denim flounced skirt and black boots. There was a young man with a red beard waiting in a van. From what I could see of him he looked nice. "Keep in touch, no matter what," I said and Jane kissed me fondly. She seemed to have forgotten all about Harry.

The war between my kids and the Whites was still going on and the house prickled with animosity. Most of the time they sulked in their various rooms. Danny, loitering like a lost soul in the hall, was the only person except myself to witness Ruth's arrival.

She came in via the back door.

"Ruth!" I greeted her with false enthusiasm. "How on earth! – Sit down, sit down. I'll make some tea. Did you meet Jane? She's just gone."

Ruth appeared indifferent and trotted out some details about a nurse she didn't like. She was wearing a heavy navy wool coat that looked as if it had belonged to a reverend mother.

"I want to speak to Clive," she said harshly after a while.

"Do you want food? I can cook some eggs," I said. She looked half-starved.

She ignored my offer, saying, "Help me, Dixie. Help me to see him." She perched pathetically on a stool, wringing her hands.

"He's not here, he won't be here, he's going away," I said uncomfortably.

Ruth looked dazed.

"Hi!" Beth, bouncing into the kitchen, was stopped in her tracks. She looked askance at me. "Mum, I can help you to sort out stuff if you like," she said with that desperate sincerity people display when they're embarrassed.

"Not now, Beth." The palms of my hands were clammy. I was puzzled and disturbed by Ruth's appearance.

Ruth eyed me suspiciously. "Why are you keeping Clive away from me?" she asked.

"Ooops!" Beth backed, bobbing and scarlet-faced, out of the room. I signalled to Danny to follow her but he remained rooted, scrutinising his mother.

Ruth turned and looked at him. "Danny, you've got huge!" she said. "As big as a house." Her voice cracked and she couldn't go on.

"Are you better, Mama?"

"Just about." She pulled a face. "You're getting more and more like your daddy." She appealed to me, "He is like Clive. Do you see it?"

"Hush, Ruth." I ignored Danny as he grabbed a

figroll from a plate and began to munch it with frantic uneasiness.

"He's old enough to know who his father is," said Ruth querulously. "Aren't you, Danny? You're Clive's son. Don't let anyone tell you otherwise."

"Stop, Ruth," I warned.

"Stop, Ruth. Stop!" She mimicked me. "Who do you think you are? Another member of the thought police?"

"Run along, Danny," I tried, but he ignored me and went on chewing biscuits and staring at his mother.

Then Clive was there, a smile slowly fading from his face.

"I've got the money for the house already." His voice was brusque. "One of those lucky things. A builder with cash in hand who'd been let down on another deal. He jumped at the chance of getting his hands on this place." He addressed himself to me as if Ruth wasn't there.

"So you and I can take Danny with us and go and live somewhere else, Clive. That'd be nice." Ruth sprang to stand beside him, resting her arm on the sleeve of his jacket, stroking his arm. Her eyes were heavy-lidded and dazed and her lipstick was applied crookedly and too bright. She was clearly on medication. We should ring the guards, I thought. It was dangerous for her to be here. Dangerous for everybody.

"Dixie..." Clive's voice was uncertain.

"It's all right." I tried to be calm. "We'll all have a cup of tea." What I needed was a large brandy.

"Oh, I've got a migraine," Ruth said in a

petulant voice. She sat down quickly on a kitchen stool. Clive looked at me over her head, then wheeled around and hurried out of the room. Danny ran after him.

Looking down I saw some silvery threads in Ruth's blonde hair. We were a pair of middle-aged frumps, I thought gloomily. Ruth pulled her dark coat more tightly around her and studied the floor tiles as if they contained the secret of the universe.

"You've got to hide me, Dixie." Her voice sounded quite lucid. "If you don't Alan is going to have me put down."

"Put down!" I managed to speak easily. "Not a chance, Ruth. That's for animals."

She looked up at me and said, "You know what he's like," in a voice that chilled me to the marrow.

"Oh, come on!"

"Hah! He has given them permission in the hospital. They're all on his side. I've heard them." Her expression grew cunning. "They think I can't hear them, but I can. I pretend to be asleep but I'm not. I stay awake all night. I know what they say when they come and whisper around my bed."

I should have done something for her. I should have kept her there. She was in no fit state to be handed over to anybody or left by herself. But all I could think was that I wanted her out of the house.

"Why don't you and I go up to the hotel and have a drink? It's a fine evening," I said.

She looked at me enquiringly and in a flash her mood changed. "Great idea!" All at once she was ready for anything. I could have suggested a trip

to Outer Mongolia or the moon. She was all
action, rubbing her hands together and jiggling
her feet.

"Wait here while I go and fix my hair and so
on," I said carefully.

She nodded, docile and pleased as a child going
to visit Santa.

It took me much longer than it should have to
return to the kitchen. Upstairs, I phoned the
hospital and they confirmed my suspicions. Ruth
had slipped out without permission. She hadn't
been discharged. There had been talk of it but her
husband was against the idea because of the
unsettled state of the home situation. "If you
could just keep here there we'll have an
ambulance out in a while," I was told.

"No problem," I said although I knew in my
heart that I was lying. I dreaded the scene that lay
ahead. I saw myself watching Ruth being tied into
a straitjacket. She'd blame me. Mad people always
had to blame someone.

Then I couldn't find a scarf, or gloves, or
proper shoes. I became caught in a mind-stopping
lethargy. It was only when I realised that twenty-
five minutes had passed since I left Ruth that I was
electrified into rushing downstairs again.

The kitchen was empty. I put my head around
the sitting-room door. Clive was reading the
newspaper. Anne and Danny had the television
on. Suddenly I was pounding down the driveway
calling Ruth's name. A full moon cast a pale gleam
over everything. On my left the new walls where
Evergreen had been rose up like giant tombstones.
Across from our entrance the Dalys' trees were lit

279

up with coloured lights. The night was perfumed with laurels and rotting leaves. Dogs barked in sharp staccatos. Maybe they were barking at Ruth. I ran in one direction and then another. After a time I began to yell. A hall-door or two opened but nobody ventured out. Eventually I raced back to Bella Vista and routed out Clive.

Driving along in his car, him at the wheel, me peering out into the shadows, a sort of kinship sprang up between us.

"This is horrible," I mumbled at intervals.

"It's not your fault," Clive offered as comfort.

I shook my head. It was my fault. It was, it was.

"In fact," he said after a fruitless half-hour, "it's my fault if it's anybody's. I should never have let anything happen between us in the first place. I should have controlled myself. She didn't want to, that time in Paris. She said it would only make everything too difficult. But I wouldn't...I couldn't!" Suddenly he was sobbing in great, choking gulps. The car wobbled to a halt. "Christ! She was so damned gorgeous. I couldn't help myself and I wrecked it all."

"It's nobody's fault," I said painfully. My heart was a trapped moth.

Clive's expression was grim. "I should have got out of here years ago. You'd all have managed much better without me."

"You know that's not true," I protested. But there was no point in reasoning it out. I knew that moment, for a fact, that Clive was going to leave and not come back.

4th December: I don't think that they ever will

find Ruth. There was a high tide on the river that night. She could have been swept right out into the Atlantic. There have been some messages from cranks who are convinced that they have seen her in this place or that, but we have been told to discount such reports.

Grief has made our children and the Whites into firm friends again. They are all pleased that both our new houses are going to be close to each other. Yesterday Clive left for the Middle East. Monsignor Patrick has not come up with the final documentation for annulment but it is supposed to be imminent.

"There's no rush, really," said Clive as he and I stood looking at each other rather foolishly in the airport foyer. I was sorry that some of the young ones hadn't come with us to fill the silences.

"I hope it doesn't take too long, for all our sakes," I said. I wanted to have everything tied up and out of the way. I, too, was ready for a clean break.

I waited to watch Clive's plane take off. He was travelling Aer Lingus to London where he would change flights. As his plane taxied down the runway I was picked up.

"Seein' somebody off?" said a voice and I turned and found a jolly-looking, camel-coated, brown-hatted man watching me closely.

"Just a friend," I said.

"Boyfriend of course."

I laughed, tickled at the idea of being considered part of that juvenile scene.

"What I think you are, darlin', is a lonely man's delight," said my new admirer. I was feeling light-headed and fuzzy around the edges and didn't refuse his offer to buy me a drink. It would be a small private celebration of the new order, better than driving home to a semi-dismantled household.

As I sat at the bar drinking a gin and tonic with him a thread of music coming over the piped tapes was a tune that Tristram used to play. My lips twitched. It seemed to be nostalgia time.

"A handsome woman like yourself should have no trouble finding herself a man," said my companion. I knew that his shrewd blue eyes had spotted the wedding ring on my finger.

"I don't know that I like men," I said and he roared with laughter.

"Still, it's good to live in a Catholic country," he fished meaningfully. "It keeps people on the straight and narrow. I hate to see a couple break up. A widow now, that's different."

I hastily finished my drink and stood up. "Sorry, but I really have to rush."

"You wouldn't by any chance fancy a spot of lunch?" he suggested.

"Couldn't. I'm a busy lady," I said. Then I froze. Watching us, from a table further down the bar, was Harry Mercer. He clutched a large briefcase in his lap.

I was compelled to make my way towards him as awkwardly as a schoolgirl. My eyes bulged and my face was burning.

"Hi there! I've just been seeing Clive off," I said uncomfortably.

Harry quirked an eyebrow. "I'd never have guessed."

My brain felt as if it had been clamped in a vice. Speech was impossible.

Harry put out a restraining hand and held his head to one side as an announcement came over the loudspeaker. "That's mine," he said. He touched the tip of my nose with his forefinger. "Mind yourself anyway," he said. "There's some nasty bastards hanging around this place."

I turned my head and watched the man in the camel coat who was scurrying towards the exit.

"How about a goodbye kiss?" asked Harry, taking me by surprise. It was more than I'd got from Clive. His lips trembled against mine and I felt the soft comfort of his tongue. His skin was sweet as honey, the nape of his neck violin strings against my finger tips. I became a suppliant moaning mass.

"Mind yourself." He had me at arm's length. Then he pulled me close again and gave my bottom a smack.

"Harry..." I couldn't let him go. He couldn't leave me like this, with tears running down my face.

"Oh, Dixie. Come on now, hush. It's OK." His kiss this time was brotherly and brisk. "I'll have to run for it. Sorry you've had a bad time, Dixie. Sorry about lots of things. And I heard about Ruth. The craythur." His expression was kind and worried.

"Harry, stay with me!" I screamed.

He stopped in his tracks. "Ah no. It wouldn't be right, Dixie. I won't say I couldn't be tempted, but it'd be all wrong. You see that, don't you? You're a mature lady. You've got kids. You'd deserve something better than I could offer. I've got commitments and so have you."

"You can always look me up, Harry," I said frantically. "Anytime. I'll be expecting you. I'll be counting on you."

But he was moving away from me calling, "Don't say anything you wouldn't swear to in court. I might take you up on it, you see. And then you might regret it."

"Don't go," I wailed. But I knew by the jauntiness of his step as he turned and headed for the departure lounge that he was already out of reach.

# EPILOGUE

We have just moved house. The last few weeks have been hectic, but the girls have all rowed in and done their best. We even have a Christmas tree decorated in our new sitting-room.

This morning Jane's letter arrived. Reading it I wished that I was young enough for a completely fresh start myself. But I'm managing much better than I expected I would.

Monsignor Patrick is coming to tea with some IMPORTANT DOCUMENTS. That's the way he referred to them, in capital letters. I suppose what he means is that he has found his way through the labyrinth of Church law, wound the thread spun by Clive and I back to the starting point so that nothing resembling a marriage is shown to exist.

He wanted to ask me some questions. I

agreed at once.

"God bless you, Dixie," he said. "I know this won't be easy."

My own laugh surprised me. "I don't foresee any problems," I said and hung up before he could reply. The action felt like a minuscule victory. I savoured it for a second, thinking all I have to do is keep a little ahead of the posse.

Most days I feel like somebody who's recovering from a major operation. Huge sections of my person have been scraped away leaving painful scars and hollows. But I'm still functioning. I hope I can keep it up. I hope that tomorrow I'll be even stronger, able to do something truly positive.

Or that I'll walk down the street and out of the blue a voice will say, "Wake up, Dixie!" And I'll stop in my tracks and blink and he'll be there. We'll face each other and do a soft shoe shuffle before linking arms and skipping off into the sunset with all the happy children frolicking behind us.